# TRUE FAILURE

# TRUE FAILURE

# ALEX HIGLEY

**COFFEE HOUSE PRESS**

MINNEAPOLIS

2025

Coffee House Press books are available to the trade through our primary
distributor, Consortium Book Sales & Distribution, cbsd.com or (800) 283-
3572. For personal orders, catalogs, or other information, write to info@
coffeehousepress.org.

Coffee House Press is a nonprofit literary publishing house. Support from
private foundations, corporate giving programs, government programs,
and generous individuals helps make the publication of our books possible.
We gratefully acknowledge their support in detail in the back of this book.

LIBRARY OF CONGRESS CATALOGING-IN-PUBLICATION DATA

Names: Higley, Alex, author.
Title: True failure / Alex Higley.
Description: Minneapolis : Coffee House Press, 2025.
    Identifiers: LCCN 2024017401 (print) | LCCN 2024017402 (ebook) |
    ISBN 9781566897136 (paperback) | ISBN 9781566897143 (epub)
Subjects: LCGFT: Novels.
Classification: LCC PS3608.I3728 T78 2025 (print) | LCC PS3608.I3728
    (ebook) | DDC 813/.6—dc23/eng/20240515
LC record available at https://lccn.loc.gov/2024017401
LC ebook record available at https://lccn.loc.gov/2024017402

PRINTED IN THE UNITED STATES OF AMERICA

32 31 30 29 28 27 26 25    1 2 3 4 5 6 7 8

For Brad Watson
1955–2020

# TRUE FAILURE

**1.** BEN RECEIVED A small severance package. He had worked in the office for four years and for those four years would receive two months' pay. He was fired on an idyllic Friday morning in June in the city of Chicago. Ben's back faced the shining lake as he sat in his boss's office and learned the details of his departure. He knew as he was being fired that he would not tell his wife. He would avoid telling Tara for as long as possible. He would lie, then continue to lie and deceive to perpetuate his original lie of not telling her he had lost his job. He didn't want to lie to her, but the alternative, honesty, did not occur to him. He didn't want to disappoint her, fill her with more doubt, cause her to worry about him more than she already did. Not that he was afraid of Tara—not particularly, not any more than was reasonable, not any more than any man is afraid of his wife. Ben's hope was to find another job, another solution, and present it to Tara as good news, a surprise, obscuring the deception and however long it would have lasted. But he was not afraid of her. There were disagreements, sure, but those were due to being human, dropped like rag dolls into the daily churn, rerouted and scuttled by eddies unseen; often much less than that. TV. Impatience. A hot room. An awful childhood face remembered. Ben could rarely recall what led to their disagreements and was bested in every argument, ultimately resembling a neutral spectator in a dazed late-afternoon crowd, leaning against the counter in their kitchen. Defeated but present.

Ben was not uncommonly dim. He could make quips about passersby. He wasn't fixed in his thinking on most topics. But he did have a submerged quality, as though his disposition were formed by a daily dunking into a surging river and a concurrent grasping back toward the surface. Momentum from elsewhere always seemed to guide him; this was true of his consciousness, his interest in any conversation, his pursuits, his attitudes, his ability to love. Ben liked it that way. He liked to claim that everything was beyond him because he had accomplished, to his thinking, nothing. He knew he could not actually carry out a scheme of his own devising, whether it be an attempt to change, an attempt to win, or a lie—any lie. It was easy, though, to live embarrassed, and allow yourself to be misunderstood by those who didn't really know you as humble, patient, wise, content.

* * *

"I WANT TO get on *Big Shot,*" Ben said as he and his newly former coworker, Thuan Nguyen—whom he called Nguyen—ate lunch.

Nguyen swallowed a too-large bite. They had not been talking about *Big Shot*—a reality show in which entrepreneurs pitched their businesses to celebrity investors—or anything even remotely related. Nguyen had been speculating in a free-associative way about vinyl flooring options and their relative efficacies in "completing the kitchen."

They were eating lunch in a narrow Mediterranean restaurant off Jewelers' Row, peak business crowd, plates on red plastic trays, wedged into a tight little mustard-colored table, of which there were many, elbow to elbow with strangers. The restaurant smelled of roast chicken and also distinctly lemon-scented cleaning solution in a way that was not unpleasant. It was a popular lunch spot located in the back of a jewelry store on Wabash, between Washington and Madison, downtown, the Loop. The Chicago of tourists and corporations; in some ways, not Chicago at all. Ben could tell Nguyen was tolerating him because Ben no longer had a job, and because that development was an hour old. They were eating lunch as they would have if Ben had not just been fired. Ben had helped Nguyen get his job around three years earlier. Nguyen had been a friend of a friend at the time, and Ben had lobbied for him to his boss, saying, "We grew up together. Played Little League. I love this man." None of it was true. Ben was capable of instant and enduring loyalty. Instant, enduring, and inexplicable.

"Now that I'm fired," Ben said, "*Big Shot.* That's what I want."

Waiting for Nguyen in the stone lobby of their building in the gap-hours between getting fired and lunch, numb scrolling on his phone, Ben encountered remembrance posts for a former college classmate who had been on *Big Shot.* That was what had put the show in his head at all. Ben and Tara watched *Big Shot,* but had never had a conversation about the show outside of the occasional half hours it stole from them.

Ben didn't want to be tolerated. He wanted Nguyen thinking with him, helping him. He needed the help. He didn't want to be walked through COBRA and the ins and outs of his other health insurance options. He wanted help to get on the show. He took a different tack. Ben read the definition of the word *lottery* aloud: "Lottery: a process or thing whose success or outcome is governed by chance," he said. "You see?"

Nguyen said, "Using that definition, everything is a lottery."

"If you put billionaires on TV, show them giving away money, you're creating a lottery system. That kind of wealth disparity, having the chance to be brought into close proximity to that kind of wealth, that's a lottery system."

"It's the illusion of a lottery. And you're missing the fact that they aren't giving away money. They're investing it."

Ben could tell Nguyen was enjoying this, that he had a chance to hook him. "Tell me the difference. To an audience. What's the difference?"

Ben was playing the role of a man who wasn't worried, a man refusing to talk about job prospects, plans, how he was feeling, growing credit card debt, the student loan debt that between him and Tara topped seventy thousand dollars—that is, anything related to the parts of his life that held consequence.

He was unwilling to talk about or attempt to develop a next move regarding a new job, or to think about why it was, really, that he had been let go. Why he had become unnecessary. He felt numb. Numb in his chest, in his thighs, in his feet, in the center of his forehead. But it was comforting to pretend to have a plan. A goal. An idea. His only ideas so far were to not tell his wife he'd been fired and to attempt to get on *Big Shot*, two more ideas than he had woken with that morning. His waking thoughts had been of not wanting to leave bed, of Red's Pizza over on Maple in the southwest suburb where they lived, tavern-style thin-crust beauties, and then wishing the bed he did not want to leave spanned the entirety of their bedroom instead of the standard width of a queen. Ben thought about this kind of thing often, the needlessly altered everyday item.

He needed a job, of course, but he couldn't bring himself to think about that yet. Eventually he wouldn't have a choice, but right now, he felt he had time.

"I need you to keep this a secret," Ben said. "Can't tell Hank either." Hank was Nguyen's husband.

"Getting fired? Or the show?"

"All of it," Ben said. He thought of trying to get on the show and losing his job as one and the same development. Both would be very troubling for Tara. Wanting to be on reality TV, much less actually appearing on reality TV, would for Tara reveal a new layer of intrinsic stupidity.

"If you really are putting time into getting on the show, I'm not sure how you're going to keep that from Tara. Paperwork, auditions. Do you have a plan?"

Ben wasn't sure.

Nguyen said, "And what the hell are you going to pitch?"

Unclear.

He'd told Nguyen explicitly to keep his secret because Hank would certainly tell Tara. Text Tara. This exact chain of information delivery was ever present in Ben's mind, related to an Illinois vs. Iowa under bet he'd made that had hit. He'd won four hundred dollars on a bad bet that had somehow worked out. No value, only certainty. More than two years had passed, and yet Ben still was galled that Hank had asked Tara via text where Ben would be taking her for their four-hundred-dollar victory dinner, only to receive the same question from Tara shortly after, very much in person. Ben remembered his anger as mostly directed at Hank's generous misunderstanding that all their financial decisions, his and Tara's, even those related to college football gambling, must have been made as a team; what a world.

But Nguyen was right, Ben was only capable of hiding so much from her. Linking the show to getting fired was his own personal guilt assemblage. It was a matter of when Ben would tell Tara he'd been fired and what exactly he'd be able to stack in his favor during the interim.

He knew his desire to be on the show was a misdirection. Ambition as misdirection, achievement as misdirection. A misdirection from the reality that he was no longer employed, had no real prospects for the immediate future, and frankly could account for less of what had happened to him than was acceptable for a person his age; he lacked answers to questions he had never even thought to ask. But this misdirection, trying to get on the show, would be a bright light foregrounding the show itself—its shine and promise, the accomplishment of participation, the action of participating in the show's existence, and not the person, Ben, not the person who'd existed before and would continue existing after. Not Ben, who was lacking a job and an adult agenda. And so Ben's plan, his whole plan, would be to get on the show. And to not tell Tara he'd been fired. What the show, its existence, had done for Ben in the past hour, the hour-plus he'd been unemployed, was make the idea of winning the lottery, *a* lottery, seem attainable.

Ben needed that right now. A magic trick.

The restaurant seemed like a made-up place—to enter, one had to walk through a jewelry store, straight through an aisle between glass cases holding rings and watches and bracelets, into a cavernous narrow room that opened up, the ceiling suddenly twice as high, a two-register counter with an illustrated menu above, color pictures of falafel specials, shawarma, hummus plates. Business Lunch Special with Rice. Combination Feast. The oddness of the physical space made the restaurant seem like a secret, but it was the opposite; that's what Ben liked about it.

Nguyen said, "You aren't giving these people on TV enough credit."

"Which people?"

"The people coming in with their businesses, inventions. The contestants, if that's the word. Those aren't people who went down to the gas station and bought a ticket, then checked numbers later that night. I mean, that's pure chance. Right? And maybe even then, I mean, I remember reading about different lottery winners with strategies. Only playing when the prize money was over a certain amount, like, three hundred million. Doing a quick pick and also playing a specific set of numbers. But even then, with a strategy, I'm arguing against myself now, that's still chance."

"You're talking about how to operate within the lottery, which is what I'm talking about too. I'm equating the businesses, the inventions, the ideas—I'm equating all those to a lottery ticket. I think they are just as cheap. Just as easy to come by."

"You're wrong," Nguyen said. "And the part you're most wrong about is thinking that the system is as pure as you're imagining. That's like thinking the world is devoid of sex and instinct. It's not a merit-based structure. You have to get on the show. Getting on the show is the ticket, not any idea. And getting on the show is not based on merit. At least not based on merit alone. And an idea by itself, hell, even a thriving business by itself, is not enough to get on the show. We don't know what's real. We see an edit."

"That's true." Ben smiled and they both ate, heads down, as

if they had to catch up to some tacitly understood lunch-eating pace. He'd miss these lunches with Nguyen. Future lunches together would take planning, scheduling, coordination, and would rarely, if ever, take place. They no longer worked together, and so to be together would take work. The restaurant had tall, waxy fake plants in corners, rectangular hooded security cameras, mirrored walls, hazy yacht rock coming from bad speakers. Behind the glass jewelry cases stood several husky brown men with mustaches and gold necklaces who might have been brothers, or the owners, or both. Ben believed the space reflected someone's idea of Miami, someone who had never been there and who disliked bright colors. A Miami of the Middle West, but not the actual Miami of the Middle West.

"You think some people luck their way onto the show?" Nguyen asked.

"That's what I'm saying."

Nguyen shook his head. "Really what you're saying is that you think you can luck your way onto the show. Which is going to take a lot of work. And it won't be luck. It will be work."

"In part luck."

Nguyen exhaled toward the ceiling. "Like: in part we are lucky that someone doesn't come into this restaurant and gun us down. My god, the luck."

Ben thought, that is luck.

Ben didn't tell Nguyen where the idea had come from. That the most caustically stupid man he'd ever known, Trevor Crant, a man who had lived on Ben's floor freshman year in Champaign twelve–thirteen years ago, had been on *Big Shot* and gotten a deal. Ben wouldn't have needed to give Nguyen that much backstory for him to understand who or what he was talking about, because Crant's product had become ubiquitous. An inexpensive natural odorless spot eraser, N.O.S.E., packaged in tiny orange keychainable bottles. Crant's tagline, one he'd repeated on the show with maniacal zeal: "You see spots with your eyes, but if you don't want to see them, use your N.O.S.E."

Their freshman year, still children, Crant had drunkenly kicked the glass out of a fire extinguisher cabinet in one of the dorm's broad cement stairwells and sliced his calf into a trip to the emergency room. Ben remembered blood everywhere on the slick gray walls, on the stairs. He remembered Crant screaming like a struggling animal being butchered; most of the floor huddled in the stairwell gawking as the EMTs arrived. Ben hadn't been able to sleep that night—a wide-awake eighteen-year-old thinking of all the blood inside himself he'd never considered. Blood rushing within him as his mind sat still like an undiscovered and insignificant Appalachian lake. He remembered Crant on crutches for what seemed like a year, swearing at most of what passed him under his breath. Smiling with his small teeth in deep Illinois winter, puffy-coated on crutches like some demented quarterback, the boy had become obsessed with literally being able to erase blood as some kind of totemic victory over his drunken stairwell incident. The two had not been friends, but many colleges are small villages; everyone knows the idiot. Crant was dead—suicide, but that was beside the point. Minor acquaintances from that time in Ben's life were posting on this day, the day Ben was fired, also the anniversary of Crant's death, "If you need help, reach out. RIP Crant."

*Big Shot* had never been appointment television for Ben and Tara. They'd let five or six stack up and watch the pitches that held their interest, skip the rest. Fairly common for them to see a face coming down the hall to pitch and instantly fast-forward to the next offering. Some people were wrong, it was clear immediately—on this the couple agreed.

Ben watched a bug-eyed man at the next table set down his fork with an odd focus, as though his hand might begin mutating. The man had been staring at Nguyen from the words *gun us down* onward. The small mustard-colored tables were inflicted on all; minor shifts in attention from the next table over felt seismic. The bug-eyed man was eating a large pile of brown rice, scooping spicy red schug into the rice before each bite; Ben didn't know what to think of this diet. Certainly a choice. Ben wanted to know how much the restaurant charged for a plateful of rice.

Ben said, "Or think about how lucky we are to live in a city with a restaurant in the back of a jewelry store."

"But see what you did there? You made the conversation about something different. You hinged what you said on a different—valid, but different—conception of luck. We were talking about something else."

Ben turned to the bug-eyed man and said, "Good?" to encourage him to stop staring, and turned back to Nguyen, who kept talking. "Okay, I'm going to do the same thing to you. Lottery. Think about this. We both won the lottery, right? Born here. Parents with jobs. Men. Not to mention, you're white. Divorced parents, both of us, sure, but supported through childhood. Went to college. And then we denied our lottery winnings. Denied our luck—"

Ben started shaking his head and said, "Debatable." He didn't want to know where Nguyen was going. He didn't want to hear criticism at lunch. At any meal, for that matter. Especially from Nguyen, who still had a job.

Ben stood up and gathered his tray; Nguyen did the same. They began making their way through the crowd toward the trash bins. Ben spoke to Nguyen over his shoulder: "So far, you are acknowledging only one lottery operating at a time. I think there are several. Maybe infinite lotteries occurring at all times."

"That doesn't mean anything."

Behind them, still seated, the bug-eyed man started choking. A few people turned toward the sound, and one man in a black turtleneck stood and yelled *Medic!* Ben thought, premature. He thought, here we yell *doctor.* Then the bug-eyed man slammed both his hands flat on the table and stopped coughing. A student in a stocking cap began clapping as if magic had been performed. The student clapped for far too long. The bug-eyed man looked across the restaurant, directly at Ben, put his hands to his throat, and mouthed a word that Ben could not make out. Something round and threatening. Ben said, "Marty Feldman–looking choking motherfucker," but Nguyen ignored his comment about the stranger.

Ben and Nguyen kept walking out through the aisle between the jewelry cases, out toward the shrieking day, the L rumbling by above them. Nguyen said, "Infinite lottery." Ben nodded. Nguyen added, "Doesn't mean anything."

They headed in the shared westerly direction of Nguyen's office and Union Station. Away from the lake. Ben with his satchel and a small box containing personal items from his desk. He considered dumping the box into the next trash can, and then did. Nguyen kept pace next to Ben with his hands in his pockets, a posture of uncertainty.

Ben said, "I wouldn't lie to her about anything that really mattered."

Nguyen made a face, then a sound like he was going to speak, but he said nothing.

"Not in a long-term way, I wouldn't."

"When she does find out, she's going to wonder what else you're lying about."

"There's nothing."

"And what else you're capable of lying about."

"Like I said."

# 2. TARA

THE THREE KIDS were each standing on their own plastic step stool so they could reach the kitchen counter. Taking turns with the hammer. Tara was letting them tenderize the pork chops with a real hammer, yellow handled, from the garage; she'd washed it in front of them with dish soap so that if any of their parents asked about the day and the hammer came up—inevitable—she could be sure its cleaning had witnesses. Pounding the chop, Billy was grunting in a way that reminded Tara of Monica Seles. She couldn't think of a good way to share this with the boy. The girls, Micah and Jules, had very different hammer styles. Micah was firm gripped and too focused on the strike, the downward momentum of her arm, and as a result was repeatedly missing the pork and striking the cutting board with a loud bang. Jules was loose and wristy with the hammer, distracted by the birds arriving at the feeder hanging outside the window. Tara ended up getting her pork in shape while guessing at the names of the birds: "Sparrow, that one's a grackle, yes, mud sparrow—"

Tara had been running a day care out of their home for the past three years. Day care had occurred to her while she was pregnant and they still lived in the city. Before then, never. Before then she was concerned with the painting at hand— paintings with titles like *Local Disaster, Look Skyward; Solemn Buried Commercial Fishing;* and *Parsnix*—making enough money waitressing for rent, and little else.

There had been the brief, shattering pregnancy. Seven weeks. She never told Ben. She thought of these as two distinct secrets, the pregnancy and the loss of it, and this understanding was important to her. Important because her own personal tally of hardships survived had to mean something. The knowledge that she could endure what she had alone was important to her. Speaking some of these secrets, some of what she was holding onto, telling Ben, would seem to allow for the actual cruelty of the world to more fully enter—like water seeping into and permanently filling the basement of the home that was her life. Still water sitting dead. It was better to pretend; it was better to lie.

She hadn't known about the baby herself until five weeks. Not uncommon, five weeks, the opposite actually, but still staggering, she thought, to be able to live even one day oblivious that another life was there with you. Think of one whole day spent evading effective advertising, selecting a bagel, considering an attitude modulation for work purposes, thinking about seasonal clothing and where to get it cheaply, getting horny for a TV doctor, refilling a coffee mug, getting horny for a TV lawyer, dropping a coffee mug, refilling a large fountain-drink cup filled with half Diet Coke and half Dr Pepper, being particular about the ice, filling with hate for strangers riding with you on the Brown Line, all those decisions in light of a baby coming. Five weeks of that. It was beautiful and silly and as common as another day. Oblivion. Daily, oblivion.

The three kids, not her own, were sitting with Tara in the green yard eating lunch, back behind the detached garage in long grass. There were mature trees quietly surrounding them: a bur oak, American linden, a ginkgo, all massive and beautiful, each over a hundred years old. Three trees can be enough to fill a yard, especially less than a quarter of an acre, and that's to say nothing of any of the bushes, shrubs, or several twenty-five-foot-tall wooden posts that held drooping electrical wires loping toward neighboring homes. The trees took some effort to notice because much of Harks Grove was full of the same; one could easily be tricked into not seeing them at all, though Tara had always marked them. The four were sitting next to each other eating pork schnitzel sandwiches on the fake steel girder that Ben had built them earlier in the summer. Micah, Jules, Billy, Tara. Loosely, it was Czech week at Tara's. The girder was made from leftover sixteen-foot precut deck planks from Nguyen and Hank's house that Ben had painted gray. They'd redone their deck and were now worrying their way around the kitchen. Tara felt both renovations were needless—the house she'd seen once was flawless—but was glad to enjoy what their overbuying had provided.

The need for a fake steel girder came from one of the kids, Billy. He'd become fixated on the photograph *Lunch atop a Skyscraper*, the famous shot of the eleven ironworkers eating lunch suspended in the air on the sixty-ninth floor of the RCA Building under construction—the photograph nearly as old as the trees in the yard. Billy could not take in the information the photo provided as real, and as a result began concentrating his attention on its component pieces; as if the disparate units that comprised the picture might form its magic instead of the plain shock of men eating lunch in the sky. Tara had asked Ben to make the kids the girder for outdoor lunches. The girder had given their outdoor lunches a ritual quality they'd previously lacked. Head outside, sit on the beam, eat.

When Tara thought back on the pregnancy, that is what she thought of most: not the two weeks she'd known her child was there with her, but the time before when she hadn't. She couldn't have known, of course. She had done nothing wrong. Tara wanted a child more than she let Ben know. Her line was, if they got pregnant, she'd welcome it. Not that this was a line she rehearsed or delivered regularly. Opportunities were wanting. Not a lot of sex, and even less talking around the sex they did have. Tara's sentiment was not punctuated by a smile, it was flat, it was true; if they got pregnant, she'd welcome it. She was a natural with children and that made her want one. She didn't feel she had to alter who she was around kids; her desire for a family wasn't complicated. Her reasons were alive to her. She didn't think Ben would be able to handle knowing about the miscarriage and she was also unwilling to find out whether he was or not. He was too sensitive, defensive, moody. And about nothing. Say, if he were wearing a hat backward, indoors, folding laundry, listening to *Led Zeppelin IV*, a muted basketball game on the TV, intently watching the screen, folding his T-shirts strangely, consistently, but strangely, she might laugh at him. Maybe she'd tell him that with his current technique, there'd be a diagonal fold-line striping each shirt. And she might also be laughing at how deeply mass popular music touched him combined with his inability to prepare T-shirts for storage, his dumb hat; the totality. And he'd be hurt. He'd tell her he hadn't listened to that record since he was fifteen; to leave him alone. She'd coo and kiss and pat his back, but still the hurt could last a whole ten minutes. Longer. She'd say, you can't laugh like that at a man you don't love. And that might be true; but it was also tiring. If you loved him, it was hard not to laugh at the man he was, unguarded. He arrived in rooms, a career, in conversations, without planning or cunning, as one would expect. And that was nothing. If there were stakes, my goodness. He could not modify his moods and reactions as she could. He could not hide. The more hurt he was, the more she had to be present to fix. The more she kept private, the more she was able to control. Tara was often more aware of Ben than Ben himself—his emotional state, his presence in a room, how he was being received, what he was actually thinking. And as a result, she was responsible for his care in a way that was not reciprocated. Ben could not sense what Tara hid from him, not in the way Tara could for Ben, and this in part meant he was burdened with less.

She didn't want to always have to guide him: here's how you make yourself happy, here's how to be a better partner, here's how.

Micah began singing on the beam, schnitzel sandwich in hand, and Billy shushed her. He'd started enforcing a "no talking" policy when they ate on the girder, and the girls respected it because Billy was the youngest of the three and this was fully his game that they were playing. Micah stood and wandered the yard, loosely holding her sandwich, self-possessed in her singing like her audience was somewhere floating inches above her head. Jules had her eyes closed with her face in the sun, still sitting on the beam. Tara could not see evidence of Jules's sandwich anywhere, her plate, napkin, anything. In the past week Jules had hidden two pairs of shoes, three forks, and now a pork schnitzel sandwich.

For the two weeks she had spent planning her new life as a mother, making decisions with that knowledge, joying in the secret of the pregnancy, Tara had been preoccupied with finding a way to make money that allowed her to stay home with her daughter. She'd always worked. She'd waitressed, bartended, while going to school and then full time after, and had felt done with it. Nearly ten years of that work. She did not want to give her patience to customers ordering drinks, give them her kindness, and then go home and feel depleted of anything she would need to give her child. That she would want to give her child. Not if she didn't have to. Yes, Ben had a job, but it was not enough. They needed to maintain two incomes like everyone they knew and everyone else those people knew. Student loans and a mortgage, credit cards, those three to begin, and need it even be said?

For those two weeks, still, Tara had thought of the unborn child as her daughter. It had never occurred to her that she could be anything else.

Tara lay prone on the beam in the sun, the trees looming above her as the three kids circled, running and shouting, "Dead, dead, we think she's dead!" Tara had named this game "Is She Dead?" and the unfortunate answer for the kids was always yes. Playing dead was Tara's forever tactic within this activity. The game as Tara defined it was that she lay on the beam and the kids ran around her while determining if she was alive or not. Either choice allowed Tara to close her eyes and not be touched for around a minute and a half. She'd lie on the beam until the kids got sick of circling and pushed her into the grass, ending the game. To call this set of actions a game was incorrect, there was no winner and no firm rules; that didn't stop them from playing. Whatever it was, this nongame, was a continuation of the ritual created and sustained by the presence of the fake steel beam. The kids stopped circling like a mob before the final violence. Micah pushed at her shoulder and Billy pushed at her ankles and Tara allowed herself to be thud-flipped onto the ground. She let her face settle into the earth, flattening the wet grass. Jules was doing the same, face down twenty feet away in the yard, though no one had noticed.

Tara had spent two weeks sizing up home childcare in the near suburbs. Looked at the websites, cruised by the low houses in a borrowed car, parked at the storefronts, read endless online reviews. She'd looked at the women—it was all women, their bland and direct operations—and known she could do better. Or, more importantly, was positive she could do at least as well in a new and more interesting way that would not resemble the efforts of others.

Tara and Ben had been living in an Uptown studio apartment then. They were planning a move to somewhere they could afford to make a down payment on a house. It was hard for them to define what the word *afford* meant. Both wanted a house, kids or not. Houses in the city were cost prohibitive. Owning anything anywhere in the city where they were interested in living was cost prohibitive. They did not have the wherewithal or ingenuity or basic skills for a home that needed any serious fixing up, which was the only option they could manage in neighborhoods they wanted to live in; this was a belief and not the truth. They'd been renting south of the Wilson Red Line stop. This was the apartment where Tara lived with her pregnancy and her miscarriage, alone. Alone with Ben. Only her mother knew: a piece of information she seemed to take in like a repeatedly canceled lunch date.

In this Uptown stretch before, during, and after the pregnancy, they had no car, no dog, did not eat out. Did not eat out as much as they'd like: Sun Wah at Broadway and Argyle. Moody's for hamburgers and draft specials. Cut-rate BYOB sushi by the Sheridan stop. Gyros at Windy City off Irving Park.

Tara had been nannying for twins of married lawyers in Roscoe Village then. Two large-headed boys. Looked like fraternity brothers already. The boys had loved Tara. The lawyers had not known what to make of Tara, beyond the husband being fixated on the fact that she'd gone to art school. This was a detail that had been included on her resume, but never spoken by Tara. She claimed a degree on the resume but in reality had dropped out. The husband had asked for her thoughts on Frankenthaler, Hartigan, Carrington. He had asked after her current studio space. She'd said she had one she didn't use. A lie. She didn't know if she wanted to paint anymore and didn't know what that meant for her making future. Tara had recommended Neo Rauch. *Heillichtung* (2014) or *Kühlraum* (2002). And Robyn O'Neil. *The Mercy Quartet* (2016). But mostly she'd evaded the husband conversationally by providing minutiae about the children. Speculative and often baseless minutiae. "They respond differently to me when I wear green. Have you noticed that? And yellow? They seem happier." There was a framed Gale Sayers uniform hanging in the husband's home office, and so Tara would return to yellow and green as capable of boosting the boys' morale as often as she remembered to. She was sure he wanted to bed her. Nothing happened.

Even after the miscarriage, she was decided on day care. Her own, once they had the space. Tara's private understanding was that the baby had given her this new vocation, and for that she was thankful.

They chose Harks Grove, near the Metra, far enough out that they could afford a small home. Three bedroom, one-and-a-half bath. Dated, worn, but their own.

A home day care was ideal because Tara wanted control of

her work, control of her days, and no boss. She didn't want anyone to know the particulars of what the work meant for her. When researching home day cares on a Canadian mom-blog, Tara encountered the idea that kids' menus were inherently condescending. That limiting a child's food options to chicken nuggets, mac and cheese, and the like was not based in rational thinking. Equating a kids' menu to a children's book was lunacy, stated the Canadian. Language proficiency and eating proficiency, unrelated. Tara was not a true believer in the Canadian, did not share in her hatred for bland American staples, but the woman's idea gave her something. The idea had opened up all her thinking at the time, though it felt distant and problematic in memory. She had started the day care with a focus first on the meals that would be provided. The meals would stem from a light curriculum she would devise that centered on various foreign countries. She would quietly play the country's music throughout the day, cook the country's food. And sometimes she'd play the music loud, and the children and Tara would run around in the living room. Sometimes not. She was concerned not with authenticity, but with honest effort. She'd attempt to match one region's music with that region's food. Illuminate how complicated each and every country is; dignify these places in their particularity. Show the country's cartoons, which were now so easy to watch online. But homey too. The curriculum would not be taught in a clinical, academic way. It would not be taught at all. It would be shared. And if a child instead wanted to kick a ball, scream until the cords in her neck appeared, sing the same song forever, so be it.

And what Tara had imagined was more or less what she was able to make real. What she was able to form was a less wholesome, less consistent, less striving version of what she'd initially conceived. Tara never watched more than three kids at one time, though she did have a short waiting list, friends of past and current customers, and could easily have expanded her business. She kept a handwritten notebook for each child in her care, and at the end of their time together, she would give each notebook to the parents or parent. The painting had stopped and the note-taking had begun. She'd cared for seven different children, total, over the last three years. The idea behind the notebooks was to mark down a couple happenings from each child in her care, each day. Sometimes the entries were a line long, sometimes pages. Tara had half a dresser drawerful of in-progress and still-empty notebooks, empty on the left, in-progress on the right.

- *Micah believes that bats thrive in countries other than the United States because it is less distracting to sleep upside down if you can't understand what everyone is saying. I told her bats don't speak English, or any human language.*

- *Jules took off her glasses today when we were outside and held them at her side. She put her head back and watched the clouds. I told her she looked very beautiful and she pretended not to hear me so I told her again and she turned saying, "I appreciate you saying it twice."*

- *Billy asked me if it was OK for him to sit in the bathtub today when we heard thunder. When I went in to check on him he was sitting naked in the tub. Once he was dressed and the rain had stopped I took him outside to watch a tree service, one man in green and goggles, section the seventy-year-old white oak that had fallen. The man in goggles was deftly using the end of his chainsaw to make the cuts. Part of the tree was in the street, and occasional traffic would creep around the shrouded man with the chainsaw. I know the tree was seventy years old because that's what the man in goggles told Billy when he asked.*

The journals had begun as an earnest vocational practice but became increasingly difficult for Tara to keep up. So she didn't. She began to invent, instead. The wholesale creation of imaginary events, imaginary conversations with the kids, wasn't at all difficult for her. Easy as breathing. The lying did not come from feeling the need to catch up in her notes; the lying came from Tara having trouble parsing her days with the kids for their contents. Even inside the days while living them, she was hitting checkpoints. Breakfast, outside, books. Music, snack, outside, books, cartoons. Sometimes, field trip. Lunch. Outside. Quiet time. Nap. Playtime. Pickup. Repeat. There were moments, hours, where she was alive to what was happening, reading or singing or playing dead or cooking with the kids, but still, this was her job. Work. She felt protective of her time with the kids—wanted it to be a practice, practice! Jesus, wanted it to be time she was awake for more completely, which it never would be. But she did love those stupid kids; at least Billy. She did love Billy. He seemed to need it most. She felt guilty about missing so much, her inattention, and the more guilt she felt, the more she wanted to do better, the more possessive she became. But there was nothing to possess. What she owned wholly, what she could possess, was what she put down in the notebooks. That which she could create and so control.

She was a caretaker, not a parent. She did not confuse the two despite any feelings. Tara felt ready to shift. She also knew she might be needing less of a change than she imagined; maybe she needed less, period. Less work, less to maintain. Different work, maybe. She didn't know what was possible, how much she could reasonably shed and still be herself. Or, unbeknownst to her, how much she had already shed. She was thinking of the kids, of Ben.

No amount of shuffling or change would leave her less busy. That was not an American option. Not one afforded to her. This understanding was another she'd invented, though she did not know it. She lived it. Everyone she knew did.

# 3. BEN

ON THE EARLY Friday Metra home after lunch with Nguyen, Ben clasped a tallboy between his shoes. He'd drunk half the beer in his initial gulp, eyes closed, right as it was handed to him. Fired. Let go. We're going to let you go. We have to let you go. No, it's not about the Milwaukee deal. No, not Renshaw. Contribute? Sure, it contributed. But this is a more global look, a global decision on your presence in the building. Which we appreciate.

Ben felt relief at having a secret. A secret could be substituted for purpose, filling that void. For years Ben had bet on football and basketball through an Oak Lawn bookie and not told Tara. Minor bets. Money line parlays, puck line shots-in-the-dark, three-team teasers. But the Nguyen-Hank-Tara slippage had ended that. He'd felt real guilt. Not at the gambling, but at being found out. Everything had moved online/offshore anyway. Now the sportsbook was another shiny game on your phone, no secret needed. That reality hit Ben, and he downloaded one of the sportsbook apps as he sat on the train. In five minutes he'd entered his personal information, put in his credit card, and laid twenty-five dollars on a single bet. Simple, Sox at home -1.5 runs. Reason to care about the game later, some stakes for the night.

Ben still wore his tie and had his satchel and jacket tucked between himself and the green-tinted commuter train window. Nguyen and Ben had messaged the rest of the work day after lunch; Nguyen from the office, and Ben from Union Station, the station bar, the train. The small cave of a bar only took cash, no cards and no tabs that could be vacated quickly as trains were leaving the station, and Ben found himself with no paper money as he went to pay. Without ceremony the bartender had gifted Ben the beer—"Can't deny the face you're wearing a drink"—and it was this beer he'd gulped thankfully and now had standing a quarter full at his shoes as the train carried him home. Nguyen and Ben's messages were single-minded in focus. They were attempting to figure out what might be an invention Ben could use to get on the show, despite both agreeing the invention was not the most important component.

desktop coffee reheater

already exists

automated tool that silently opens beer cans

no idea what that means

why are these all beverage related?

what do they say on the show

what

identify a problem

yeah but our problem is how to get on the show

right right

A business was out of the question because a business would take time to prove. Without analyzing whether this feeling was true or not, Ben felt that inventions were put under less scrutiny than businesses; he remembered Crant, his spot remover. When Crant pitched he had not yet had any business, only a proven invention. Ben understood that "invention" and "business" were not mutually exclusive categories, and that to succeed on the show in the traditional sense, the blending of one with the other—no, more than blending, complete overlap between "invention" and "business"—might be necessary. But still, on the show there were people who were more "invention" people and people who were more "business" people. Those weren't the only two categories, they weren't categories at all, but by presenting himself as an "inventor" as opposed to a "businessman," Ben felt he would be graded on a curve.

The train gently rocked side to side. A woman across the aisle was atonally singing the popular chorus of the song playing in her earbuds. And in many cases, Ben thought, the product or service was hurt by having existed and failed for too long. Both Ben and Nguyen agreed the invention was not the make-or-break element to getting on the show, and certainly not the most important piece in getting an investment. As Nguyen had said, the structure was not pure. When it came down to it, the show was humans talking to each other, Ben had pointed out in a message. Nguyen said it wasn't helpful to reduce the problem at hand to "humans talking to each other," because that revealed nothing. Ben disagreed; he believed what it revealed was that they had a chance. Keep them talking and we have a chance. Still, regardless of tactics or understanding, one needed a ticket to play, an invention, a business, something to pitch. But he'd worry about that another day. Instead, on the train Ben began a list in his head:

1.  Confidence
2.  Belief
3.  Ability to convey 1 and 2

Ben thought, CBA. Ben thought, Collective Bargaining Agreement. Ben whispered aloud, "Confidence, Belief, Ability to convey 1 and 2." His whispering sounded like a man attempting to remember the names of relatives before entering their home. He hoped he appeared to possess urgency to the other passengers on the train and peeked to see if anyone was watching him. No. Ben's phone buzzed with a flurry of texts from a thread he was on with friends from college. The thread was titled "Somebodies I Used to Know/dads." One of the dads was going on about some recent penny stock success. Ben muted the thread. The singing woman had her eyes closed, humming through the verses. She appeared to have recently cut her own bangs. She had a flat dot of mustard on her lower cheek. Ben realized she was beautiful and tried to stop looking at her. Ben thought of the phrase *furtive glance*. He tried to focus on his mnemonic device. He finished his beer and set the empty can back between his feet.

Ben and Tara Silas lived in Harks Grove, Illinois, a south-west suburb of Chicago, in a split-level built in 1963. They'd been in the suburbs for three years. The house sat on a street called Prairie Avenue. The trees were old and sprawling and reached across the street to one another. Many of the homes were new, tear-downs; many were not. This suburb was a green one, literally, green and brick-schooled and populated by trains, both commuter and freight. A town divided in its support of Chicago's professional baseball outfits, but Midwestern in a way that was less overt than you might be imagining. Maybe be-cause so many of the townspeople worked in the city and came from the city. Or maybe because the internet is not Midwestern. There was, however, the neighbor boy who had died of an in-curable disease at age seven, and the red ribbons wrapped around every tree on Prairie in his memory. Closer to the boy's house, the ribbons had come down after a couple weeks. But farther on, blocks away, the neighborhood obliviously contin-ued to mourn, the trees wrapped red for months now. Weather made the ribbons a sagging tribute. And even then, they re-mained. Ben was unable to not make a face, a demonstrable frown as he passed these trees. He couldn't understand how these people could pay so little attention and at the same time be so concerned with the appearance of their grief. He did not know if this was Midwestern or human. He did not understand he was one of these people.

Ben walked into the house and said, "Hello!" No one was home. This was not unusual. Neither was Ben taking an early train home on a Friday. But not this early. Tara took the kids all sorts of places in the summer. But not zoos. Tara was anti-zoo. Not because of any animal stance—solely because zoo trips often became raw walking in heat. They could be anywhere—well, not at the zoo, or McDonald's, or the mall, probably at the library or the park, but, reliably, they would be home by four thirty, well before the first of the Friday pick-ups began. Ben knew the schedules of the various children, parents. A thought entered and spoke to him, I know the tendencies of a set of adults, I know who will be late, who will be early, I—

He determined he was not actually identifying a problem that could lead to a business idea, and stopped. He tried to make permanent the realization that knowledge of one's own particular life does not necessarily have use in any business sense. He took a shower and in the shower drank another beer. He said aloud, "Not an alcoholic, but I drink too much beer." This was a problem, a problem he felt would be shared by millions and potentially one that needed solving. He did not know how to make this thought relevant to getting on the show.

Ben got one of Tara's empty notebooks from the bottom drawer of her dresser in their cluttered bedroom upstairs. He was impressed by her note-keeping regarding the kids; he didn't understand it. He knew that her journals were partly fictional. He did not know the full extent of their untruth, though if he had he wouldn't have been bothered. He loved the idea of her inventing, embellishing the lives of these children, and would never out her, would lie for her without a thought. His loyalty was a form of optimism, though he didn't know it.

Ben was in the living room with the lights off, sitting near the broad front window that looked out over the street, rectangular green lawns, all these front yards with real depth, the trees. His hair still wet from the shower. The wonderful empty portion of an afternoon. He wrote across the front of the notebook:

AMERICAN MAGIC

He wrote the two words without thinking and without conscious hope, though hope was surely the root of their being chosen. He proceeded without reflection.

His first entry:

1. Confidence—look into how confidence helps/hurts contestants
2. Belief—related to confidence, but also, how obvious signs of dedication/self-sacrifice can help contestants
3. Ability to display 1 and 2—how are confidence and belief shown to the investors

Below that Ben made a double line and wrote down the word: IDEAS.

He paused for a moment because he had no ideas. Not one that was plausible. He thought, if he didn't have any ideas, could not think about how to approach this problem from the perspective of someone pitching, what if he attempted to think of his dilemma from the perspective of a Big Shot—that is, from the perspective of someone hearing pitches? If he were a Big Shot, who would it be that he would most want to give money to, to invest in? He crossed out IDEAS and wrote IDEALS. He would think of IDEALS in place of having any IDEAS.

Who was the ideal person to invest in? A woman? A beautiful woman who needed money? That seemed like a possible version of right.

No woman came to mind, the woman on the train with the speck of mustard on her face, no, no one. What did he have? TV? That was the subject here. The show that entered his thoughts was the one that was on in their bedroom most nights, or that Tara watched, and Ben tried to block out: *Law & Order: Special Victims Unit*. Tara only ever called it *SVU*. If Tara went upstairs to bed before Ben, she'd put it on, rolling through the seasons on repeat. Ben could only handle so much. Frankly, it was too brutal. But if he was searching for a woman who was confident, embodied self-sacrifice and dedication, and had the ability to have these qualities be perceived and understood by those around her, Ben had seen enough to know that such a woman was Olivia Benson, was Mariska Hargitay.

Ben knew Mariska Hargitay only from *SVU*. He wasn't aware

of any of her roles that preceded her playing Olivia Benson, which, based on the sheer amount of time she'd played the role—over twenty years—seemed undeniably her life's work.

Mariska Hargitay was ideal in a way. Beautiful, but not oppressively so. Older than she looked. Familiar. That is, Ben thought, returning to his original drift, Mariska Hargitay could believably play a woman starting a business later in life as a second career, her kids now grown, pitching on *Big Shot*. Someone you'd want to invest in, someone you'd want to help. Maybe someone who had dumped her life's savings into her new venture. Someone emboldened by self-belief and determination, yet vulnerable; Olivia Benson walked that line.

The ideal was to invest in someone the audience wanted to see gain help. A vulnerable person but not a helpless person. A person with quiet strength. A person millions of viewers would potentially want to support. Ideally, that vulnerability would be present immediately; even as the person pitching made their way down the hallway toward the Big Shots. You'd want the person's speaking voice to cut against that vulnerability, as well as the person's business, current sales numbers, plans for the future—all would hopefully stand in opposition to obvious vulnerability. And yet, this vulnerability would always be present, reminding the viewer, almost existing as a physical reality: I need help. Ben thought of how that overt vulnerability might exist within this woman being played by Mariska Hargitay in his thoughts. He began a list:

*Mariska Hargitay, limping (crutches?)*
*Mariska Hargitay, stuttering (hard to imagine)*
*Mariska Hargitay, nervous (unfocused? rambling?)*
*Mariska Hargitay, attacked*

Ben stopped and looked out at the green world. *Attacked* didn't mean attacked. He meant assaulted, and even there in his thinking he was avoiding the word. He'd meant raped. That was what he'd had in his head after writing down the word *attacked*. A woman wearing all black sprinted by pushing a stroller. Ben said,

"I made it worse," to the empty room. "Much worse," by which he meant what he'd come up with was worse than having nothing at all. He crossed out what he'd written except three words.

~~Mariska Hargitay, limping (crutches?)~~
~~Mariska Hargitay, stuttering (hard to imagine)~~
~~Mariska Hargitay, nervous (unfocused? rambling?)~~
*Mariska Hargitay, attacked*

He did not like what he was doing. He'd imagined Mariska Hargitay in the role of a woman starting a second career, pitching on *Big Shot* wearing all the marks of having been assaulted; he didn't want to use the other word, *raped,* more truthful and wounding. How was this related to his instinct on how to get on a reality television show? He couldn't say. But it had been his instinct. This was the person he'd most want to give money to. This hypothetical contestant. A woman that looked like Mariska Hargitay, was Mariska Hargitay physically, but was not famous, not an actress, and somehow emanated that she'd been attacked. Is that what he meant?

He could not imagine a more ideal—it was sick to use that word in this context—a more ideal person to make a pitch. If it were up to him, he'd give her everything he had. But why would she be pitching to him? What was he thinking? He would be making the pitch; that was the whole point. That was the goal, for him to pitch. And in any case he didn't mean the actual Mariska Hargitay, did he? She didn't need his money, anyone's money. She could buy and sell Ben a thousand times over. More than a thousand times over. Did he mean a copy of Mariska Hargitay, with drastically different life circumstances? And if he did mean a copy of Mariska Hargitay with drastically different life circumstances, why did he mean that? Why would anyone mean that, ever? What the fuck was he doing? Why had this thought stepped into the void that was his thinking? Tara.

The instinct felt real. A beautiful thriving survivor; the idea felt innocuous when stated that way. Who was more powerful, more deserving? Who deserved more to be listened to? To be given a chance.

But Ben was not beautiful, had not been abused, was surviving nothing. Was not a woman, much less a beautiful woman. And he was not the person hearing pitches. He was trying to make a pitch. How would understanding his own predispositions aid him in making a successful pitch? How would thinking about ideal contestants be of use to him? He didn't know, but it was where he'd begun. How often was anyone's ideal conception of anything relevant to their actual life? But, he thought, always relevant to see your mistakes clearly. And this, clearly, was a mistake. Right?

No. It was a thought. He'd done nothing.

He understood that his instincts about an ideal contestant were tied to vulnerability. If the investors did not feel the contestant needed help, why would they help? It seemed obvious. Then he thought, in most cases, *help* was not the relevant word. The relevant word was *profit*. Money. But it was more complicated than that; the decisions were not made that cleanly. As Nguyen had said, this was not an arena devoid of sex and instinct, just the opposite.

Profit was important, maybe most important—but not necessarily monetary profit. These investors were already wealthy, and a large portion of their desire to be on the show was to curate their public personas. These were investments being made on television, manipulated events designed to portray the contestants and investors in specific ways. So, providing "help" was a part of the equation because of the existence of the television audience. The viewing public wanted certain people to gain an investment. Wanted the right people, certain people, to be helped. Vulnerable people.

Ben looked up the definition of vulnerable on his phone: *susceptible to physical or emotional attack or harm.* Right, he thought. And if the person seemed like she had been at one time even more vulnerable and had then placed herself in a less vulnerable, yet still precarious situation, even better—he stopped. That was not the ideal. The ideal was safety. The ideal was beginning your train of thought absent the exploitation of another human.

Why was he making this so theoretical? Tara. He was thinking of Tara. It was her. He didn't know where the Mariska Hargitay thought had come from, not exactly, but he did know what was behind it.

Tara and Ben had met in the crowded lobby of the Vic Theatre at a Gillian Welch and Dave Rawlings show, waiting in line for drinks, Tara behind Ben in line. Ben had turned around looking for the friend he'd come with and saw Tara. He'd turned around again. And again. Again, pretending to look for his friend. Tara had finally met his gaze, and Ben had told Tara she was beautiful instead of introducing himself and Tara had let him guess what she was thinking for the next several days. Then they were together for the last year of college, at different colleges, Tara at SAIC and Ben down in Champaign. When Ben graduated, he'd moved to the city, to Chicago, to find an accounting job and be closer to Tara. They did not move in together, but despite that, Ben could sense the new relative closeness felt strange for her immediately. She told him that the daytime was when she got her work done. By "work" she meant painting. Usually these were medium-sized canvases, flat colors, recognizable urban and suburban relics placed in a welcoming disjunction. A stainless-steel thermos the size of a water tower set down on a high school soccer field. The dark-gray interior of a new sedan seen from the perspective of the driver, with anthropomorphized ants performing Shakespeare in period dress on various tiny stages on the dash, in the cupholders, under the gas pedals, and so on; that painting was called *Shakespearean Ant Festival Toyota Corolla*. Ben would be struck joyful whenever she showed him new work. She told Ben she was accustomed to having her space, and Ben didn't know what to think. He wanted her to paint, though. Ben gave her space. The space grew. They took a break.

Ben had never heard the details of the assault from Tara directly. Not in one straight shot. Over the years, seven years now, what he'd pieced together had given him the following understanding: After closing, Tara and another bartender had been alone in the bar about to lock up. The man had made a pass, tried to pin her against the wall. She'd pushed him away and he had grabbed her by the hair, slammed her head down on a high-top table, thrown her against the wall, and dragged her, still standing, into the kitchen. Ben knew that Tara had never been taken off her feet; this detail was important to her. Ben remembered that Tara was adamant the man had not thrown her to the ground, that he had never been able to knock her off balance. Ben knew that in the kitchen there was a further struggle and Tara had grabbed a steak knife as the man had tried to get behind her, stabbing the man up through his armpit and out his shoulder. That she had begun to crank the knife, as if to attempt to dig flesh out of his body. Ben knew that at this point, with the knife still lodged deep in his shoulder, the man had fled. Ben knew that Tara had sat on the kitchen floor, taking ragged deep breaths, yelling as loud as she could, screaming, not for help, but to release the rest of her instinct to kill the man. That had stayed present with Ben, Tara screaming from the kitchen floor. If for some reason Ben was forced to speak this memory, he would not be able to. He loved Tara. Ben was awed by her; she didn't really know the extent to which he watched her go about her days thinking, goddamn. Ben had no idea how she'd done what she'd done. He did not know what it meant for Tara to be so strong and capable and willing to do whatever it took to live. Ben did not know that most women were like this. That they had to be.

Ben had received the initial pieces of this story days after the assault. Another work day done, he'd found Tara waiting for him in the gray stone lobby of his office building, a red cast on her broken left arm. People were streaming out of the lobby around them. She told him a man at work had attacked

3
1

TRUE FAILURE

her. Tara said, "Didn't work out for him." Ben didn't know what she was talking about in the sense that he knew exactly what she was talking about and couldn't believe what he was hearing. "Couldn't take me. Not a fucking chance." Tara was speaking quietly into his shoulder, tremoring with rage. Ben had held Tara in the lobby, his suit coat and satchel on the ground at his feet, both looking over the other's shoulder as they talked into each other's necks. Ben was crying. Ben told her he wanted to get married. He didn't ask, he said it like that, I want to. And they did the next day at the courthouse on Randolph. Tara with her red cast and Ben in a T-shirt. Their families were elsewhere; other states, other lives. Ben and Tara had each other.

\*\*\*

BEN COULD SEE now how limited his imagination was. Ben thought, maybe the point, the actual relevance of the Mariska Hargitay instinct, was sex. He thought, I'm fucked.

He debated adding to his mnemonic device: Confidence, Belief, Ability to believe in 1 and 2, Sex. CBAS.

If nothing else, he believed he must remember where he had started. He thought, because I am not Mariska Hargitay. And neither is Tara.

Ben wanted to stay within the bounds of what was real.

\*\*\*

THE WOMAN IN black running behind the stroller passed in the opposite direction, on Ben's side of the street. She did not notice him, scheming and dazed in his living room. Ben couldn't imagine anyone else being similarly lost; he hoped not. But who knew? Who knew. Scary breed, humans.

He could not account for the level of guilt he felt. What had he actually done? Arranged the wrong words together in his thoughts, written down the wrong words? His words weren't going to be published in an article, in a book, anywhere. His handwriting was mostly illegible. But he did feel guilty.

He felt guilty because he knew he couldn't explain any of it. He'd thought what he'd thought, written down what he'd written down, and there was no hiding from himself.

Ben stood up in the living room and looked out at the green world and imagined the sounds he would hear if instead he were standing on the lawn. He wondered if the woman in black would have noticed him if he had been out front. Could one inconspicuously stand in one's own front lawn, doing nothing other than attempting to understand how sex and bias function in gaining an advantage on reality TV? Maybe if he'd also been staring up at the trees. People do not suspect much of the man looking up at tree branches. His concerns seem ineffectually aimed. The AC whooshed on in the living room. Ben tried to feel the grass between his feet, hear cars passing at thirty miles an hour, ignore the grip of the enveloping heat, be unbothered by the insects locked into their frenetic clicking language, the birds swooping and sitting. His mind was weak. He knew that. Of course he'd been fired. He'd been distant and drifting, dead in the office. Made the same soft, lazy mistakes over and over and over. Successes there brought him no joy, didn't even register, and the failures did not sting. Punch the clock. He'd been fired and there was no mystery.

Undeniable public success on his own terms: the only situation he could imagine that could make him happy, that could allow him to begin to change his life.

The problem, as with everything, was that there was no middle, no balance. Either continue to endure your day job quietly and perform to a level that will result in not losing that job, or attempt to get on a nationally televised reality show that is giving away millions of dollars. A middle way did not occur to Ben.

What would Tara think if she saw what he'd written? He didn't know. He believed she'd understand. He believed she'd see he was trying. But trying to do what? Get on the show.

Of course, she'd only have partial information. She did not know he'd been fired. Not yet.

In the living room, dazed, he knew it was a distinct possibility that his instinct held no meaning; and if that was the case, he'd have to find another place to start. But he couldn't start over, could he? He couldn't really run from how stupid his starting point was; in creating distance from where he'd started, he'd constantly be reminded of what he was separating himself from. He could only try to see his start, and acknowledge how limited his control over his thoughts was, and attempt to do better.

He knew this all to be reductive thinking. The kind of thinking that so often succeeded on TV, in this country, always. That might be what he needed to get on the show. He wasn't sure yet. He wanted quantifiable proof that the show was as fucked as his instincts told him it was. He was willing to be wrong. Wanted to be wrong. That's not true, he didn't want to be wrong. He wanted to find that the show was as fucked as his thinking was, which might mean his chances for success were improved. He walked into the kitchen and opened drawers until he found a highlighter. He wanted to remember the hole he was starting in. He highlighted: *Mariska Hargitay, attacked.*

For most people that would be more than enough: the regrettable thought recorded and considered. That would be the end of it. But Ben was not most people, despite appearances. And more importantly, neither was Tara.

# 4. TARA

"I AGREE WITH you. If any of this matters, it's on the casting side," Tara said as they both lay in bed, lights on. A Sunday night two weeks removed from Ben initially telling Tara he wanted to get on the show; a conversation she had walked away from, out of the house and into the yard with her beer to watch the sky pink and gray into darkness, because she'd thought Ben was joking. That this was a conversation she could reasonably abandon to catch the last of the day. She'd realized Ben was serious as he followed her outside. He stood barefoot in the grass and asked if she wanted to get on the show. Tara hadn't known how to respond. Last burning pink light behind him, Ben had smiled at Tara in a way she found charming: completely undeterred. He smiled at her like that now, in bed, and said, "Is there still ice cream?"

Tara stood within the narrow hall of light created by the open freezer, not aware of its labored thrumming. Ben was on his knees digging through bags of frozen mixed vegetables, potstickers, boxes of samosas. He announced, "Mint chip, decent amount, and a heel of chocolate walnut fudge, and your unfortunate popsicles."

"Unfortunate popsicle," she said, watching Ben palpate the ice cream container containing the chocolate so its contents were now a part of the bulk of mint chip.

Their bedside lamps shot huge symmetrical hourglass shadows up to the ceiling. Tara had her green popsicle, Ben a large spoon and objectively too much ice cream. Nothing stylish about their bedroom; too white and unadorned. Tara had hung one small Diebenkorn print and Ben a picture of Tony Eason sitting at a bar in Champaign. The room was crowded with squarish stacks all slightly too tall: clean laundry, unread and reread books, pillows, pristine magazines, folded blankets. No dog and no kid, so stacks like these could stand undisturbed for months. A home renovation show was running, closed captioning down below and the sound off. Tara went on, "Casting assistants—I mean, I don't know this for a fact, but if that many people have that title for single episodes, one, two, it must be a catchall. A way for people to get paid who aren't long-term employees. Not decision-makers."

Tara had seen enough episodes to know what the initial questions would be for a business the size of her day care. How would you scale it? Since you are not able to be in multiple places at once, and you are the business, how would you train franchisees? What about your business is proprietary? Is your pricing too low?

Ben had asked again in the grass, Tara laughing, why she couldn't go on the show. She hadn't even responded. The reason she couldn't go on the show was that she thought the show was ridiculous. They'd watched the show together, Tara half paying attention, but this was something else entirely. Watching the show while looking at her phone in bed versus taking the real business she'd created in the real world into this fake arena to ask for an investment? No. Never. She hated all the fawning over the Big Shots; the endless parade of small, stupid ideas. But she couldn't tell any of this to Ben, who had been scribbling in a notebook for two weeks, having Nguyen come over the past two Saturdays to watch the British and American versions of *Big Shot* in the basement, both taking notes. Nguyen could barely look at her. As if he were ashamed by his enabling of Ben. The two men would sit on the carpet in front of the couch, their notebooks and laptops spread out on the floor. Tara couldn't even begin to guess what it was they were writing down. She felt particularly uncomfortable being in the same room with Nguyen as he watched TV, which he always did with his mouth open. It seemed to reveal him as a former latchkey kid. As if his particular childhood had primed him for this dumb pursuit—all that TV. This was more Nguyen exposure than she was used to; he seemed eager to be with Ben, to encourage him. It was baffling to Tara because Ben had nothing to pitch. He had no idea, no business. He'd said as much when he told her he wanted to get on the show.

Out in the yard, sun gone, Tara had eventually asked what he was going to pitch, the obvious question, and Ben had responded by saying, "I'm less concerned with what I'm going to pitch than with how it is I'm going to get on the show." At that point Ben had turned his attention to the blank night sky. Tara had allowed Ben's response to go unremarked upon in hopes he'd hear what was potentially problematic within his answer: you must have something to pitch to get on the show.

She was unclear on what Ben considered to be the true hurdles in his path at this juncture. She wasn't willing to do the work for him, especially when it would not ultimately matter. He would not succeed.

Ben's fixation for the past few days had been the credits for the American version of the show. He'd talk to Tara about his theories at night in bed. He'd told Tara he was attempting to determine who on the production staff had the longest tenure. Tara told Ben he needed to find who had risen through the ranks of the show's behind-the-scenes hierarchy, regardless of tenure. Ben told her there were hundreds of people credited for a single episode, or for a handful of episodes, as a "production assistant." But under that same title, "production assistant," were around a dozen names that were credited online for working on, ballpark, eighty to ninety episodes. Of the roughly dozen people in this category, many were later credited as stage managers, head stage managers, staging supervisors. Tara's thought was that if finding out who was an actual decision-maker on the production staff this early in the process actually did matter, they needed people who had risen, recently, and not people who had started at the top; those were the people Ben would need on his side. She felt that regardless of where Ben landed with what it was he'd be pitching, he needed someone who had at one time known far less than they knew now and was conscious of that progression. Such a person might be sympathetic to Ben's exact capacity for ignorance.

Tara rested Ben's open notebook on her stomach. "You don't have a business, an idea, nothing."

Ben had his arm over his eyes. Tara knew he was resisting creating a pitch because he was anxious. Stalling. Once he committed to what it was he would pitch, he was that much closer to being rejected and eliminated from the process—back to real life. The most effective way for Ben to live in that hopeful phase was to do nothing, or, as he was doing now, very nearly nothing.

From cross-referencing recent credits against IMDB information, there were five names Ben had isolated as having ascended through the ranks of *Big Shot*'s casting department and that were still currently working on the show. Ben had the five names he'd arrived at in his notebook, and Tara began reading the names aloud. She was interested to see what else it was Ben had written down during his bull sessions with Nguyen. He kept his arm over his eyes, and Tara looked through the notebook. On the TV two men were standing in the empty frame of a house, pretending to cry. The closed captioning read [*sobbing noises continuous*]. Tara looked again at the names. Ben had printed out small photographs of the people he was able to find pictures of and Scotch-taped them next to their names in the notebook.

*Beatriz Chew*

*Andrew Wagner*

*Pipes Nusbaum*

*Marcy Lon*

*Jabaree West*

For Beatriz Chew, Marcy Lon, and Jabaree West, Ben had been able to locate social media profiles and worked from there, despite all but Ms. West's being private. He studied profile photographs. For Pipes and Mr. Wagner, no luck. The only information on Pipes was a linked personal IMDB page Ben was able to access from the main *Big Shot* page. Same for Andrew Wagner. And no photographs. General searches on either were fruitless; *Pipes* was not a real name and *Andrew Wagner* was too real, a name shared with thousands of people.

Seeing the faces of the people who would potentially be making the decision on Ben was helpful; Tara was surprised. There was power somehow in recognizing these were regular people doing a job. Maybe a job they didn't even want. They weren't wealthy. They had bad haircuts, forced smiles, insecurities. Had married wrong. They were hiding. Looking elsewhere for fulfillment. Looking for other work. Tara held onto the notebook, flipping backward and scanning the pages of what Ben had written, ramblings, and Ben kept his arm over his eyes and continued speaking to her.

"Should I call the production office and ask for these people by name? Try to get some sense of who they are? Use an alias." Tara ignored this question.

But even from the small photographs available of the five who had risen through casting, Tara had to admit, there seemed to be obvious leaders and decision-makers. There did actually seem to be information to take in from these pictures. Beatriz Chew was too retiring in her photograph to be someone who was making calls that held any weight. She smiled with her mouth closed and had glasses that hid her face entirely. Her photograph was poorly cropped from a larger group shot. She stood in the back row of those gathered, and this configuration was not height related. She reminded Tara of an adolescent cartoon bear. No one professionally credited as "Pipes" was making decisions. A nickname like that, used professionally, revealed you to be a mascot. A lovable mascot. It was either Andrew Wagner, Marcy Lon, or Jabaree West that would be the gatekeeper Ben would have to get past. Maybe all three. Some combination. Ben hadn't found a picture of Andrew Wagner. Marcy looked tall and deadpan, especially for a professional photograph. Jabaree looked like she would have no problem correcting you in the pronunciation of her name, thank goodness.

Tara considered these strangers' faces. Their bedroom was loud but indistinctly. White noise machines were running on either side of the bed, and their ceiling fan had a consistent rolling wobble. Ben still had his arm over his eyes, and Tara had his notebook open and then tented again on her stomach over the covers. The men who had been previously crying on TV were now upset about the color of a house they had seen for the first time ten seconds earlier. Ben mumbled something in his sleep Tara couldn't make out. She considered punching him in his softening belly. Hitting him, at least she'd know he was conscious of the moment at hand. She let the thought pass.

Tara walked around to Ben's side and turned off the lamp on his bedside table. Distracted by the TV, she knocked over an ankle-high mound of folded bath towels soundlessly. She did not restack the towels. She stood for a second watching rain-soaked contractors stepping onto a newly poured concrete slab somewhere in the American South. The closed captioning read [*traffic noise from street*]. Tara got back under the covers, clicked her lamp down to its lowest setting, turned off the TV, and began looking more closely at the notebook.

She began reading the pages of Ben's rushed half-cursive half-blocky lowercase writing. His printing was difficult to read completely independent from its content. Within the sentences themselves there was lots of garbled, repetitive talk about confidence and belief. Her eyes went to a highlighted phrase and stayed there: *Mariska Hargitay, attacked.*

Tara said, "What?"

Her question did not wake Ben. She watched him to see if he was faking, like maybe he'd been waiting for her to find those words and was pretending to sleep, wanting to register her re-action. That didn't make sense. How could those words be the result of anything? But, no. He was actually asleep. There was no prank. She didn't actually know what she meant by "prank." She didn't know what he meant by "attacked" either. Whatever he'd meant, Tara thought rape. Mariska attacked, to Tara, meant Olivia Benson, and in that case we're talking *SVU* and rape. She watched Ben for a moment longer, came to no understanding, and kept reading.

# 5. MARCY

Marcy Lon was in her boss's office as rarely as possible. She was there now in an all-orange outfit, "construction orange," she had anticipated hearing her boss say as she entered, but thankfully the room was empty. Bright tangerine was more accurate, earthier. She had planned on telling him when she'd be taking a vacation, which for her was the equivalent of requesting time off. His office, in a tucked-away corner of the studio lot, had preserved the accoutrements of a particularly garish vision of masculine idealism. Midday bourbon and wood grain; desperate, grim silences; and profound one-note simplemindedness. She wrote the following on a legal pad resting blankly on his desk:

"I'll be on vacation from the last week of August through Labor Day. I'm leaving LA. Heading up into Canada. Nova Scotia. The cabin sits on a cliff overlooking the ocean."

Up into Canada was misleading; it suggested Vancouver. The line she gave her boss was the same she spoke at the rest of her coworkers. Even after including the follow-up coastal cabin information, Marcy believed she could read in her coworkers' faces a misunderstanding that where she was going was due north, to Vancouver. She believed her coworkers lacked the ability to imagine the reality of her Canadian vacation. Her coworkers did not know the country's variance. They knew Vancouver, they knew Toronto. They knew the Maple Leafs, the blue and white, they may have heard of bagged milk, ketchup chips. Of course, none of them had been there. There was no need. Americans did not and will not take in Canadian data. Much less Californians. Marcy felt, quickly, if her coworkers' comprehension and ability to envision her physical surroundings during her vacation was a concern of hers, and it wasn't, she would have said: I'll be off the coast of Maine. Her chief concern in articulating the vacation to her coworkers was to use the word *Canada*. She wanted to be clear that she was traveling to another country. Another country increased psychic distance. And she wanted, most of all, to increase psychic distance. In place of increasing actual distance, this was necessary.

She had planned on telling her boss as she left his office that next to the cabin there was a wheat field that grew right to the edge of a cliff. For some reason, this detail, which Marcy had invented, was the one she often repeated to the few coworkers who chose to stay present in the conversation she had caught them in. These words were spoken to listening faces she outranked, nodding chins and concerned mouths, but also these words had been addressed generally toward the refrigerator in the smaller break room, the far end of the mirror in the women's restroom, the dazed earlycomers hiding on their phones before a meeting: "There's a field, tall brushy wheat, right next to the cabin. All the pictures I've seen, it's full sun and this field. And it's not safe, but it's true, this field, this wheat, grows right to the edge of the cliff. There's no fence. You're standing in the field looking toward the ocean, you see only these spikes of wheat swaying, waving, and then blue." She'd spent four seconds looking at an exploded-view image on her phone separating wheat into its respective parts to arrive at the word *spike*. If she felt Canada had registered but then saw doubt on a coworker's face at the mention of Nova Scotia, she'd reassure the person, say, "No, you know, you know. New Brunswick, Prince Edward Island. You know. East coast." The other invented detail she'd add about her trip was that she would not be bringing her phone. She'd repeat and combine this lie with Canada in a line she gave everyone who made it this far: "Foreign country without a phone." Some laughed at "foreign," but most did not. If given the chance, she said too loudly that the point of the trip was to unplug, forget her work, forget the networks and reminders and messages and notifications and further reminders that made up her days in Los Angeles, and take some time to relax. To read, and sometimes she'd mention books she planned on reading, or rather, authors, because she planned on doing so much reading that it was more efficient for her in conversation to mention authors. She'd say, "Annie Dillard, Duras, Malcolm Lowry." When she mentioned the reading to coworkers, the authors, no one asked any follow-up questions or had any problem in appearing to be unfamiliar. Marcy didn't know if this was because no one read anymore, or because no one in her office, relatively speaking, had ever read. She herself was not a big reader, and had taken the three authors she mentioned from an interview with a filmmaker whose name she'd forgotten; the director had listed favorites, probably also stolen. Marcy would say, "I don't care what anyone thinks. I'm heading up there and I'm not bringing a phone." This statement was untrue in at least three ways. One, Marcy would not be leaving the country. She would not be traveling to Nova Scotia. She was headed to a rental in Venice, meaning she wasn't even leaving Los Angeles. Two, she would be bringing a phone. Maybe two phones. Three, she cared very much what people thought, most especially her coworkers, the people whom she had given the opportunity to believe she was the person she claimed to be, the kind of person who took solo vacations to Nova Scotia to read. But she was not. No one was. Vacations taken solely to read are not real.

On her way out of her boss's office, she told the boss's secretary, a delicate froggy-looking boy with wet eyes, that she had left a note for her boss. The boy had let her walk into the empty office, had pretended to not even notice her, maybe out of fear or a general lack of understanding. He seemed unsure what he was allowed to say. What restrictions he was able to enforce. The boy said, "I'll type it into an email and send it to him today. Nice to see you again." Marcy said, "We haven't met," though

4
3

TRUE FAILURE

they had maybe four times and she knew it, and made her way out into the hall. The offices in this part of the studio lot felt particularly vacated today. Friday, unremarkable.

Marcy wanted to be the kind of person capable of fulfilling the lies she laid out so meticulously, making these lies the events of her actual life, but she was not.

Enduring a conversation with her boss was the only work Marcy had planned on doing, and she had managed to avoid even that. She took the stairs down one flight to the fourth floor, passing the open-cubicled middle section of Big Shot Productions, passing Caryn, Charlie, Michael, Roberto, none of whom would have guessed she knew their name, and stuck her head into her own office until her dog, Jet, noticed her. He rose yawning from his blue bed. A standard black poodle with a workmanlike haircut. The dog followed two steps behind Marcy, unleashed. In the fourth-floor break room she filled a clear plastic cup with ice and carried it with her as she began making her way out of the studio offices into the shining day, Jet trailing. They walked the back lot. Narrow blacktop alleys led between hangar-like studio buildings as they headed toward the enormous pale-pink concrete parking structure, Marcy loosely holding her cup of melting ice. She did not bring work home, as a rule. Not in a way that was obvious.

There was no set of people whose opinions Marcy cared about more than her coworkers. She knew this in a way that made her feel like a small animal in her stomach was attempting to scrabble its way out of her chest. Mistakes had been made to arrive at this place; mistakes, yes, but not concessions. She did not concede. She won. And she lied. Layers upon layers that formed whole systems of untruth. The deepest and most damning structures she'd fabricated and continued to maintain were wholly internal. Her spoken lies could never rival those repeating in her head, the repetitions reminding her of the minor additions she'd have to voice for her invented personhood to continue. Remind them: I read. Remind them: I am different away from work than I am at work. Remind them: I am sharper and more focused and more isolated. Remind them: I am able to leave the country, willing to leave the country for quiet, for focus, for study. For time with books. Remind them: I am different than they are. Remind them: I can act however I want in this office. She enjoyed much of her job, it should be said, but because of deceits small, simple, and also labyrinthine and total, she could not relax into the standing she'd earned. The performance was all-consuming and as a result no longer a performance in the minor, sheddable sense, but instead had become a part of the ongoing series of decisions that formed her. As if there were an alternative.

No relaxing, but Marcy could speak too loudly about a vacation, real or not, to people or not, refrigerators, bathroom mirrors, because of what she had achieved in this office. Fiercely respected. So much so that her dog was allowed. Only her dog was allowed. Mostly Jet slept splayed on his bright-blue dog bed in Marcy's office. For a dog, he was private and sentinel-like. He was never on a leash. In addition to dog privileges, Marcy was granted two interns; the most experienced one, Callie, had been centrally occupied in recent weeks by a side project Marcy had given her.

For interns and newer employees especially unfamiliar with Marcy's rhythms and only versed in the bullet points of her success and the dark dog, she was pre-deified a lesser goddess. For these underlings, the route Marcy had taken to her current standing was hidden. A path that had been swept away, covered with recently felled and still full branches and now years of springs, winters, and rain. She was always hiding. It was not initially obvious to these gofers, but the person still employed in the office who most resembled the type that had enabled Marcy to rise was now Marcy herself. She was given time, tolerance, office animal privileges, benefit of the doubt, because she was proven in a specific and quantifiable way. Marcy was needed. She gave the show its echo.

Marcy always left her car on the top level of the studio's parking structure. She opened the glove box, which was full of tiny green airplane bottles of Tanqueray. Jet pretended not to notice. Marcy opened two bottles and poured them into her cup of half-melted ice. She took a drink and reclined her seat all the way back, letting the AC hit her. Jet yawned.

She was able to identify the contestants viewers remembered. In focus groups over and over, this was borne out. There were several women and men in the office with similar gifts, with a good eye, the right eye—it was part of the job, its essential quality, maybe. But Marcy was unrivaled. She understood when niche tipped over into obscurity. She knew when persistence began reading as shrill. She understood the relationship between posture and likability. She thought about speed of speech, walk, gesture; held private beliefs about eyebrows, shoes, modesty, sideburns, volume, squinting. Online, her contestants—she thought of them as her own—her contestants were the ones people posted pictures of. Without fail. Poorly cropped pictures of their own TVs shared to affirm something about themselves: that they too had a chance, maybe. Her contestants were the ones viewers wanted to align themselves with. The human contestants. She had used this language early in her time with the show, it was language she had found on her own, that she'd invented, and it had infiltrated to the highest and lowest levels of the operation. We need a human contestant. We need a human. Is this the human. Is this the human? Marcy, find us the human.

She should have grabbed two cups of ice. She could have made Jet a drink. She needed to start keeping a bowl for him in the trunk. Still parked, Marcy dialed the general studio number and asked the right questions to be connected with the froggy assistant—"It is your job to make me aware that you are alive in a way I should take notice of." She hung up.

Luck was part of it. The color of her skin, white white, tall, with a name people remembered. Marcy Lon. Other privilege too. She repeatedly got the opportunity to make the decisions that she would later be praised for and that would allow her to make similar decisions in the future. The majority of the show's other contestants were polished, prepared. Not difficult to observe a homogenous group and then point at some others. Her position was less complicated and less worthy of praise and awed speculation than, say, the camera operator, in her opinion. This was also a private opinion. She did not edit the program; only infrequent editorial notes on her contestants after rough cuts. *More closeups, need her eyes more visible. Eyelashes, show them.* She was occasionally on set for shooting. The work she was paid for was not what she viewed as her actual job. Her actual job, Marcy believed, was to direct her coworkers' thinking regarding who she was at any given time. Doing her actual job enabled her to do what it was that she was paid for. She did not believe she possessed any exceptional skill. She believed management to be taxonomy. The rest could be inferred. Management, of course, was not a real job. Casting was, but she had loved this work in a way that did not allow her to apply the ugly word: *job.*

The thoughts she was attempting to prevent her coworkers from having were, at present, mainly related to the people Marcy had come from, or, as she phrased it to herself, the people she had fled.

Marcy's phone chimed an email alert. Callie had sent another update on her project, the murder that Callie had been investigating, or rather: the murderer.

A man had been killed on the front lawn of Marcy's childhood home nearly thirty years earlier, and Marcy was worried the killer, a man named Walt Hillis, might try to drum up some attention around the anniversary of his crime. He was in prison for life, but the impending anniversary made all this urgent for Marcy. For the past thirty years she'd been afraid of acts Walt Hillis had not carried out. The murder he'd actually committed rarely occurred to her; it was the possibility of other violence that had stalked Marcy. Nothing had yet come to pass. Hillis had sat in prison and watched baseball, is what her intern had told her at the very beginning of her investigation into the man. The intern, Callie, had been tasked by Marcy with determining the killer's current state of mind, mental acuity, daily routine, and interest in causing further death, particularly as it related to Marcy. Callie had told Marcy she'd gotten the baseball detail over the phone from a former guard at San Quentin she'd been able to track down via a social media group for retired San Quentin staff. Marcy wanted more, though—she needed Callie to learn everything. Marcy was allowing Callie to be out of office on Thursdays and Fridays indefinitely, for the sole purpose of conducting this project. There was little oversight as to the goings-on of her interns by Marcy, much less her supervisors. If they did as she asked, she had no questions.

"The people Marcy had come from" makes it sound like her family was large, shambly, infirm, and they were not. No red-rimmed uncle with long fingers. No fat fuck crazy addict aunt. No NASCAR, no rape, no meth, no toothless mouths, no beatings. One mom, one dad, one sullen, pudgy older brother. The brother, a veterinary assistant, believed his unhappiness was caused by others, and by others, he meant his wife. Marcy had called her brother on his thirty-ninth birthday, roughly two years prior to the prospective false Canadian vacation. He'd answered, drunk, seemingly already midconversation, "Found the perfect description of Charlene today. In my field guide. Perfect write-up to the point I'm suspicious. Here it is: 'a songbird with a strong, sharply hooked bill, often impaling its prey of small birds, lizards, and insects on thorns.'" He'd read Marcy the definition of a common shrike. That was the last time she'd spoken to him. To make your wife a bird so readily was terrifying. And yet she was not running from her sunk brother.

"The people Marcy had come from" had nothing to do with how this one mom and one dad conducted themselves, spoke, thought, or interacted with each other in the present, or the past, really—if you understand the past not as most readily available memories, but as a totality, a fixed ocean that you can't grasp whole or in part, unmappable, that can only be conjured through absolute lies and ridiculous failing gestures. But, in a way that was real and not solely in Marcy's thinking, her one mom and one dad were infamous. Loving and private people who lived cocoon-like in their one-story in San Jose. A white house with brown shutters and richly rounded green shrubbery. White, brown, and waxy green—those three colors together made Marcy sick.

There would be no foreign vacation, but there was also no one waiting for her, no boyfriend, husband, girlfriend, wife, or kids—a dog, yes, but she felt sure Jet knew her patterns and trusted them. In her mind, having no one waiting was a gift. She could do as she pleased always, without being checked. And she did.

Marcy lived in flat pinks, crumbly rusty reds, shiny sky blues, black-blues, oranges. Throwaway beauty colors worn with the knowledge and flash of impermanence. Colors that made up her rugs, towels, few plates, two mugs, all silly bright or full colored in ways that allowed no blending, no mistaking. And Jesus that sounds like painful curation for a daily life, but the truth is she simply dismissed anything that was wrong and let very little in the house or on her body. Impeccable vicious instincts she trusted to such a degree that alternatives rarely occurred to her. The older version of this is not the woman with art director/ museum trustee glasses. The older version of this is a woman who saves herself for necessary moments. No small talk but warm passage through days regardless. Slowly walking through stores. Slowly making dinner. Uncoupled in a city new to her. A retirement city. Distant but not drifting. Reachable for some. It's important to say: a lying past doesn't necessarily lead to a contrived, boxed-in talky life. Dazed, routine grace is possible.

By the time she felt ready to leave she'd had five of the airplane bottles, which for her meant two car drinks, or one real drink; she'd had one drink. She patted Jet, half asleep in the passenger seat, and asked, "Do you care if I put on music?"

Marcy began driving down the ramps of the winding parking structure. The music reminded her of adolescence, Cyndi Lauper—the radio was playing that perfect first record in its entirety, and the music made her feel that that which mattered was ahead of her and undecided. She would be as she wanted to be. She would.

# 6. CALLIE

CALLIE WAS PARKED in a Target parking lot in Burbank, the sunshade still up on her windshield, listening to a podcast called *Murder Girls*. The parking lot was littered with stumpy palm trees, at her back the low Verdugo Mountains. Target, the state of California where she never felt at ease, the mountains like bunched hills behind her, and the space-shuttling of her sedan by keeping the sunshade up—all those together brought to Callie's mind the end of the world. That, and the deep con she was running on her employer. She was not doing anything she'd promised to do in pursuit of information about the man who'd murdered another man on the lawn of her boss's childhood home. Hillis. The event was so chancy, so made-up sounding, that Callie fed into that notion and embellished the man further, his specific interests, language, traits.

Callie knew that even without seeking murder, a specific killing or in general its actors, aftermath, tools, distortions, believers, all were bombarding her. It is our TV, our politicians, our news, the fear behind our decisions—her decisions. Callie was seeking to learn of murder, just not about the one Hillis had committed. She could not care less about Hillis, Marcy, any of these people.

Callie took a melted granola bar from her glove box, same as she'd eaten as a nine-year-old in Minnesota, and focused back in on her podcast: "Speck is seen in the video that this anonymous attorney sent to Bill Kurtis, with literally a mound of cocaine, fearless. Absolutely no fear of getting caught."

"Stateville," the other host spoke, "Stateville had Gacy. Chicago Rippers. We need to talk about them. Jesus, those ones are brutal. Potentially too much—" Callie rewound the episode in fifteen-second increments by stabbing her phone with her middle finger. She ate the granola bar in three bites and ground the melted chocolate from her fingers into the palm of her opposite hand. She'd listened to some of the episode on the drive over from her apartment and was going to sit with the AC running for another half hour finishing. Callie could have walked from her apartment to the Target in nine minutes. She'd never even considered doing so. Instead she'd gotten a McDonald's drive-through Diet Coke and then parked in the Target lot. This was the routine for Thursdays since her out-of-office assignment had begun.

The episode was over, and she called her mom on speaker. Her mom lived in the Twin Cities, a widow, and their routine was to rehash details of the episodes together. Her mom listened to the new *Murder Girls* episodes the night they were released, Wednesdays, and took notes for their calls.

"You hear about Speck, I mean, he's a name. I've never dug in, though."

"You do hear about him."

"And the drugs in prison. At that quantity. What's to make of that?"

If someone had seen Callie sitting in her car, they might have thought she looked like a grown Girl Scout; if they'd heard her speak, that would not be the case. Her hair was parted down the middle, a shineless blond. When she spoke, you could only focus on her voice being a creation. A kind of artificially flat, unimpressed tonality that was pulled from some movie performance that unfortunately had affected the course of her character permanently. This self-styled voicework paired with her being from the real Midwest made her a tough one for coworkers to have a shorthand for, mentally. Here she was, the favored intern, and who the fuck was she?

Visiting a prisoner on death row was more difficult than Marcy had initially understood, or was interested in knowing, and Callie used that to her benefit. To visit a male prisoner on death row in the state of California meant you were going to San Quentin, but first you had to be invited via California Department of Corrections and Rehabilitation Form 106. The form needed to be sent by the prisoner that you wished to visit and contain their signature, meaning that, pending approval, they would like to add you to their visiting list. And death row meant an extra layer of vetting and observation. The dense bureaucratic reality was complicated and stringent enough that Callie's not even attempting to participate within its bounds was fully tolerated by Marcy. There were so many impediments to visitation and actual contact that what Callie was really tasked with, though Marcy did not know it, was to curate ancillary information regarding Walt Hillis as he was now, living on death row. For Callie, this meant that she could take a throwaway detail in an article on Hillis from around the time of his sentencing and extrapolate outward, forming his current reality as it was now, something completely of her own creation. There was no check on Callie's work, no way for Marcy to know what was real and what wasn't beyond simply asking for sources, which Callie knew Marcy would absolutely never do. Marcy wanted to believe.

The work that Callie was doing on Hillis took the form of emails. She'd send Marcy weekly emails with her findings.

Callie was very well versed in true crime speak, had kept three-ring binders on various serial killers as a teenager, made printouts of GeoCities websites, watched *Law & Order* growing up with Mom, experienced a long Zodiac phase, and when murder podcasts came to the fore, settled into deep fandom for *Murder Girls,* which in turn she got her mom hooked on. It was their version of articulating love for each other by talking about the hometown team; they chose killers instead of the Twins.

When occasionally Marcy would close the office door and ask for some kind of in-person update on where Callie was with Hillis, Callie was able to provide historical precedent citing other California killers, buoyed by the tangle of bureaucracy she alleged to be caught in regarding the state's Department of Corrections. The truth was that she was not actually tangled because she was not participating in the system; she was making it all up.

Callie said good-bye to her mom, still in the Target lot; Callie would talk to her again in a few hours, surely. She mentally transitioned into wanting to obtain the best bagged salad she could purchase inside the Target as determined by an online list, the best frozen turkey burger, the highest-thread-count sheets under sixty-five dollars. She'd linger in the dollar section by the front, walk the shampoo/deodorant/soap aisle, occasionally making notes on her phone of details to include in her email to Marcy, her ongoing invented portrait of Hillis.

- his interests didn't change—separate from the criminal aspects of his thinking, he's maintained the same enthusiasms throughout his life: the San Francisco Giants, tidiness—

Callie sometimes sent bullet points, but even more often she'd format the emails into a stranger and more complex presentation. Anything to keep Marcy's attention moving around the bright fake points of light she was providing her and not able to see the blank reality: none of this was real. Hillis was a disgusting racist murderer. He was known for refusing showers; but also he was not *known*. He was nobody. There was no collection of peculiarities that Callie could send over that would lead to Marcy's safety; she'd always been safe, nothing had changed.

# 7. BEN

BEN WAS LEANING against the kitchen sink listening to the music playing on Tara's phone—a familiar playlist. His own phone was going off in his pocket; one of the wives of the guys in his group text of college friends had had a baby. Ben held up the screen to Tara, who took the phone and double-tapped the five pictures Ben's friend had sent, a heart for each. Tara was at the table with her notebooks. It was drizzling outside, Monday evening in Harks, the kitchen cold, both drinking canned beer in Koozies. Billy was playing upstairs, though you'd never know it from the scene in the kitchen.

Ben was zoning out thinking about his inane clandestine routine. Baseball entered his thoughts, meaning gambling on baseball. He had lost nine consecutive bets, singles, nope, and none of the parlays had hit, not one, after hitting on his initial return to betting. Yet, again, he had action. D. J. LeMahieu over 1.5 hits at +300, Rockies on the road in LA +2 runs at -200, Sox home money line against the Twins at -250. $25 down would pay $185 if it hit. He'd constructed his parlay with a game in three different time zones, so with any luck, Ben would have something to distract him for the course of the entire night.

He'd been pretending to go to work for the past two weeks as if he hadn't been fired. He'd worn the same gray suit he would have if he'd been employed, carried the same brown leather satchel, rushed to the train with the same empty purpose. He'd sit with his satchel on the Metra, surrounded by the same faces and routines and public decisions he'd witnessed as a man with a job. Weary fuckers with haircuts. Ben probably appeared the same. He'd listen to the same music in his headphones: Lucinda Williams, Doug Paisley, Aimee Mann, among others he had in long rotation. Maybe all of them had lost their jobs, and in spite of this continued with their commutes, grooming, clothing choices. When he'd get into the city, he'd make his way up to street level out of Union Station, then east toward the lake, before heading south to the Harold Washington Library, not far from his old building downtown. This had become the new routine. Once inside the library, he'd find a nook and continue watching every episode of *Law & Order: Special Victims Unit* on his laptop. Initially, this had been a countermeasure for his false start, his *Mariska Hargitay attacked* beginning. But what the routine had become was harder to determine.

Ben's nook today had the following message carved deeply into the desktop: GET FUCKED. He recognized the affirmation. Yes, he thought, get fucked. There was often a man who wore navy-blue coveralls in one of the nooks and resembled Lightnin' Hopkins, and Ben understood that proximity to this man represented a kind of luck. Today, the man was nowhere to be found. Instead there were librarians avoiding eye contact, and other hunched lunatics, like Ben. For the past weeks he'd been watching every episode of *SVU* in chronological order. Everything was online. If he felt he had missed something, he'd rewatch. Even when he'd move on to the next episode, he was sure he'd missed something. Ben was fixated on the first episode of the series and would return to it as he made slow progress. Some of his season 1, episode 1 notes:

- *Benson and Stabler meet for first time at crime scene in opening seconds in downpour. Crime scene is cab, cabbie stabbed to death dick cut off.*
- *Benson in Giants hat, Stabler in Jets hat. Can barely tell because hats are soaked w/ rain.*

- *"Are you obsessed with sex, detective?"*
- *"This is an all-volunteer unit, isn't that correct?"*
- *"Yes, it is."*
- *"Could you tell the court why you volunteered?"*
- *Multiple instances of suspicion about why someone would be on the sex crimes unit at all, as if acknowledging existence of such crimes is a problem in and of itself.*
- *Diner waitress, great*
- *Acknowledgment of reality is often problem*

Ben had a checklist he was working through, copied into his notebook, crossing out as he went along.

- *Law & Order: Special Victims Unit* (TV Series) (1999)
  - ~~"Payback" (1999) ... Olivia Benson~~
  - ~~"A Single Life" (1999) ... Olivia Benson~~
  - ~~"... Or Just Look Like One" (1999) ... Olivia Benson~~
  - ~~"Hysteria" (1999) ... Olivia Benson~~
  - ~~"Wanderlust" (1999) ... Olivia Benson~~

The act of watching every episode of *SVU* repeatedly reestablished the correct relationship between Ben and Mariska Hargitay, which is to say, no relationship. Ben was a viewer of a television show she appeared on. That's all, and don't forget it, Ben.

Ben knew this was all in his head, was entirely a problem of his own creation, but it felt essential for him to face. And, most importantly, he needed something to do with his days. On some level, Ben knew that staring at his computer screen, regardless of the content, could not actually make his life better. And yet.

Daily, after his time with Benson, Ben would watch *Big Shot* on his computer. He could watch the show and become skilled at watching the show, but that was not research. He'd watch interviews with the Big Shots themselves. He'd watch interviews with past contestants, which were harder to track down. Even harder to find were any written remembrances or insight from past contestants. An exception being the following post from former contestant Bruce Magnus, a man with a squared goatee, answering a question difficult to ascertain—and one he was definitely never asked—that headlined his own personal website's "Frequently Asked Questions" section. Magnus had successfully pitched a dog comb that also applied flea repellent. The FAQ section of his website opened with the following general address, which might have been an answer to a question Magnus had been asked in his head: "What is the moment when you're pitching on *Big Shot* like?"

"The contestant walks down a dramatically lit false corridor to a set of doors that swing open. Through the doorway and the contestant stands in front of the Big Shots for a full minute for what is referred to by production as 'the staredown.' The contestant is told not to speak. Off-camera, a production assistant holds a large countdown clock that runs down the minute sixty seconds to one. I'm told this opening gaze portion is essential in the editing room. In past seasons, methods were attempted to rig the shoot, tipping off certain Big Shots on certain pitches, making specific details available to certain Big Shots, providing specific angles of entry to the Big Shots ahead of actually hearing the pitches, but apparently it very much dampened the liveliness of the room. The concession became that each of the Big Shots wore an earpiece and was fed limited information during the pitches. As simple as 'Keep pushing on recent sales,' or 'Ask about mother,' or in my case maybe it could have been 'Mention that you don't like dogs,' trying to trigger me.

"Since no notes are provided to the Big Shots before a pitch, or during, the origin of the information fed to them through their earpieces remains largely mysterious to them. They know the size of the preproduction staff, have some sense of the depth of the preshoot research, but not the source or context for the information they are being fed. These are very wealthy, very part-time participants. Remember that. They come in and do the job. Where the information they are being fed is coming from and for what purpose is mostly out of their purview and realm of interest. This is my opinion. And it's best this way. The Big Shots need to be in the moment and not mired in a larger strategy related to getting footage that will be easy to cut into an efficient narrative. That is for production to worry about. And so each shoot they are being goaded, but they do not know to what. They not only are receiving the pitches blind, they are asking the questions they are encouraged to ask blind.

"Edited, the pitches are between ten and twelve minutes. This usually means an hour or more is cut out from every pitch. The bulk of that editing eliminates detailed financial talk, much of which is repetitious and involves the individual Big Shots coming to a fairly complete understanding of the purported reality of the contestant's past earnings, potential earnings, prospects, and planning. Often what is cut is discussions of origin or family life, contestants praising Big Shots, reshoots for clarity, a director yelling 'again' if a question is unclear, garbled, or contains profanity.

"After each pitch, successful or not, contestants are required to sit with a psychiatrist hired by the show. Depending on the state of the contestant, the psychiatrist attempts to place the person's pitch within the context of their life as a whole, of their successes and failures as a whole, and reiterate, most importantly, that this pitch is an early step in the process, regardless of the outcome. Should the contestant be offered a deal, the psychiatrist reminds the contestant, because this will be the fifth or sixth time the contestant will be hearing it, no deal is finalized until the Big Shot's individual team has vetted the contestant and reviewed financials, legality, and the veracity of their claims made within the pitch. Around 15 percent of deals are called off due to this process. I'm surprised it's not more. The psychiatrist is there to comfort, reframe, protect.

Encourage honest reflection. There may be little correlation between what you feel in the room while pitching and what you see on TV. You may not recognize the tenor of your voice. You may not recognize your face, your reactions, the Big Shots' reactions to the pitch you just made them. You very well might not ever be on TV."

***

THERE WAS A delay in starting dinner Ben couldn't account for. He grabbed another beer and slotted it into the Koozie. No, he could account for it, he could: he hadn't started cooking yet. He would wait another five minutes and then suggest picking something up. He was considering how insular his routine, his life, had become. He'd placed a seven-dollar bet on a Czech soccer match while at the library earlier, a live line, and lost within minutes. He'd never heard of either team, and had told no one of the bet. There was no joy in it, and little to gain. Eleven dollars. He'd bet on a draw, and as soon as the universe had his seven bucks, a goal came. He'd deleted the betting app from his phone after the loss. It felt like shamefully throwing away a nearly full pack of cigarettes, because he knew the deletion was not permanent. Your routine becomes your life, no matter how stupid. And he was committed. He was not planning an exit from this routine; the opposite, actually—he would attempt to hide more completely within it. Tara was still at the table inventing days for the kids. Alone in their thoughts together. Drinking in the kitchen nine feet apart, listening to Tara's music and waiting for the next thing to happen. The room didn't feel tense to Ben, but he also didn't know what was happening.

Their kitchen was pale blue and white. Inviting and dated. An inherited and passed-down heavy round kitchen table. One that had been made in Canton, Illinois, a hundred years earlier: Tara's people. Mugs hanging under the cupboard. A green hummingbird feeder outside the window over the sink. The music playing was from a playlist Tara had created called "Hundred Again," made up of songs Tara believed she'd heard over a hundred times. Conservatively. The playlist had little personal associative runs in it—a clutch of Gillian Welch songs, a Bill Fox song, a Bill Callahan song, Gill-Bill-Bill, and so on. Tara always listened to it straight through, not on shuffle. Ben believed their kitchen, their whole house, felt more like it should belong to people their parents' age. It seemed like a house that they had inherited, though this was not the case. Their small alterations and paint and clutter/knick-knack removal had done nothing to lessen that feeling in him. The appliances were hanging on. The washer was in its death throes. An eerily purring refrigerator that could not form ice. The house was wrong, all houses really, but that did not mean he didn't want one.

"Do you hear Billy?" Tara asked.

Ben shook his head. He hadn't heard or thought of the boy since Billy had finished the quesadilla Ben had made him and gone upstairs to play in the guest bedroom. Tara and Ben had reassured him earlier that it wasn't supposed to storm badly. A little rain is all. He'd asked them to warn him if that became not true as he took small bites of his quesadilla. Billy was consumed with knowing the truth of situations and near futures. Recently he'd learned that truth could easily become untruth, and he'd been asking for warnings of this possibility. Ben watched Tara walk over to the split-level's five stairs to check on him, watched her face register that she could hear him inventing brief scenarios for flying ships and spacemen, space-dogs.

Billy was staying with them for two weeks while his parents climbed mountains in Africa. This was day three. Ben had been surprised Tara agreed to watch the boy for that long; felt it might have been her testing him. $220 a day plus expenses, sure. Billy's parents' trip was connected to a charitable fundraising endeavor in a way that was hard to understand. Ben was thinking about Africa dumbly, could picture only vast plains like a harshened and vacated American Midwest, the occasional giraffe, and heat. Listening to Tara's music, Ben was wondering whether there was anything redeemable in vacations of the sort Billy's parents were on, curated performative vacations, was there any other kind, when she spoke: "You realize how stupid it is to ask me to go on the show, right?"

Ben hadn't mentioned anything about the show in a few days. Nothing he could remember. He hadn't spoken in minutes. Ben said nothing, waiting for Tara to lead him out of confusion.

She said, "I run a three-kid day care out of our house."

Ben watched his wife. He wanted to understand where this was coming from. He didn't know if she was upset because of something specific or in a more general way. Didn't know if she'd found out he'd lost his job. He'd felt from the minute he'd been fired that she already knew.

Tara went on, "And I didn't want to bring it up because I trust you, but I want you to think about what you're doing. How it is you are going about trying to get on this show."

"Didn't want to bring up what?"

She said, "Billy," loud, to see if he would respond from up-stairs. He did not respond. Ben began turning on the remaining unlit lights in the kitchen, as if for protection.

"He's doing LEGOs, say it," Ben said, flipping the last wall switch in the now fully glowing room.

Tara put her head down, laughing. "What the fuck is 'Mariska Hargitay, attacked'?"

Ben could not tell how Tara meant her question. She was exasperated; he could see that. As if this had been weighing on her. The moment stretched. Despite Tara saying she trusted Ben, she was clearly becoming more irritated than she had been seconds earlier. Ben thought that not instantly laughing along with Tara, not having an immediate explanation, was making all this much worse, resharpening the gaze Tara was now applying to the words he'd written down, the words it seemed she'd initially been able to dismiss. Ben ascribed an intensity to her gaze that caused him to consider the women several generations previous that she was descended from. Women who had endured real winters unprepared. Women who had kept children alive through sickness, exposure, pursuit; through daily life. Abandoned women. Women who had traveled oceans, mountains, rain-soaked hills, deserts, frozen earth, and not stopped. Ben didn't know anything about her ancestors, was inventing these bleak lives with the guilty portion of his subconscious imagination, but such lengths seemed possible. As if this question, this now-incredulous laugh, was coming from all these women, not only his wife. Not any part of this was funny; that's what her laughter was telling him.

Ben was shaking his head. His eyes were closed and he was saying, "I didn't even think before handing you the notebook. I should have said—"

"Should have said what?" Tara was speaking with her hands now. "You would only have to say something if there was something you'd need to apologize for. And that's where I'm at." She had both her hands in front of her in what could have been some casual church gesture, "and also with you," if witnessed through the window from the street, but inside the bright kitchen it felt imminent that she would make fists and hit him.

She lowered her voice slightly, maybe remembering Billy. "In this notebook is all sorts of made-up shit. All made up. Of course a woman can use a man's sexual interest to her advantage. Of course a beautiful fucking actress would have an advantage in doing that. Your small speculation adds nothing. Then you go on and on about each of these Big Shots. Sam Mackaday. Suzanne Reinhart, Bill Brunswick—on and on. Each of their investing habits. Prefers young white men with Ivy League background. Prefers brown-haired white women, in general.

Prefers mothers and daughters. Prefers immigrants with im-perfect smiles. Prefers non-whites with heavy accents. Prefers simple. Bucked teeth. And even more reckless, I see now, you're finding names in the credits and trying to murder-map out their supposed career growth, of which you know nothing, to see who you can exploit for your gain. And now, thanks to you, these names are in my head. Jabaree West. Fucking Pipes. Marcy."

Ben nodded. Tara's level of frustration matched his initial guilt, but still her response surprised him. The intensity of her attention, though negative, made Ben feel incredible—like he'd won a short foot race against a stranger and had no obligations left for the day, could celebrate the victory in a dark bar by himself, taking down draft after draft.

He'd thought she'd understand what his intention was, even more than he himself. That she would be able to ex-plain to him what his intention was, why the thought had appeared in his head, what it was exactly that was wrong with him; that she would know. Tara had seen what he was guilty of, clearly: exploitation. At any cost, get on the show. An American impulse.

Ben said, "I was trying to remember where I started. That's why I wrote that down."

"I don't care why."

"I'm trying to get on the show. Prove that I can do it. Think of it like a painting—I'm making sketches"—Tara grunted—"okay. Actually, no: think of it like your journals for the kids. You write them and spend all this time and then who the hell knows if the parents read them?"

Tara shook her head, ignoring his explanation, and went on, "Ben. Attacked? 'Attacked' doesn't mean attacked. Then you highlighted those words—"

Tara asked, "Is this a porn thing? Do you watch rape shit?"

"Jesus, no." He didn't. Ben motioned for quiet, pointing to-ward the guest room upstairs.

Tara said, "What part of this is my fault?"

"Nothing. Nothing."

"Right. I didn't think any of this was a big deal, but now I'm in the kitchen here thinking, here's what is *your* fault: thirty-year-old married man writing 'Mariska Hargitay, attacked' in a notebook, in an attempt to understand how to get on *Big Shot*. That doesn't even make sense! You don't have a business. You don't even really have an idea. You had an instinct. A fucked instinct. You don't have anything. You have the trees outside that you stare at. That's what you have."

Ben did not say, "I have you to help me," because it did not occur to him.

Seemingly on cue, Billy tiptoed dramatically into the kitchen in an oversized green T-shirt and tall white socks saying, "Mariska Hard Day?"

Tara gave Ben a vacant face as she scooped up Billy easily and said, "From a murder show." She vampired the boy's neck as she took him back upstairs. Billy was shrieking.

That night Tara left a sticky note on the bathroom mirror for Ben. She was asleep in bed the next morning as he read it, readying for his fake commute that she still did not know about.

*You may be right re: beautiful-resilient-taken-advantage-of women being the most successful on the show, but you are not such a woman. Neither am I. And if you're right, why would you want to be on this show. If it is that important to you to get on then I would suggest you think about who it is that you are and go from there. Think about what it is that you have. Trees outside to stare at. A wife who loves you. An opportunity to do something else. Adler Planetarium during the day and will be back early-ish. I love you but you're being fucking stupid. Choose something else.*

Ben read the note three times, then crossed out the lines that he felt weren't relevant, taking with him what he could.

# 8. TARA

ON THE METRA into the city with the kids, Tara was texting Nguyen's husband, Hank. He had started the exchange, sending Tara pictures of seemingly identical white farmhouse sink options for their renovation. In the seat in front of Tara on the train, Micah and Jules were sharing headphones and making huge eyes at each other. Jules had hidden all the forks from the silverware drawer as Tara had made pancakes that morning and so they'd eaten the pancakes with their hands after spoons proved difficult. Syrup everywhere. Tara did not want Jules to win. Couldn't let her know she cared about these thefts. Smiling at Jules as the girl raised the sopping pancake to her mouth with bare hands. On the train, at Tara's side, Billy was napping with his hands in his pockets like some 1950s drifter, his head against the window. Clarendon Hills, Western Springs, Brookfield, Berwyn.

Tara put her phone under her leg and looked at these three kids that were not her own. The train rolled on. She wanted to scream until everyone on the train car was killed by her scream. Billy could live. A piercing note that would burst passengers' bodies at different times, depending on personal weight, depending on individual density, a scream that would continue after the passengers were dead, exploding the train's windows and blowing out its metal frame, flattening the landscape, emptying it for Tara to walk privately—that is how complete her solitude would be on this plain, it was a privacy. Eventually she'd encounter wildlife her scream hadn't affected, and this wildlife would speak to her in a language they shared, hums, mutterances, she was thinking of a broad-leafed plant, deep waxen green, the plant asking her in a hushed rounded tone about her plans. No, she did not want that. She saw the scene from outside herself. Day care. Jesus Christ. Day care in the southwest suburbs. She hadn't painted anything in three years. This was barely an exaggeration. She was ready to try again. She wanted to already be trying, to be the person who had never stopped trying, but she wasn't.

Tara sometimes texted Hank, empty jabs at their spouses, and had never texted Nguyen. Tara and Nguyen had a cautious relationship with each other. Tara felt that Nguyen was attracted to many of the same qualities in Ben to which she was most attracted—his boyishness, stubbornness—and yet, Tara resented Nguyen. *Resent* may have been too strong a word, but she was aware that Nguyen was able to participate in Ben's life, benefit from so much of what was good about him, and yet experience none of the consequences. It occurred to her most surface friendships were like this. Tara sensed their link to be conditional. She wanted to ask Hank outright if he'd heard any of this Mariska Hargitay talk. Are you encouraging this? If this somehow was a part of regular conversations that Nguyen and Ben had, and if it had trickled down to Hank. She did not ask.

Why make this reality show, one you only sedately watched until a few weeks ago, what you fixate on? Was there even a reason? If there wasn't a reason, that would be most troubling: that Ben could be so fully captured by trash caught in the wind and blown into his face. She was open to coincidence leading to meaning, but garbage must be seen for what it is and rationed within one's life so as not to take over. Her own life was filled with small junk heaps, many that she loved, but they would not lead her.

Tara could tell Ben had been particularly unhappy at work the past couple weeks, and that must have been in part what this reality show obsession was about. The show was some distraction that had occurred to him and that he had now leapt into; and there was a consequence right there. Nguyen could be a part of all this front-end planning and hobbying, but he would never have to reckon with watching his husband on national television being made to look like a fool. Not that she would either. It would never get that far.

Tara didn't begin a painting without having an image in mind. She worked from photographs, usually ones that she took in search of the vision she was striving toward. She wasn't capable of forcing this process. Thinking and returning to the idea that she wanted to begin a new painting was enough. She'd have an increasingly specific impulse toward an object in a particular space that would gain magnetic power: a yellow Mr. Coffee floating in a fogged alley, the heating unit on the roof of a grocery store creating its own dark weather above, a pile of orange construction cones in a shallow pit at center court of a dramatically lit high school gymnasium, and then she'd take a photograph either approximating or documenting the image she was compelled toward. Often her work was a layering of objects into new locales. Familiar set on familiar made unfamiliar. She knew something would come to her and would be ready when it did. She didn't have another way to work, unwilling to force the process.

On the train the girls were asleep in front of her and Billy's head had slumped more severely against the window. Tara pulled him into an upright seated position and he didn't even open his eyes. Their train car was quiet now that the girls were asleep. Swaying. Everyone else was bent on their phones, heading to work, or sleeping. Offices with lax start times and those with enough clout for it not to matter, the underemployed.

Tara could not intuit the meaning of the Hargitay thought. They never talked about sex, Tara and Ben, not sex between them or sex in general, and certainly not after she had been attacked, though there had been no rape, no nothing, never mind that rape had obviously been the man's intent. Tara believed that night loomed larger in Ben's thoughts than in her own. Clearly. It had changed the way Ben related to Tara physically. After the night Tara was attacked, which had undoubtedly accelerated the end of their separation, their reunion, their marriage, Ben had let Tara take complete control of initiating sex, and during, it was always her lead. Usually Tara on top. Always Tara on top. It hadn't been like that between them previously. Variance had been normal before their separation and her attack. Since that night he'd never, not once, been the one to lead her to bed, or the couch, or anywhere. Even drunkenly, he'd hit some wall, and wait for Tara to guide him. And so they had less sex, by a lot. Once, twice a month was overstating it; it was much less than that. Six times a year? Tara couldn't say, other than: almost never. This was an unspoken reality, not one Tara dwelled on, but still, its consistency and form were qualities that were set and that she had not put words to even in her thinking. She understood Ben was distancing himself from this man who had attacked her, but Tara didn't want to have to tell him that there was no relation. She did not want to have to tell him, "You can fuck me from behind." She didn't want him to think of himself in relation to her attacker at all. Be my husband. Love me. Nothing's changed. She didn't want Ben to contextualize their physical relationship as having any connection to her attack. There was no connection. And nothing had happened. She had won. She'd stabbed this man through his shoulder, handled him without hesitation and could have killed him, knew she could have killed him; she was not a victim. He hadn't even taken her off her feet.

what does Nguyen tell you they are doing when he comes over trying to figure out how to get Ben on Big Shot whatever that means

She put the phone back under her leg. She also felt Nguyen did not want to betray any confidence of Ben's; for that reason Nguyen purposely set himself apart from Tara, more so lately, and, simply, she had always gotten along much better with Hank. Hank was not questioning. He was a tall, baby-faced real estate agent who lifted weights. Before they were married, Hank's last name had been Ngo, but Hank had wanted to share a last name with Thuan, and so Hank's last name was now Nguyen. Hank and Tara had never hung out alone. There had been double dates and surprisingly similar levels of frustration over their husbands, and that bonded them. But they didn't hang out—they texted.

> I think it's just a weird hobby. You're frustrated he's bad at it
>
> you don't even know how bad
>
> eh how many people do you know are good at hobbies? I mean GOOD your last several cakes were failures
>
> I don't know people with hobbies anymore I know people who watch TV

The line for the planetarium stretched thirty yards out of the grand entrance into the sun. The planetarium sat right on Lake Michigan. At their backs was downtown, to their right columnated Soldier Field, to their left, to the north, the Natural History Museum. All teeming with groups of children in brightly coordinated T-shirts. Lake Michigan's water near the shoreline was island blue. Tara pointed out the water to the kids, and Micah said, "Is that exactly the same color as the water in Belize?" Tara said she believed that to be possible. Then Jules, with the red glasses always falling down her nose, added, "Near Ladyville, maybe." They'd found Ladyville the day before on a map of Belize on Tara's computer. Listening to Wilfred Peters and Mohobub Flores and laughing. Again Tara agreed, maybe the water near Ladyville was exactly the same color as the water near the shore in Lake Michigan. She regretted her pancake behavior from the morning and squeezed Jules's shoulder.

The line was slow moving. They tottered closer to the entrance, the enormous copper doors. Children were wincing in the heat, wiping sunscreen out of their eyes, screaming, running in tight loops out from and back to the thick line of soon-to-be planetarium visitors. Billy held Tara's hand, as he usually did when there were this many people around. She thought, for $2,800 I can hold his hand like this the whole two weeks. She resented the thought, wondered why it even came to her. She always held his hand like this. And also, what was the difference? She was never not being paid to hold his hand. Any situation where holding the boy's hand was a possibility was one for which she was being compensated. Why was she thinking this way? She couldn't help it.

A skinny red awning covered the final ten yards before they actually reached the entrance to the planetarium, and when they did, wide and proud Micah and aloof Jules were holding hands too, standing in front of Tara and Billy.

On the train ride home, the kids couldn't stop talking about the chairs in the planetarium, the deep reclined angle. The loud "space music." Jules adjusted her glasses by scrunching her face and said, "I could sleep forever in those chairs. If I didn't have to pee. I mean like, if peeing wasn't a thing." Tara had fallen asleep in her chair, remembered nothing of the music, the fake stars, and awoken with drool ringing her chin like curved fangs. Micah said nothing but put all her weight into pushing her train seatback into a similar position as the planetarium chair. She was straining, standing as she pushed her body into the cushion. Her round face turning red. Tara could feel other passengers waiting for her to say something; she said, "Micah," and was ignored. Another twenty minutes and, of the three, only Micah was awake in the green train car. The child lifted her head from her phone, a limited old-tech and parent-rigged hand-me-down. "There are McDonald's in Belize, so—" She used this argument, an attempt to get Tara to take her to McDonald's, for every country Tara had highlighted—over the past two years, thirty-seven different countries, she was persistent. Doggedly hunting the fast-food burger.

That night in M I C A H, Tara wrote:

*I want her to want different things.*

Tara looked at what she had written and regretted it. She hadn't invented this entry; it was true. What she'd written, the specific criticism, was not for the girl. And even if it was, she was a kid. Not a thirty-year-old. The wants of this kid, ultimately, would have no impact on Tara's life. She looked again at what she had written. She changed nothing.

Tara glanced around the kitchen and felt old. Here in this house taking down notes late into the night in her blue kitchen. She'd felt old all night, especially since putting Billy to bed. She could not have envisioned this life for herself, even ten years earlier. Twenty, twenty-one—at the time she'd imagined her future would be painting, living in the city, with a day job that paid the bills. Barely paid the bills. She had anticipated years of that, a life of that, hoping maybe something would break. Get in some shows, get to know some of the gallerists, who knows. Maybe eventually some kind of teaching to supplement an increasingly steady income from selling her work. She was in the wrong city for that kind of life. The wrong century. No, those were excuses: she was the wrong person. She was interested in half of what it would take to make a living painting. Less than half. That is to say: she was interested in painting. She'd known it at the time, in her twenties.

She went upstairs and Ben was reading in bed. One of Tara's books. Mary Robison. He was grinning like an idiot until he realized he was being watched. He'd been quiet all night before heading upstairs. He'd said he was sorry, and she believed him. He was. She waited for him to put the book down.

Tara said, "Why don't you ever want to have sex with me?"

"That's not true."

"When have you tried?"

Ben set the slim book on the nightstand without marking the page. "Walk back out. Close the door. Come in as if you hadn't said any of that."

# 9. MARCY

THERE WAS AN ice rink, a massive rectangular brick building with a white dome top, that Marcy passed on her weekday commute. The building brought to mind for Marcy a half loaf of sliced bread. The dome top seemed to her to be a signifier more than a functional necessity, though she knew little about architecture, and even less about the structural needs of an indoor ice rink. For a reason unknown to her she pulled into the lot one day, slipped the SERVICE ANIMAL vest she'd ordered online onto Jet, walked into the rink with the dog, and sat in the stands. She sat with her phone and watched a youth hockey team practice. There appeared to be only parents and a few bored siblings in the stands. You could hear every word the coach was speaking: "If you feel bunched, you are. Powerful to gaps, powerful to space, and then keep it. Own the space. Head up with the puck." His whistle sounded mic'd. Sitting in such a cold, enormous room was wonderful. *Room* felt wrong. *Hall. Valley.* No one cared about the dog in the vest.

At the rink, Marcy was going over Callie's most recent Hillis email:

**The Number 30 and What We Know of Its Importance to Hillis**
In my note from two weeks ago I went into why I feel like numbers are a worthy area for us to explore in regards to understanding Hillis and what he will do or continue to not do. The only artwork hanging on his cell wall is a lined sheet of paper listing every retired number in the San Francisco Giants organization, one of which is 30, for Orlando Cepeda.

Thirty years since the murder and nearly as long in jail, and that means nearly thirty years of safety for you. We can stretch that number

73

to include the totality of your life, but the threat of Hillis surely is why we won't. Hillis's main focus, as we know, is the Giants, and numerical importance and reverence arrives to him through that lens. The number 30 has been retired in the SFG organization since 1999. Oddly, and I'm sure Hillis knows this, twenty-nine players have worn the number for the Giants. All the names pre-1958 being New York Giants:

Dante Powell (1997–1998)

Jacob Cruz (1996–1998)

Marcus Jensen (1996–1997)

Dan Peltier (1996)

Jamie Brewington (1995)

Jim Deshaies (1993)

Jim McNamara (1992–1993)

Chris James (1992)

Mark Thurmond (1990)

Donell Nixon (1988–1989)

Rusty Tillman (1988)

Chili Davis (1981–1987)

Bob Kearney (1979)

John Tamargo (1978–1979)

Derrel Thomas (1975–1977)

John Boccabella (1974)

Don Carrithers (1970–1973)

Jim Johnson (1970)

Billy Hoeft (1963, 1966)

Orlando Cepeda (1958–1966, RET)

Dick Littlefield (1956)

Bob Lennon (1954, 1956)

George Spencer (1950–1955)

Kirby Higbe (1949–1950)

Ray Poat (1947–1949)

Hooks Iott (1947)

Bill Voiselle (1942–1947)

Sid Gordon (1941–1943, 1946–1949, 1955)

Tip Tobin (1932)

I will work on obtaining a photograph of the sheet of paper where he lists all the retired numbers for the team, but if that is unattainable I will make sure to determine if there is anything noteworthy about the paper or anything else we can glean from its contents.

**Further Notes on Hillis's Family on the West Coast**
Due to Hillis being an invented surname, the name I have been searching for and researching is Hillis's last name at birth: Dracker. There are only four Drackers alive in CA as of the writing of this email, and three live in Grass Valley. The fourth is a Mary Dracker, currently residing in Duarte—

The email continued for another five sections.

A father in the stands was attempting to start a chant based on the first names of the children on the team: "Jes-se, Ni-sa, Burk-ley, Ty-ler-B., Ty-ler-R., Jace . . ." There was no order to his naming, he was including the children in his call as he saw them, and so it was impossible for anyone to join in. And now he was clapping, his neck turkey-strutting in place. It occurred to Marcy that he was not trying to start a collective cheer of support at all, but instead just shouting names in a familiar cadence. Jet and Marcy watched, embarrassed for this ridiculous dad. This was practice. Someone needed to explain to him what practice meant. This dad had not grown up playing sports. Her own father would never.

\*\*\*

MARCY HAD FLED a regionally infamous couple. Her parents. The murder they'd witnessed was known in the Bay Area by a few names, or had been known, but the most widely reported and repeated headline was *PEST CONTROL KITTY GENOVESE*. Marcy's parents' infamy was much amplified because a teen-aged bass player in a once-nameless San Jose hardcore band, high on big drugs in a Denny's booth, had been struck dumb by the headline, holding the newspaper to his face. He'd taken from the headline none of the content but instead formed an empty and unpunctuated acronym, PCKG, and so they were. A nice rhyming four letters that looked great on a black shirt in several ways. Four letters that could be spittle-shouted at the opening of PCKG's first record, *South Bay Fuckin.*

> *PCKG that's one way to be*
> *Empty dead to me*
> *That's you that's me*

And she was fleeing the bug man. The killer. That's what this vacation was, regardless of whether it made sense or not, existed or not. Or she was fleeing who it was she imagined him to be.

Marcy had invented a whole life for him and mixed that invented life with the actual facts into her understanding of the killer: The bug man had previous convictions. Walt Hillis. Pest control was not his initial career path. But he took his training seriously. The company did too. Training was what the company was built on. Training on the care of his uniform. Training on how to conduct himself while driving the white company van to a customer's home. Eyes on the road. Play the radio only if it will help to put you in a focused and pleasant frame of mind. If music excites you, consider silence. Demeanor training. Do not interrupt while in a home. Ask before using the bathroom. Compliment cleanliness when you can. Walt Hillis memorized and could differentiate the following: confused flour beetle, cigarette beetle, drugstore beetle—those last two are very similar—black carpet beetle, furniture beetle, rice weevil, wheat weevil.

He was a born talker. A tall man who slicked his hair straight back and maintained his mustache seriously. A program of decisive clipping. Sometimes he said his own name to himself in the mirror while grooming. Walt Hillis. A name of his own making. Admiring the thick brown half cruller that did not extend past his top lip. He swam laps daily at the Y. Crisp freestyle sets with flip turns. The man had a very small ass. Speedo. He nightly shaved his legs and he nightly shaved his arms and chest and stomach and then entered his bed like a virgin. Folded-down sheets and flat-on-his-back sleep. He felt this fit with pest control. Sleek entry into a house and arrowlike through the water. Efficiency in rooms and in sleep practice and in the pool. It made sense to him. He rarely brushed his teeth. This also made sense to him. The mustache was in style. His hair, the same. He was susceptible to trends and false thinking and was not educated. This was fairly late in the twentieth century in California. The reading he brought into his studio apartment was motivational scam literature. He began addressing the people around him with lines from the book that ultimately took his thinking from him. *The Power and the Way and You.* "There is no chance. There are events, but no chance. There is action and inaction. Let me ask you, why have we been brought together?"

Following a run-in with the manager of the YMCA where he swam laps daily, the run-in being that the manager would not answer his question, "Why have we been brought together?" Walt Hillis grabbed the manager, a man named Darnell Poole, in the parking lot as he was leaving the Y, headed to his car. Walt Hills had Darnell Poole bound and gagged in the back of his pest control van for fourteen hours total, from his abduction to the time of his death in front of Marcy's childhood home. Throughout the fourteen hours that Walt Hillis spent driving the van around San Jose getting gas, stopping to eat at two separate Round Table Pizzas, leaving Darnell in the van each time, he referred to the manager as "Donny" because Hillis felt he looked like a young and hale Don Baylor—he did not.

Marcy was not there, not home; she and her brother were in Ohio staying with an aunt, sweating in the Midwest for a week. Swim, Dairy Queen, the lesser Hollywood Video with its earnest pro-wrestling aesthetic—these activities allowed them to avoid the murder. It would be making an assumption to say that Walt Hillis wanted to be caught, but it is hard to dispute that he wanted the manager's death to be witnessed. He was scheduled to service the Lons' home the following day, in the afternoon.

HOUR FOURTEEN, WALT Hillis backed the van onto their front grass. He jerked open the back door of the van and threw Darnell onto the ground. Then Walt Hillis took off his button-down shirt and draped it over the top of one of the van's back doors. The sound of a running vehicle on their front lawn brought Marcy's parents to the window. They smelled intensely of sunscreen. They stood next to the window and gawked through the blinds at Walt Hillis taking down his brown pants. They watched as he urinated on Darnell, on the man's clothed stomach. They were at the edge of the window, hiding, watching as if what was happening in their yard were scandalous television. Television broadcast from Real Hell. And also watching as if it were not life. Mr. Lon could not help but think this was some of God's punishment for him. He had a guilty conscience despite being mostly silent and sedentary since birth. Mrs. Lon didn't believe in punishment of that sort. She was not nearly that stupid.

From the ice one of the volunteer coaches, a bearded man in his twenties, made the slash-the-throat gesture at the still-chanting dad. The dad gave the young man an earnest double thumbs-up, "Evan, yep!" and sat down. Marcy and Jet both felt thankful for Coach Evan.

Five other neighbors had witnessed some portion of the murder. But because the van had been backed onto the lawn and its rear doors flung open, the view mostly was reserved for the Lons. It was as if Walt Hillis had arranged a makeshift stage solely for them. They were the audience.

Marcy's mom did not fear for her life. In her mind, as he peed, she thought, the appointment stands. She came to understand that urination would not be the culminating act.

Done peeing, Walt Hillis stood watching Darnell. The man began shrieking. Until then he'd been stoic. He'd been attempting to conserve energy in case an opportunity arose for him to escape. But with the piss and the following silence, the heat of the day, the grass below him, he lost control of his temper.

Darnell was grunting from the center of his being, the veins in his forehead popping, squealing like his stomach would rip open from effort. Walt Hillis watched. He was impressed with himself, the knotting of the feet, hands, the fully wrapped duct-taping of the lower part of the man's face, the blindfold. Walt Hillis began mumbling. The couple prayed, literally prayed to their God, that this was all. Peeing was all. We can recover; a little pee, thought Mrs. Lon. They did not move. They did not speak. How could this get worse. As time stretched, and Walt Hillis made no move, the couple made noises to each other like needy dogs and Mrs. Lon decided to ease herself down flat on the floor of the living room. She still wasn't scared for her own safety; it was more a question of how much waiting she could do at her own window. Very little. Two minutes had passed since the van had arrived.

Still mumbling, Walt Hillis grabbed a shovel that was clipped into one of the van doors. He looked around and then directly into the home as he held the shovel, as if through the blinds and into Mr. Lon's skull. The placement of his gaze into their home seemed to articulate neutral acknowledgment. He took a step toward the house, a final confirming look, and then was back to the squealing man. Darnell had not let up. To the last. "Quiet now, Don."

Walt Hillis hefted the shovel. His shoulders tensed and with a motion as if he were starting to dig a hole, he cleaved Darnell's head off. The sound was a wet crunch. Mr. Lon urinated on himself. He tasted iron. He passed out. Mrs. Lon played dead, thinking for some reason that her husband had been shot, and that she would likely be shot next. Continuing the scoop, Walt Hillis walked with the man's head in the blade of the shovel and into the gray asphalt street. Many witnesses now. Not including the kids on the street, there were five others at windows, and others gardening, pushing strollers. Walt Hillis flung the man's head trebuchet style into the air and off briefly into the sky. It landed two houses down, partially exploding like a water-logged firework, near a ditched Huffy bicycle.

And so Marcy was also fleeing Walt Hillis. Still alive, still in jail. Or she was fleeing her imagining of him. The murder, its weapon, its victim—she'd invented none of that. The mustache, the daily swimming, the book, the specifics of her parents' witnessing, among other pieces, that was mostly her. She couldn't remember what was her own making and what had actually happened. But, regardless, interviews travel, and attention travels, and the thirty-year anniversary of the murder was fast approaching. PCKG. It had been the last Friday in August all those years ago. Marcy feared a thirty-year anniversary would bring renewed interest, new coverage, new interviews with Hillis—and she did not want to be linked. Or Marcy wanted enough people, maybe only Callie, to believe she was linked, so Marcy could display to her that she did want to be linked. No one in her current life, outside her family and Callie, knew about her family's connection to the murder, to the best of her knowledge.

A woman was speaking to Marcy in the stands at the ice rink. Marcy stopped reading Callie's email and looked at the mother. The mother looked Mormon—deathly white, deathly straight teeth, blond, clean, heavily scented. Marcy made a face that meant, say it again.

"Which one is yours?" the woman repeated. The woman made expectant eye contact with Marcy and then Jet, and then back to Marcy, the same look for both.

Marcy scanned the ice and pointed. "That one."

"On the Zamboni? Glenn?"

"Glenn on the Zamboni is my dad," Marcy said, standing. "Stepdad. Now you know."

"Did you get lunch?"

Marcy stared at the woman's soft chin. "It's our time and we use it how we want." Marcy went down the stairs to the glass against the rink, Jet tight to her, and circled to the other side, finding a place in the stands in the uppermost row where they wouldn't be bothered.

Marcy wanted her coworkers to believe that her aspirations were different from their own. But that her past was maybe similar. That like theirs, her youth had been flat childhood days, divorce, swim lessons. Not vanilla ice cream in a cereal bowl, sitting with her parents and friendly TV and a brother shut into his bedroom listening to industrial music that made everyone worried about what would become of him. Not the soccer team, the volleyball team, the school newspaper. She wanted her coworkers to be positive she was the difference. That Los Angeles meant something different for her than it did for them (it did not). She wanted to make movies too. Always had wanted that. That want had brought her to LA originally. She'd worked on sets as a production assistant and ended up in casting by accident. Had been introduced to a casting director whose dog she'd admired. A three-legged beagle named Nájera. She'd run into this woman and Nájera on sets. The woman would ask after Marcy's clothes, and Marcy would pet the dog, play dumb. As if the clothes had materialized onto her body instead of having been hunted and meticulously selected. She'd ask questions and pet Nájera. A job opened. A normal route into a career. She later ran into the woman and found she'd changed the dog's name, and her own name, to Pat.

Marcy watched the woman stiffly leave her seat and follow the invisible trail left by Marcy all the way to her new perch in the stands. Together again. The woman did not want to travel through her day with even the faintest sense that she had caused harm. Marcy found it unbelievable such a person had lived as long as she had, maybe thirty-five, thirty-seven years in the world with that disposition, remarkable. Do no harm.

"I'm sorry if I offended you. I didn't mean to pry."

Marcy didn't want to stand again. "It's fine." Jet had closed his eyes at her feet.

"I know Glenn isn't your stepdad. Which kid is yours? He's mine," the woman said, pointing to the shortest kid on the ice. If you'd never watched hockey and had been asked to pick out the least talented, the worst skater, the kid most unable to hold their stick, it would be her stumbling runt.

Marcy nodded like a bored aristocrat, looking elsewhere. "None of the kids are mine."

"I love dogs," the woman said.

"Trying to think of a generalized way to say this so the brunt doesn't come down entirely on you."

The woman's smile did not waver.

Marcy said, "I want to know less about you than I already do. Less about everyone I've ever met."

The woman's demeanor still did not change; she was intently listening, "Yes, except who?"

"Except for my dog, actually. I want to know much more about my dog."

"What is the dog's name?"

"Jet."

"What do you want to know about Jet?" Her knee was nearly touching Marcy's.

"I want to know specifically what Jet can sense in the rooms we live in together. And about his memory. I do not want to be told by a documentary on dogs what my dog knows, and I do not want to be told by a veterinarian or a scientist or an animal behavioral researcher what my dog knows, because, despite what anyone in any of those categories of people might say, they have no fucking idea, I'm sure; these people are only fantastically educated guessing creators. At best. And the knowledge I'm after, the information about my dog I want communicated to me, is information only my dog could ever provide. When are you most afraid? Do you know when I'm most afraid? Do you care to make me feel better? You do, don't you? I'm interested in the information I'm unable to receive. Information that does not exist, will never exist. Staggering, the amount of animal knowledge that cannot be converted into information we can understand."

"I'm an animal," the woman said. "In that way, I am."

Jet said nothing. Marcy looked to Jet.

"I'm an animal too," said Marcy.

She watched the woman as she retraced her steps back to the other side of the rink, yelling, "Give 'em heck, Jo-nah!" at her boy, splayed on the ice for too long now, as if waiting for the rapture. Please, fuck you Jesus, take me.

Marcy returned to her email without lingering on what had just taken place. Charged interactions were normal for her. She made them so.

The executives favored Marcy because she had advocated—*urged* was a better word—for several contestants in the past that no one else had seriously considered. Her peers, at this point, could pick out the men and women Marcy would fight for. "Hopeless and emotional," a Ryan had told her, "that's what you like." Marcy disagreed with this characterization of her taste, which was far too narrow an understanding.

They were all Ryans to Marcy. She'd particularly hated the construction *what you like.* Those three words in that order made her think it possible these Ryans had talked about her sexual preferences, though in their talk it had probably been phrased darker, she imagined. She had yet to meet a man she worked with whom she trusted. She cared what some of the men thought, she knew she did, but if pressed, she could not actually think of a single example.

There had been the man pitching a dog cremation kit for home use with a conventional oven. $19.99 retail. He'd worn transitional lenses while making his pitch. A man from Holland wearing transitional lenses still heartbroken by the loss of his own dog appearing on American TV earnestly selling a way for people to cremate their own dead animals. His pitch was fear based; the Dutch man claimed most pet cremations were faked, the pets' bodies dumped, spoke of "pervasive gray-sand substitution." There was the overly muscled and falsely direct man selling a dog comb—there were too many dog pitches—that also evenly distributed flea repellent. There had been the woman selling an Oreo-sized printer able to produce nail-art adhesives bearing personal photographs. Nail Pix. During her pitch she had mumbled, "Photographs on nails unexplored," and then had been forced to enunciate the foolish thought with volume. There had been the awful shark-looking man with the pocket-sized stain remover, feverishly stating, "You see spots with your eyes, but if you don't want to see them, use your N.O.S.E." He'd walked onto set holding his nose as if it were bleeding, and then actually dripped real blood onto his white shirt before using his product to make it completely disappear. There had been the man claiming his proprietary spice blend was the key to seventeen unrelated Atlanta restaurants' average sales growth of 13 percent over a nine-month span. Wong's Versatility Original Hot. He could not account for the source of his data when pressed for evidence. He could, and did, sing a song he'd written that he let the Big Shots know was called "Versatility Now, Versatility Forever." Wong had stood pigeon toed, eyes closed, singing. His clothes hung loose, as if on a wire hanger. He was drunk on gin, though nobody had known it. Marcy had given it to him.

\*\*\*

THE KIDS WERE trudging off the ice like little space explorers with walking sticks. The labor involved in playing hockey, the sheer amount of specialized gear each child required—Marcy liked how inane and apart-seeming this sport was from the rest of life. To excel at hockey seemed only hermetically valuable, which made Marcy like it more. She did not desire to play herself, did not want to watch any NHL, doubted Jet could somehow participate, but her private esteem for the game had grown in her half hour of witnessing. Marcy and Jet let the rink empty and stayed in the stands as the Zamboni again began making its passes.

None of Marcy's contestants represented themselves well. Or, they all represented themselves very well, and lacked any sense of how to add varnish to their desperate, tottering, sweaty attempts. Human.

# 10. CALLIE

CALLIE WAS WATCHING a woman and her husband shopping for sweaters in the women's section of the Burbank Target. Callie was carrying a basket and setting it down on the floor when she picked up an item, which was often. She'd pick up a top, a pair of pants, set her basket down, and watch the couple. The woman with the husband was seeking sweaters, medium, in bright colors. The woman had not said as much out loud, but Callie was watching closely, and once she realized what the woman was after, began her own search for the same. Callie held up a light-blue sweater from the rack, like holding a gem up to the light, and with no partner to speak to, addressed the vicinity: "Hard to find a nice bright medium." The woman looked at the sweater Callie was holding, looked at Callie, and smiled nervously. The husband was not paying attention, he was on his phone. Probably texting another woman, Callie thought.

The man had a knobby quality, lanky, and Callie thought if he were a serial murderer she'd refer to him as the Ichabod Killer; this made complete sense to Callie, this assignation, naming, hypothetical homicide. She was sometimes conscious of slipping into murder-brain, playing the constant detective, but not as often as she should have been. The couple walked to another part of the store, the woman guiding the man as if he were blind, still on his phone; Callie dropped the blue sweater into her basket on the ground and left it there. Callie was not conscious of the expression on her face that had caused the couple to walk away. Later the wife would tell her tall husband that the woman who had been following them in Target had reminded her of someone lying about her age to retake high school classes again, some kind of second chance at a lost youth. Her husband told her she was thinking of a movie, and she said, yes, but it's still what I mean.

Callie made a note in her phone as she wandered the Target:

- Hillis has been known to ignore questions and conversation directed his way even while in captivity. He has nothing tangible to distract him in any of these situations where communication with another person is made possible, and yet, he still manages to be distant and very much living in a different world.

Callie was utterly disinterested in working with Marcy in any kind of future. It was in her best interest to keep this fact veiled as long as possible. And to maintain Marcy as a reference. Callie wanted to move to New York. Wanted to work on *Good Morning America*. Wanted to be up early on the East Coast, making real money and buying tasteful understated décor for the life she wanted to create. To wear modest, inanely priced sweaters, show virtually no skin, ever, and yet be cleanly desired by many, by members of all genders. Wanted a husband with parents who were boat people. A husband with a beautiful and welcoming sister. A thick-eyebrowed welcoming sister. She could learn from the sister, but without judgment, only encouragement. Domestic learning. Self-care learning. Her husband would have an ageless but wrinkled mother. No dad. She realized she wanted her husband to come from a boat mother instead of boat people. She was editing her future always. A husband with a career like dentist, actuary, financial planner, dermatologist.

To have lived and worked in Los Angeles and New York on TV shows and then return to the Twin Cities to start a family, there it was, nirvana. These hypothetical future conversations were always with her: all the rest of her life at dinner parties, with other moms at an Eden Prairie playground, getting drinks with new neighbors. "Before kids? I was in TV. Out in LA, yes. New York too. That's right."

# 11. BEN

THREE WEEKS HAD passed since he'd been fired. Tara still didn't know. Trees. Seasons. Change. Seasonal. Seasonal specials. Nothing. He had nothing. Ben had lost around $1,900 from betting on baseball, a figure that was not that difficult to hide temporarily but was becoming increasingly real on his credit card.

He'd been watching five episodes of *SVU* a day at the Harold Washington library, five days a week. Some days only four. Five episodes a day was two hundred minutes of *SVU*. He had watched seventy-two episodes of the show since being fired. His notes on episode 72, or season 4, episode 6, "Angels":

- *western-style breast pockets for bus driver/no snaps*
- *"Dead kid now."*
- *"We're constantly kicking out street kids and hookers."*
- *Belzer Matrix*
- *"sodomized" at least second time jfc*
- *"What kind of sick bastard are you?"*

Good question.

This episode exemplified what Ben now felt was so impressive about Hargitay. She was an actress, yes, not a real detective, but still the material that she was engaging with every single episode was relentless. Moments of levity existed on the show, but only within the framework of crushing systematic human evil. Her performance did not ever lag. It was clear that viewers, and Ben now, drew strength from Olivia Benson because of the absolute fight in Hargitay's performance. Benson was insistently human, driven to do right for the victims of these crimes, and generally dignify the lives of the people she came into contact with. That is to say nothing of Hargitay's choice, outside the performance, to be an advocate and vocal spokesperson for victims of sexual crimes. She was making an impact psychically on TV, and then in possibly an equally substantial way through policy and action in the real world.

Several librarians had noticed Ben over the past weeks; he stood out in his suit, calmly angling for nooks mostly coveted by the underemployed and homeless. There was no librarian consensus on what Ben's deal was; he was noticed but never discussed beyond an exchange of concerned glances between tired coworkers. Increasingly, Ben felt that he was stepping into a bunker divorced from the real world. Fake New York on his computer screen, fake detectives in fake New York.

Ben's viewing pace had slowed because he had slid into a deepening glacial panic. He was desperate to get on the show to justify all the deception he knew he would not be able to keep secret much longer. And he needed a job. His anxiety manifested through a persistent low-grade buzzing in his clenched jaw. Ben was bracing for being found out; that is, bracing for when Tara learned he'd been fired. He didn't feel he'd be able to specifically admit to the complete *SVU* viewing. It was too hard to explain, not the kind of thing one could easily incorporate into a story, an apology, especially one you were delivering to your wife.

After watching seventy-two episodes whole, what struck Ben was that had he been paying attention to any of the episodes that Tara had watched over the years in the bedroom, he'd never have had his Mariska Hargitay thought. Olivia Benson was powerful, which is to say, Mariska Hargitay was powerful. Vulnerable, yes, but that would never be the first word said. Ben felt reverent of this character and the nobility of her questing. It was biblical, vengeful, but big-hearted work, encased in TV policing. Network TV, yes, but the character herself existed on a more real and textured plane. Many interviews with Hargitay brought up how fans often conflated her with the character of Olivia Benson, and how she welcomed this. She encouraged the blending. Her real-life mission had come to mirror the character's. Hargitay had altered how rape kits were processed in the real world due to her activism for the cause. Ben was a fan, pure and simple, a complete convert to the series and its motives.

Ben's time at the library not spent with Hargitay was occupied with trying to further understand what he could about the arbiters of casting on *Big Shot,* and searching job listings. He'd return again and again to *Big Shot*'s credits. Fixating on Jabaree West, Andrew Wagner, Marcy Lon. Fixating on the strength of a "W" or an "M" at the start of a name. West. Wagner. Marcy. Letters that made space for themselves, would not be crowded, were never silent, but also asserted themselves without any volume needed. *wwwwwwwww-wwwwwwuuuuhhhhh. mmmmmmmmmmmmmmmuhhhh.* Ben would quietly moan in his nook, emitting his fevered-sounding hum unconsciously as he did his research, fucking jaw. When he'd maxed out his abilities in deciphering the portent of letters in the names of strangers, the faces and expressions of nobodies in tiny photographs, he scrolled through jobs. Accounting and accounting-adjacent positions in Germany, Hawaii, the deep suburbs of Fort Worth, before shifting to looking at real options, ones in Chicago and, to use the language of car dealerships, Chicagoland. And in this way Ben had been actively avoiding looking for a job and also avoiding actually applying to audition for the show. He had yet to even look at the application. He still didn't have a pitch. But time was running out in several ways. Chicago auditions were coming, and he had less than five weeks of severance pay left, which meant two more paychecks. He needed to actually begin applying for jobs that he had a chance of getting. He fired off his resume to a credit union in Edgewater and to a nonprofit in Lincoln Square for a staff accountant position. Two realistic options. The nonprofit emailed back within minutes asking if he was available to interview the next day, Saturday, and Ben replied that he was. He had no idea what to expect. He did not fully understand what "nonprofit" meant.

Ben's lone genius might have been his ability to stall, evidenced clearly by the past several weeks, fifteen years, the amount of time he was capable of spending engaged searching for a new desktop background image. There were hours left in what he called his workday. He couldn't handle any more *SVU*, and he'd already landed an actual job interview—the dumbest luck. He needed a change, a shake-up in his routine; felt one change, to his computer's desktop image, might lead to other larger changes. Ben didn't strictly believe this but was willing to participate in broad and permanent modes of self-delusion in order to avoid more important concerns and that which scared him—often one and the same. He sank deeper into the nook, as if he were beginning to climb into a tunnel. He'd had an Alec Soth photograph on his desktop for years and had ceased to be able to actually see it. He wanted a different background in hopes it would spur some new thought; this he actually did believe. He tried a black-and-white behind-the-scenes picture of Adam West sans cowl holding a mug of Bat-coffee while wearing the rest of the Batsuit. He tried a picture of Tuesday Weld squinting at the camera. A topographic map of DuPage County. A snowbound alley on the west side of Chicago in 1973; rectangular taillights visible from within a great white mound. A young couple, farmers, the man with bad skin and a crew cut wearing a gray sweatshirt and the beautiful mother naked from the waist up, both standing, the mother nursing their baby in their small trailer's kitchen. A top-down photo of a flattop grill at a diner: bacon, sausage links, hashbrowns along the back, eggs frying up front.

He tried maybe sixty pictures, all wrong. An hour gone. He

eventually arrived at a photograph that worked by embracing what Tara had said: "You have the trees outside that you stare at. That's what you have." He took this information from her literally and put a picture of the view from their living-room window looking onto green tree-lined Prairie Avenue as his laptop desktop background. It felt right. It was a photograph he'd saved from the original online listing for their home.

Ben moved the few icons he had on his sparse desktop to the far left of his screen and looked at the familiar view. The view he saw in empty afternoons and early warming mornings, blank dead nights. His own street, there it was.

And while staring at this image, he came to know his pitch. He did not have to write it down, he did not make any note, he knew it whole, and it had been there with him all along.

Ben would pitch nothing. That's what he had: nothing. Or, only himself. "You have trees outside to stare at," and what she hadn't said was that you have the empty, raw want. Ben knew it. He would ask the Big Shots to believe in him—he'd ask them to trust him to bring their invested money back to his community and create his own local one-time lottery. No, his own *Big Shot*. He would create his own *Big Shot*. That was it. Trust me to do what you do on a local, more personal, smaller scale. He'd select several winners. He didn't want to pitch an idea or product that was ultimately tied back to an origin point he would be ashamed of, or have to reckon with later, so he'd use their own idea: *Big Shot*. The Mariska thought had led him to nothing. And from nothing he'd take what was already there. Even businesses that claim and forefront some morality, even those that abide by what they claim, are laying waste everywhere they go, be sure. Having to account for, on a personal level, bringing another object into the world, or reframing a common domestic challenge as needing a gadgeted solution, or sourcing ingredients for food—anything really, despite being completely out of his reach to make a reality—having to fully account for any of these hypothetical

91

TRUE FAILURE

products was not something Ben felt he would ever be up to. He had nothing.

He had nothing and so he would take what the show already had and offer it up as his own.

And he could couch his nothing, his repurposing, his repositioning of the idea of the show, inside a prank, an April Fools' pitch. Only the real trick would be that Ben wasn't kidding. There was no prank. If placed within the framework of April Fools', maybe his whole no-business no-idea no-nothing pitch had a chance to make some sense.

He felt he had the pitch he would have to make to the real gatekeepers, the producers of *Big Shot*, and now it was a matter of getting the opportunity.

In his mind, this was a pitch done in a similar fashion to those seen on the show, except without the set, or the music, or the celebrity Big Shots. Maybe one camera recording from a fixed position for legal purposes. Ben imagined a conference room, white walls, impatient men and women in business attire. An enthusiastic woman doing most of the talking and staying cheerful, "Okay, let's hear what you've got." Then politely being dismissed and told to wait for a phone call. Walking past a line of other hopefuls waiting in the gray hardpack-carpeted hall, to the elevator, down to the lobby, to the parking lot, the car. A shaky moment, exhale, drive home. And then months. Waiting.

Realizing what it was he would pitch, combined with his imagining of the circumstances that would surround the pitch's existence, caused Ben to finally do the legwork of reading how it would be, on a granular level, that he would get on the show. He'd avoided learning this basic information as a protection tactic; now he was ready. He stood in his nook at the library, took off his tie while several other jobless library regulars noted his standing, noticed an unblinking librarian watching him from ten feet away, and sat back down.

There was paperwork. Lots of paperwork. The initial

application was fifteen pages long and easily accessible online. Depressingly accessible. When Ben typed *how to get on big shot,* a search that over the past three weeks he had avoided making, the third search result was a PDF of the complete initial application form. Tens of thousands of other people, maybe more, maybe lots, lots more, had gone after exactly what Ben was going after right now. He wondered, how many others had analyzed previous contestants—all of them—and then found comfort in their privately held notions of what they believed could actually sway the investors? All of them. But they didn't have CBAS. 1. Confidence, 2. Belief, 3. Ability to believe in 1 and 2, 4. Sex. And how many others had a notebook that held what his notebook did? No one. How many others had commuted daily to a public library to chronologically watch all of *Law & Order: SVU*? No one. Most people weren't even capable of imagining the mistakes Ben excelled at making. It was frightening to think that the information one might need, or the information that might end one's march toward getting on the show, was instantly available. And that after typing *how to get on b* his search was correctly assumed, completed, answered.

## "BIG SHOT" INITIAL APPLICATION PACKET

**General Instructions:**

Thank you for your interest in applying to participate in *Big Shot* (the "Series"). In order to apply and participate you must fully complete and return the following attached documents to the Casting Department:

- Short Application
- One Minute Audition Video (.wmv, .avi, .mov, .mp4)
- Audition Release
- Submitted Materials Release
- Intellectual Property Release (submit only if your audition video was shot by someone other than you)

*If you are applying as part of a team of collaborators, EACH*

*COLLABORATOR must complete and submit their own Initial Application Packet; however, collaborators may appear together in a single audition video.*

**Please note**: In order to fully complete the application process for the Series, you must complete and return the Full Application Packet, which will include the following documents which will be provided by Big Shot LLC at a later date.

- Applicant Questionnaire
- Business Details Questionnaire
- Intellectual Property Questionnaire
- Audition Release
- Submitted Materials Release
- Background Questionnaire
- Participant Agreement

Please be advised that you must meet the following eligibility requirements (which may be changed at any time by Big Shot LLC in its sole discretion) in order to participate in the Series:

- You must be 18 years of age (or the age of majority in the state in which you reside) or older.
- You must be a legal resident of the United States.
- Neither you nor any of your immediate family members or anyone living in your household may be nor have been within the past one (1) year employees, contractors, officers, directors or agents of any of the following: (a) Big Shot LLC, any entity owned, controlled or affiliated with Big Shot LLC, or any parent, subsidiary, affiliated or related entity of any of the foregoing; (b) any person or entity involved in the development, production, distribution or other exploitation of the Series or any variation thereof; (c) any known major sponsor of the Series or its advertising agency; (d) any "Big Shot" or any entity substantially owned or controlled by any "Big Shot"; or (e) any person or entity supplying services or prizes to the Series.
- You may not be a candidate for public office and must agree not to become a candidate for public office from the date of the Audition Release until one (1) year after the initial broadcast of the last episode of the Series in which you appear.

- You may not have been convicted of a felony.
- You must voluntarily submit to a background check.

**Applicant Name:** *Ben Silas*

**Business Name:** *Ben Silas*

**Business Website (full URL):** *N/A*

**If applying as part of a group, the name(s) of your collaborator(s):** *N/A*

**Your Street Address/City/State/Zip:** *1000 Prairie Ave. Harks Grove, IL 60515*

**Birth date:** *4/14/1987*

**Gender:** *M*

**Occupation/Place of Employment:** *N/A*

**School(s) Attended & Degree(s) Completed (include year(s)):** *University of Illinois/Bachelor of Science in Accountancy*

**How much money have you invested in the company and in what time frame? What was that money used for?** *N/A*

**What was the GROSS income from your business last year?** *N/A*

**What was the NET income from your business last year?** *N/A*

**What are your SALES PROJECTIONS for THIS CALENDAR YEAR?** *N/A*

**What are your SALES PROJECTIONS for NEXT CALENDAR YEAR?** *N/A*

**Have you ever tried to raise money from outside sources?** *No*

**Do you have any physical conditions, special needs, accommodations or fears that we should know about?** *No*

**Have you ever had a temporary or permanent restraining order entered against you or has anyone sought a temporary or permanent restraining order against you?** *No*

**Have you ever been charged with any felony or misdemeanor?** *No*

**Have you ever been convicted of any felony or misdemeanor?** *No*

**Have you ever been party to a lawsuit?** *No*

**Describe in DETAIL what your business or product is. What does it do? Provide as much detail as possible:** *I do not have a business or product.*

*My pitch is relevant if you are again shooting seasonal specials as you did last season.*

*My pitch is specifically for the spring seasonal episode that is hypothetically occurring again this year. Last year you had a garden-ing pitch (natural soil enhancer), a wiffle ball pitch (unbreakable ball, increased movement even at lower velocities), an online dating ser-vice aimed at baby boomers, but one area of spring that was missed was an April Fools' pitch. To be clear, I am not trying to fool any-one. But I think for what it is I am trying to do, the context of April Fools' could help make what I'm aiming for more understandable to an audience—*

# 12. *TARA*

SATURDAY MORNING, TARA and Billy were in the house alone. Ben was in the city meeting up with a man he'd gone to college with, someone he'd told Tara had been badgering him to come in from Harks on the train for an early weekend drink. Tara didn't mind; Ben never met up with anyone. And Nguyen didn't count. She made Billy French toast in the dim kitchen; all the light in the adjacent living room gave the room a lazy warmth. Billy drank three and a half glasses of orange juice, an indulgence reserved for the weekend. Unlimited juice. Tara drank coffee from the automatic maker and ate what Billy didn't finish, along with three hunks from a block of New Zealand cheddar and two half handfuls of ripe, falling-apart raspberries standing in front of the open fridge. Tara ran her red fingers under the cold tap and looked around: this was her home. This was where she lived. For an instant her face appeared to indicate this realization had caused the whole house to begin lifting into the sky. She was very aware that she used to live elsewhere, but she hadn't been still enough in years to see where it was she had actually moved. The clarity left her like fog leaves a mirror.

She was listening to Ben's music, or what she thought of as Ben's music. Singing along. He loved all those Drag City records, some of which she loved too, but he chiefly loved *Viva Last Blues* in a way she couldn't really understand. Tara found it ultimately too scattered. She missed Ben this morning, somehow related to having Billy in and out of the kitchen, wandering the house, and related to being acutely aware of time passing. And the sex, lately. It had been nightly and loving and binding in a way it hadn't been between the two of them, really, since they'd met. Like early-days-dating sex, without the frenzy or nerves and with far more laughter. He'd finish and she'd imitate his grunt devastatingly. He sounded ridiculous. She would laugh for half a minute at her own impersonation. Ben would laugh too. Sometimes she'd finish. Sometimes. She'd told Ben she was off the pill, not drinking, nothing, and watched him, waiting for his understanding to click in.

She listened to Ben's music as she slowly cleaned up, singing, and Billy made his way through the rooms of the house playing. Tara was listening in Ben's dumb fashion too: he usually skipped initial tracks on records, it was a tic that for some reason carried over into much of his musical intake regardless of artist. It made sense to her when he did it with *Desire* or *Good Old Boys*, but Ben did it with almost every record he listened to. He'd said that people put too much thought into what the first song should be, and he wasn't interested in their thoughts. He wanted the music. He'd explained his thinking once when they were first dating and never again. Tara had told him what he was saying made no sense—the artist had also chosen to put a particular song as the second track, and the third—there was no avoiding "thoughts." But she had to admit, you rarely lost the best song with Ben's method. There were notable exceptions. Most recently, she'd argued for "Goose Snow Cone" off *Mental Illness* and over the years "Changes" off *Hunky Dory* and "Misfits" off *Misfits*—Ben immediately relented on that one— "Misunderstood" off *Being There,* and "Margaret vs. Pauline" off *Fox Confessor Brings the Flood,* which wasn't the best song on the record, but Tara could not stand for its exclusion. And of course "Farewell Transmission." No one argued that one. She didn't know where he'd gotten his theory; it was exactly the kind of belief, and one he'd always held onto, that made her love him. There was something hopeful about his boyish stratagems and his loyalty to his own mistakes; he believed they mattered when it was apparent to everyone else alive they so clearly did not. So she'd skipped the opening two tracks, her own extra flourish, on *Viva Last Blues,* and started with "The Brute Choir" and sung along, full voiced, in the house.

She had made no plans yet for the day. Tara had not taken a shower, brushed her teeth, or put on a bra, and she felt glad this little juiced-up kid was running around her home. He was done circling the house in the invented boy world of his mind and lingered in the kitchen with her as she sang, making faces at him. She let him watch cartoons at the table on her computer as she finished up the few dishes, still singing, and went upstairs to the bathroom to gesture toward getting ready.

The sticky note that she'd left Ben a week ago was still on the bathroom mirror, but Tara noticed he'd done something to it. He'd crossed out most of the message and left only one sentence. He'd also put a piece of Scotch tape over the upper border of the sticky note, as if this message were meant to have some permanence. Tara didn't know if this was a message Ben intended for himself, or for her:

*You may be right re: beautiful-resilient-taken-advantage-of women being the most successful on the show, but you are not such a woman. Neither am I. And if you're right, why would you want to be on this show. If it is that important to you to get on then I would suggest you think about who it is that you are and go from there. Think about what it is that you have.* Trees outside to stare at. *A wife who loves you. An opportunity to do something else. Adler Planetarium during the day and will be back early-ish. I love you but you're being fucking stupid. Choose something else.*

Tara brushed her teeth and looked at the note. The note was for her. Maybe that wasn't Ben's intention, but she'd received a message regardless. An image came to her: her street, Prairie Avenue, from the perspective of someone standing in the middle of the road and looking down its length, the trees forming a partial canopy, and overlaid on that, a large black football helmet with a bowl set into its crown for chips. A snack helmet.

A black snack helmet the size of a small car in the middle of her tree-lined street. This was the image she would paint.

Upstairs, along with the bathroom, were three small bedrooms. Their room, the room Billy was sleeping in, which they called the guest room, and then a third bedroom which Ben had intended to be Tara's studio but which in reality had become junk storage. Early on he'd been fixated on altering the room so as to provide Tara with more ventilation—oils—but he knew nothing about painting or the fact that turpenoid made this somewhat irrelevant. It was lighting that was more important, and after removing all the junk, it was lighting that Billy and Tara would have to work on before she could get started.

During her student years she'd mostly painted in rooms with fluorescent ceiling lights. Fluorescents give off a cool light, and she'd counter this with a daylight bulb in a clip-on lamp that she'd point at her canvas. But the junk room upstairs already had a desk lamp, so Tara just needed one additional clip-on lamp with a daylight bulb. One lamp on either side of her. The most important thing about the lighting setup would be that no shadows were cast from her hands onto the canvas as she was painting. She still had her pallet, a rectangular piece of glass with white backing that she'd place on her right side on a table she'd also have to buy. Pallet on the right and side table on the right so she would not have to reach across her body. She was remembering her process. Her process was still in her instinctually, but she explicated it to herself in order to consider what it was tangibly she actually no longer had and would need to purchase. She was remembering all she'd gotten rid of. Ben had not been aware of how much she'd tossed. Moving into the house was a new life for Tara in a larger way than she'd ever stopped to think about. Yes, the day care, and the latent hope for a kid that was now out in the open and regularly pursued, but as she was cataloging all she needed to reacquire, she clearly saw the loss of giving up her painting life. She wasn't being dramatic. She'd given it up. It was very hard for her to feel like she was not overreacting. But she wasn't.

She'd make two stops with Billy. Blick and Home Depot.

**B**

- *turp*
- *silicoil jar x2*
- *pallet knife x2*
- *18" x 36" prestretched canvas*
- *medium*

<u>**HD**</u>

- *bulbs*
- *clamp light*
- *tarp*

Tara and Billy walked outside into the slow, bright day. She waited several seconds until no cars were coming in either direction and then took the picture with her phone she'd seen in her mind. Standing in the middle of her tree-lined street, looking down their long, straight road; it felt like her road. Billy waited, buzzing at the end of the driveway, monitoring traffic. He said, "Yep, yep, yep." A small yellowed Mazda pickup was approaching, as tall as a mailman, and Tara stepped to the side to let it pass. She stayed in the road and took a couple more pictures. She'd take Ben's Illini snack helmet and spray-paint it black on the driveway. He'd miss it but forgive her. That is, if she chose to tell him.

# 13. MARCY

THERE WAS A pet store in walking distance from the rink. Marcy and Jet were intently looking at the fish. An associate in a blue shirt approached them and greeted Jet, "Haven't seen you in so so long, how are you, boy?" Her name tag read "Murla." Marcy was waiting for the next surprise from Murla, a woman she'd never met. Murla unhooked a set of keys from the belt loop of her khakis and held them up. "Going around asking individually because people don't listen to the announcements." She pointed toward the ceiling as some message was being fuzzily murmured out of the speakers. "Are these your keys?"

Marcy instinctively reached into her bag as if to make sure this set of keys completely unlike her own had not somehow been lifted from her. "They aren't." Murla began saying something and Marcy interrupted her: "You recognize Jet and not me?"

"He's been here with someone else."

"He hasn't."

"Seems very possible he could lead a life you don't know about. He's not even leashed. Seems to be able to do as he pleases."

Marcy didn't know what to say to that other than, "Oh get fucked," and started walking away. Jet did not immediately follow. Marcy stopped at the end of the aisle and watched Murla hold the missing keys down low as if to give Jet the chance to catch their scent. Marcy said the dog's name quietly and the dog shook himself out and trotted toward her. Murla straightened, watching them leave.

If Marcy had lost her keys, no one had a copy. The situation she'd created for herself at work was not one that fostered relationships that allowed for key exchanges. Marcy wanted people to be intimidated, curious, at a remove. She needed certain people to be motivated by fear to work hard for her, but mostly her actions at work were designed to encourage others to leave her alone, allowing her to continue to do the aspects of her job that she could not delegate. Neighbors too, though. They probably would go Murla on her as well, knowing the dog more readily than Marcy. She needed a different job, a different place to live, a different way to live. And to start, a vacation.

The vacation that Marcy would not actually be taking was during a weeklong window before casting for the eleventh season of the American *Big Shot* proceeded into its final stages. It was the period where contestants were told that background checks were taking place, which was true, though the processing time was greatly exaggerated by production. Background checks were followed by routine calls to employers past and present, landlords, banks. Minor and major investigations into social media by interns. Information was gathered and grouped. Files were made. Marcy was not involved.

The vacation she would not actually be taking would also occur during the time Marcy believed the majority of the renewed interest in the PCKG murder would begin to arise, if it did at all.

Her parents were victims of a particular kind of news coverage and their own negligence—and a very un-California willingness to be honest. They knew their mistake and would talk about it if asked, especially Mr. Lon; but it had been several years since they'd been asked. Interest in the case had waned. Had waned greatly—true crime was a completely normalized mass entertainment, and all mediums were saturated. In their responses to PCKG questions, the Lons' reasoning and thoughts had sometimes been invented but never to obscure their mistake; they often simply ran out of truths and felt impolite saying nothing. At the diner, or at church before they had stopped going, or if some odd reporter had called, they'd talk. Both felt it was the least they could do. A man had died, after all. Neither actually believed that if they had called 911 or run outside anything would have changed. Not that they ever ran anywhere. Both felt, probably incorrectly, that the murder had been inevitable.

Another headline, not PCKG, was clearer: "Bug Man Kills San Jose Father on Front Lawn as Customers Watch." But BMKSJF-FLCW is less nimble when repurposed.

\*\*\*

MARCY WANTED TO shrug off her job, her easy competence in its strictures. She wanted a job where she didn't feel she had to invent herself daily. And wanted something much closer to what she had actually planned to do in the first place: making movies. She wanted to forget everything she knew about the needs and pressures facing her superiors, and how to appease them. She wanted to forget the names of coworkers' children. She wanted to forget entire lives she'd had gummed and slurred at her while caught in expensive lunch traps.

Some lies Marcy has forgotten telling during work lunches:

- "Never had a soda at McDonald's. Say what you will about meat, and it's true, murder, but the real evil is soda. Big Mac, no middle bun, no lettuce, no fries, and a coffee. A meal I self-prescribe. Like a B vitamin."
- Claimed to have been born in the pink bathtub in her grandmother's pink house. Doused in rosewater during first shrieking breaths. The toilet pink too. Nonna sitting there tinkling clear, grandmotherly, hydrated piss as Marcy arrived. Claimed the house later burned down while her grandmother slept with the radio on. Don Everly's firm rhythm strumming pushing her into the next world.
- Said she could sing in close harmony with any living North American woman.
- Only child raised in Oregon.
- Said she "did not understand" the BBC.

She was an aspirational liar. Aspired to have gradients and alleyways in her past that she lacked.

She wanted to make dusty American movies; this was her original and renewed reason for being in LA. She wanted to make three movies and then occasionally be invited places to talk about other movies. She wanted to have made dusty American movies. She imagined herself giving a lecture on Robert Altman, the women in Altman's movies, Julie Christie, Shelley Duvall, Sissy Spacek, Karen Black, and then after the lecture in the small auditorium, let's say the Jack Baskin Auditorium at UC Santa Cruz, a 150-seater, plush, only a quarter full for her talk, the scattered audience attentive but distant, she wanted to admit to a young tan student with wispy blond hairs above his lip that for her, "Altman" meant only *Brewster McCloud, McCabe and Mrs. Miller, The Long Goodbye, Thieves Like Us, California Split,* and *3 Women.* That's it. Dump the rest. She wanted to be harsh with the boy when he protested. She wanted him to think he had a chance to fuck her.

She imagined explaining to him that she was paring down her intake to clarify the vision she was creating for her next film as she made her way back into the pet store, leaving Jet waiting on the sidewalk at the storefront's window. Marcy clarified to herself that in this projection, this waking dream, she had already made a film. Three films. She had actually made none.

Marcy found Murla near the prescription dog food and asked to see the keys again, said that she actually was missing her keys. Murla made no move toward her belt loop. Marcy stepped closer and said, "I'm sorry for swearing," turning her palms up like a minister. Murla's posture softened. As the woman began to speak, Marcy ripped the keys off her belt loop and calmly walked over to the fish. Marcy removed the lid on the betas and dropped the keys in. She knew how to leave the store, directly and as if nothing had happened. She had not yet figured out how to leave the show.

105

TRUE FAILURE

# 14. CALLIE

HER BURBANK APARTMENT was eight hundred square feet, one bedroom, one bath, and rent was $3,000 a month. There was an outdoor and an indoor pool for residents, a tight movie theater that showed three movies a week curated monthly on a theme. There were free shuttles offered and not taken as a sign of status. The branding and advertising for the building was similar to that of a sweatless gym. The building was called West Place.

Biweekly Callie was paid $1,320; she could not afford her current life. The credit cards were many, and there was money from her mom, sent via bank transfer, phone to phone, where the reality of their money truly existed. Her mom was not wealthy. She'd told Callie that debt was not real, money was not real, but the apartment was, West Place was—the job, the internship, that was real, and her next job would be real too. Even more real. What mattered was the progression—less firm realities becoming increasingly solid in the ascension.

Work and no extra spending money, no spending money at all, meant that the majority of Callie's time not at the studio or sitting in the Target parking lot pretending to be investigating a thirty-year-old murder was spent in her apartment or wandering the West Place grounds. This was her choice, her way, regardless of her financial situation. The apartments sat on top of an expensive grocery store called Borgans near other buildings that might have housed real estate agencies, anonymous marketing firms, other apartment schemes.

Callie's constant detective work had recently centered on a man she was able to observe easily without leaving West Place: the building manager, Miguel Galarraga.

Miguel was in his late thirties, two small daughters, a wife. He was clean-shaven and wore his hair parted to the side with product. He wore a navy-blue T-shirt tucked into jeans, a black leather belt, and Wolverine boots every day. Maybe five foot nine, one hundred and sixty pounds. Callie allowed she might be off on his weight.

The majority of the time Miguel was on the property, he was maintaining the landscaping. She did not suspect Miguel of any crime; nothing about him sent up any red flags to Callie, and that is why she had become increasingly focused on being aware of his activities. If *Murder Girls* had taught her anything, it was that evil was often hiding in plain sight, and once a criminal act provided new context for previously benign details, past behavior often seemed rife with what should have been clues. Had anyone ever spoken to an ex-boyfriend of Callie's, many strange happenings named would have made any number of future crimes of hers seem inevitable. She'd faked a car accident to lure an ex into speaking to her after he'd cut off contact, copied several keys without permission, and there was a missing dog. The dog had been named Slowbert.

From her deck Callie was able to see the majority of the front landscaping leading into West Place. Ovate topiary, closely clipped grass—too close, as if for putting instead of life—Southern California locoweed, buckbrush, green and white was the aim for whoever had designed the landscaping that Miguel maintained. He was down there now on his knees, cranking a sprinkler into compliance.

Callie went down the back stairs and around so it appeared she had been arriving from somewhere other than inside her own apartment as she encountered Miguel. "Who is it that picked out all this? The flowers and the shape of things?" She was standing behind him as he worked on his hands and knees.

"I did. I underbid the contract that was in place by four grand and asked only that they keep me on. Building manager and groundskeeper."

"Not a promotion."

"Not a promotion. Another job. Two jobs now."

"Admirable."

"Okay." Miguel was on his knees squinting up at Callie. Water spraying chaotically, chopping the air behind him.

Callie wanted to know what he carried on his person daily that could potentially be harmful. Nothing was clipped onto his belt, and she saw no outline of anything in his front pockets. He had no reason to be suspicious of her, so she asked, "Do you carry a pocketknife?"

Miguel reached into his back pocket and snapped open a large serrated knife, handing it to Callie, handle first. She smiled hugely at him, and he smiled back, the sun bearing down on them, beads of sweat rising on their foreheads. "Thanks, Miguel," Callie said, holding the knife aloft as if set against the sky it would be revealed more fully.

And so Callie was building her file.

# 15. BEN

BEN WAS SITTING on the crowded rooftop of Gene's Sausage Shop in Lincoln Square. Downstairs was the grocery portion of the building, the monstrous deli counter, aisles of imported wares and rare condiments, and up on the roof was a friendly bustling umbrellaed place to drink beer and eat bratwursts, pretzels, mustard. It felt wonderful to shake loose from Benson and Stabler. The rooftop overlooked the busy square—strollers, bearded dads, put-together seasonally conscious moms, the Book Cellar, Old Town School of Folk Music.

Nonprofit must have meant anything goes for an interview. Saturday on the roof. Ben wanted to order a beer, but that seemed a step too far before even looking his interviewer in the eye. Her name was Shirley Chandra, and she had given no physical description of herself in the email.

Ben flagged down a server and ordered a beer he planned to quickly down and then set on the empty table next to him. He'd told Chandra in an email he'd have a White Sox hat with him on the table, the Batterman logo, which actually had the opportunity to stand out in this part of the north side. He didn't want to say he'd be wearing it, because who the hell wore a ball cap for an interview; though maybe considering the other factors operating in this setting, he'd be fine. Other than the hat as a marker, Ben didn't know how else to describe himself physically in a way that was distinguishable. Six-foot-one, two-hundred-ish pounds, thirties, white, brown hair; that described nearly every white male on this rooftop. He'd been right, though, about the hat. Looking around, he mostly saw bright-blue hats with red Squatchees. The bandwagon had swelled; most in bright blue would look at you blankly if you said "Dale Sveum." Ben had hit on two single bets the night before and was up $54; or that was how he was choosing to look at the numbers. Actually he was down around $2,300. Understanding the minor win as a more complete victory, erasing all losses, was a delusion he did not have to force. The server set down his beer. Ben's phone dinged. An email.

**Big Shot LLC <intern19@bigshotllc.com >**
**to me**

Ben Silas,

Congratulations! You have been invited to audition for **Big Shot** casting producers in Chicago, IL. The auditions will begin August 6 at 8 AM at 9700 West Oak Road, Rosemont, IL 60018.

If you accept this invitation click the GREEN button in this email that says YES. If you are unable to make the audition click the RED button that says NO. From there you will be assigned an Interview Number in another email with further information along with information on Audition Video guidelines.

Ben looked off to his left seeing nothing, and then drank his beer in two muted veteran gulps. He felt an immediate sense of doom but, once the initial dread wave had crashed, felt it was inevitable that he would get on the show. He started laughing on the sausage roof. No one noticed. He stood laughing and still went unnoticed. He called over the same server as before and ordered two more beers. He dialed Tara, standing next to his table, feeling unable to sit.

"I'm in. Auditioning in two weeks."

"I thought you didn't have a pitch?"

"That is my pitch."

Tara said, "Essentially, you are asking them for a job?"

"Huh."

"You don't have a pitch, so the work falls to them? You see that. They have to create meaning out of your nothing."

A woman walked up to Ben and asked if his name was Ben,

she was pointing at his hat on the table. He shook his head no. He put his phone down for a second and said, "I'm sorry, my name is not Ben," as he put on the hat. Something in him wanted to sarcastically tell her, "Sorry, professor," but he resisted. He didn't know if she was a professor or what the core of his hypothetical insult really was. The server set down Ben's beers. Shirley Chandra continued walking around the rooftop pretending to look for the man she already knew full well she'd found.

On the phone Tara said, "Hello?"

"I don't have an idea; I'm using their idea. I want them to give me money so I can organize my own *Big Shot* in Harks. Local. Smaller, less profitable ventures that aren't designed to make me money but instead help the community. Help the community thrive."

"You don't wave to the neighbors."

Still on the phone, Ben held one of the beers he'd ordered and watched Chandra take one last imperious look back at him. Ben took a long drink. Chandra put both her hands up to her throat and continued to hold Ben's gaze. Then she looked beyond him, and left. Ben turned around casually and looked down at the square, strollers. He waved as if he recognized someone below, still holding the phone. Ben was waving to a blank spot on the ground. He said to Tara, "Did you take another test today?"

"Pee on the stick? No, baby. This kid loves when I say PEE on the STICK. Listen, we are checking out at Home Depot over here. But I'm happy for you? I'll tell Billy. He's excited."

He was asking for a job. He hadn't seen it with clarity until Tara had given him the thought. He was asking for money and to be given something to do; looking for work even as he believed himself to be avoiding doing so.

# 16. TARA

- *Titanium White*
- *Cadmium Yellow*
- *Naples Yellow*
- *Ultramarine Blue*
- *Phthalo Blue*
- *Burnt Sienna*
- *Yellow Ochre*
- *Cadmium Red*
- *Sap Green*

Tara started sketching the trees onto the canvas in thinned-out yellow ochre. Billy came in occasionally and stood near the door as she painted. Billy was entranced by the bright lamps and the stillness of the room, which he articulated by saying, "Like *Star Wars* parked and you're working on it."

Tara said, "*Millennium Falcon,*" and Billy nodded, smiling.

Once the sketching of the trees was done Tara would begin the sky gradient. From the darkest uppermost sky, the gradient would be burnt sienna with ultramarine blue into ultramarine blue with phthalo blue and titanium white and then adding more and more titanium white for the brightest sky directly above the tree line. Tara would do the sky gradient after sketching the trees because that way, when she painted the trees on top of the dried sky gradient, she would not have to go in and add pieces of sky where it broke through the leaves. She had little scraps of paper on her newly purchased Home Depot side table with sketches in pen and notations of color. She'd been working for only an hour or so after getting everything set up when she heard Ben's car on the driveway. She hadn't yet finished sketching the trees. Tara heard Ben come up the stairs and into the room, and when he didn't say anything, she turned from the small canvas. She was watching him, waiting for him to speak.

"I lost my job."

"When?" Tara said. "Lost."

"Three weeks ago."

"Where have you been going?"

"Downtown. The library."

"To make me think you were going to work."

"Yes."

Tara's head dropped briefly and she said nothing. Then, "How long are we okay for? Are we already not okay?" She turned back to the canvas and said, "I need you to order food. Red's. Billy is going to be hungry. I want my own. Sausage-mushroom. Well done. And get a salad. Extra Caesar."

Tara needed to let the paint dry before starting on the sky, but she wanted to start immediately. She cleaned her brush in the silicoil jar and began applying medium to the canvas to help accelerate the drying of the trees. When she was done, she stayed in the room letting the day slip. She could hear Ben chasing Billy around the first floor, growling, the boy laughing maniacally. She'd wait for the pizza.

# 17. MARCY

IN HER BARE kitchen, Marcy poured gin into a bright-orange mug filled with ice cubes and poured half a beer into a black dish for Jet. That's another one she'd ask the dog. Which of these do you prefer? Coors? Local IPA from down the street? Saison? She put the gin back into her barren freezer. She thought, Siberia. She thought the words: *FREEZER OF THE MIND*. All that was in the freezer was an ice cube tray and another bottle of gin. Jet lapped up the beer and then looked at Marcy, waiting for her to pour water into his dish, and then he lapped that up too. Once that routine was complete, she drank the other half of the beer and took a deep gulp of the gin and set the mug in the freezer. Marcy and Jet walked out into their darkening neighborhood. Marcy carried a Maglite when walking the dog at night.

She'd watched a terrible TV program that had reconstructed JonBenét Ramsey's childhood home on a soundstage, speculated about her murder, the murder weapon, everything. One of the forensic scientists was positive that the murder weapon had been a Maglite and had illustrated how easy it would be to kill a child with the heavy flashlight. He'd said, "Or kill anyone, for that matter." Marcy had purchased two the next day.

She thought of trees in LA as emanating darkness. Bent palm after bent palm, she passed them warily. Black pouring out. Everywhere else she'd been, even in the self-besotted Bay Area, trees held darkness as the night came on. Here, they *were* darkness. She whistled for Jet to catch up. She held a coiled leash in her hand in case bored police passed, or any particularly intense neighbors had had a bad day. She would not stop for other dogs, and if someone greeted her she would usually respond with, "Good night." She needed to eat.

# 18. CALLIE

WITH ONE OF her credit cards not yet maxed, Callie had ordered four baby monitors. One she positioned to record her front door. One she placed high on the wall near her sliding glass door looking out over the street, another in her bathroom above the mirror so the camera had a vantage of the entire bathroom, and the last in her bedroom from an upper corner for maximum coverage. After she'd installed the app on her phone and practiced toggling between cameras and understanding how to access the footage recorded earlier, she went into her bathroom with two rolls of paper towels.

Callie made softball-sized balls with the paper towels, ran them under the tap in the bathroom, packed them like snowballs, and then flushed them one by one. After three balls her toilet began backing up, laking her bathroom floor. Her phone chimed. A text from Marcy.

did I miss this week's Hillis email?

Callie looked at the ceiling, looked at her feet, getting wet. She had been planning on writing the email later that day, but decided to try something else:

I'm done with the emails. I'll fill you in next week. There's been a development

wow, ok. Monday

Callie dialed Miguel's work cell. "Hi, Miguel? This is Callie in 317. My toilet is backing up and I tried plunging, I was hoping you could help me?"

# 19. BEN

NGUYEN CAME OVER to help Ben shoot his audition video. The audition tape was to be a minute long, maximum. The parameters, other than the top end of the running length, were fairly open. In the email detailing how to digitally submit the file and what the file extension should be, there was language explicitly stating there was to be no copyrighted material of any kind present in the video, including sports memorabilia, food labels, vehicles with their factory badging displayed, and so on. The email also stated that the audition tape did not have to necessarily be viewed as a mirror copy of the pitch you planned on making at the audition or on the show, should you be chosen. The video could highlight what you wanted it to highlight. As the two men walked through Ben's chirping and shaded neighborhood to an empty grassy park across from train tracks, Nguyen read over these guidelines on Ben's phone. Nguyen had said he only had an hour to spare—a lie, it seemed—and was reading the guidelines as if futilely preparing for an imminent exam.

"They want you to sink your own ship and eliminate yourself early in the process, if you are so inclined. Leaving their requirements so wide open weeds out the people who aren't smart enough to approach this tactically."

Nguyen's tactic was to have Ben sit on a park bench, green expanse stretching behind him, and lay out what made his pitch different. Ben lacked an approach. He believed his lack of an approach was an approach. It was not.

Behind Ben on the bench there were children playing in the deep background of the frame, audible birds, an ideal suburban daytime scene, perfect scaffolding for a man directly addressing a camera and asking for money. Speaking from a place of neither opulence nor desperation. A request for money made from such a setting seemed like a promise to bring similar environs to others.

"My name is Ben Silas. I live in Harks Grove, Illinois. I am seeking an investment of $500,000 from the Big Shots in exchange for no equity in my company. There is no company. There is no product, no business—there is nothing, other than my request for the Big Shots to invest in me. My idea is only to take your idea. To take *Big Shot* local. I am asking for the Big Shots to believe in me, to invest in the person, as you often say—" and here the video would violate one of the key guidelines by hard cutting to copyrighted material, but, material from the show *Big Shot* itself. Nguyen would splice together six quick clips that included each of the most recent season's four Big Shots saying some form of "I invest in people." These included: "I believe in you, that's why I am making this deal," and "I may not understand this business, but I understand and can see your passion," and "My bet is on you." It was a gamble to break the rules provided, but it felt like the correct play to both of them.

In the video, Ben went on, "I want to play an April Fools' joke on the Big Shots, but also really ask for this investment. They have stated in the past that they invest in people, believe in people. If the Big Shots balk at my request for $500,000, good—I expect them to. That was part of my negotiation. I will then ask for $25,000 from each Big Shot, a total of $100,000, and with that I will create my own *Big Shot*. My goal is to project to them that I am the kind of person who has made good decisions before—I am employed, married to a wonderful person, happy. And I know I can apply these funds locally in a way that will make a real difference in my community."

# 20. TARA

TARA WAS AT the kitchen table piecing together how to share information about Portugal with the kids. She was drinking a domestic red blend from a plastic tumbler with a straw. The helmet painting mostly finished upstairs, she was waiting for the next image to arrive. Ben was at his audition in Rosemont. Audition, interview, whatever. He'd sent in his ridiculous video a week earlier. Tara was listening to her "Hundred Again" playlist. Last had been a live recording of "Bastards of Young," and now she was into solo Westerberg. Rain was speckling the window above the sink. Billy was upstairs, preemptively hiding under his bed. Tara had told him a storm was a possibility and that if he was afraid he could get in the tub or crawl under his bed. Billy had stared at her, confused. He was not afraid of storms but seemed willing to perform the behavior related to that fear. Watching the understanding that this was a game pass across his face, Tara repeated his options; Billy now received the information gravely, but not without obvious joy. Tara asked him if he wanted her to sit in the bedroom with him, but he said he wanted to be alone. His fears were in part a game he could play; whether or not they were real was irrelevant. A game he could reliably play without any companion. The first sentence about Portugal on the CIA World Factbook website had thrown her:

> *Following its heyday as a global maritime power during the 15th and 16th centuries, Portugal lost much of its wealth and status with the destruction of Lisbon in a 1755 earthquake, occupation during the Napoleonic Wars, and the independence of Brazil, its wealthiest colony, in 1822.*

She thought, how could a country's "heyday" be determined before its run as a country was over? There was a doomed and permanent past-tenseness in the common usage of the word. She read about the origin of *heyday*. Did the CIA believe Portugal's status as a country to be finished? That its current existence was some kind of afterlife, or purgatory, a shell country that existed only to produce a national soccer team? Tara acknowledged, in her thoughts, that if the CIA had qualified "heyday" with "current," the sentence would be confusing: "Following its current heyday as a global maritime power during the 15th and 16th centuries—" She wanted the sentence to be clear but also to allow for the possibility that Portugal could rise again. She ripped a piece of paper out of the back of her lesson-planning notebook and began writing: "From the country's inception to the present, Portugal's heyday was during the fifteenth and sixteenth centuries, when the country was a global maritime power." She said aloud, "Why couldn't the CIA have written that?" She wondered if the person who wrote the Portugal page on the CIA World Factbook website was considered an agent. Or was such a task outsourced? Could she be an agent?

She closed the lesson-planning notebook. Half-frozen ice dumped in the refrigerator. It was Saturday and she was only watching Billy. The weekends were days she typically did not watch any kids, but tending to Billy did not require much. He was used to being alone; seemed to prefer it more than most kids. Tara went and grabbed the three in-progress notebooks for the children she was watching, and the fourth she had just started, and opened B I L L Y. She began writing at the kitchen table.

*Billy asked why you decided to stay in Africa for another week. But only once. I told him: passport issue. We received the stuffed toy snake you sent. He has been wearing it around his neck and walking on the balls of his feet asking to be called "King Snake." I told him in this country we do not have kings.*

Tara stopped writing. He'd never asked to be called "King

Snake." She set aside B I L L Y. She grabbed the other notebook she had recently begun keeping, which she had titled O T H E R, and wrote the date as she had in her Billy notebook. She then crossed out ~~O T H E R~~ and titled the notebook ///. She wrote:

*If you tell the babysitter you'll be back at 12, then call and say you'll be back at 12 a week later, that's fucked.*

Tara closed the notebook. She had charged Billy's parents triple her usual rate for the additional week, claiming her entire schedule would have to be reworked, and they hadn't hesitated at all; she wondered if she should have charged more. They would have paid. Their decision had already been made. The money, and Billy, and her, all were secondary. Doing what they wanted to do had primacy. She almost admired them.

# 21. MARCY

"HE DOESN'T HAVE a business, and he violated one of the four rules for the audition video repeatedly," said Callie.

Marcy made a mock-pained face as she stood from her desk. She leaned on, in several senses of the phrase, Callie's adherence to standards. Out the office window Marcy thought the studio lot looked like coffee-table-book shots of brutalist architecture. She was thinking of one particular book belonging to an ex-roommate—a woman with a shoulder-spanning tattoo of what she called "Mother's horse." The tattoo was of an anthropomorphized penis. The view from Marcy's office was planar concrete surfaces and small perched boxy shadows. Beige, dusty pink, soft, forgotten brown. Unpeopled and right angles. Marcy put her forehead against the glass. Jet sighed from his blue bed. Without turning from the window she said, "Put that dog's face on a box of cereal."

Marcy could not think of which cereal brands featured a photograph of a dog on their box, though there were several. She could tell Callie did not like her outfit. A black collared shirt and bright-blue slacks with a single pleat. Callie never liked Marcy's outfits. They were expecting the other intern, Brent to come in, and so Marcy had not yet asked what the development in her Hillis investigation was. Brent was not privy to Hillis case talk.

Marcy had the potential contestant's video paused on her computer. She'd been alternately watching his audition tape— the man was sitting in a park mumbling—and making sure her email alerts for Walt Hillis were set up correctly. There'd been no news. But, the video: Ben Silas looked like any fucking white guy. He looked like one of these middle whites that said they hated buying clothes and defaulted to packs of gray T-shirts from Target, Levi's with stretch, sneakers for which he probably had a whole personal mythology he used to explain his brand loyalty, and so on. He looked thoughtful in a possibly annoying way. Clearly discontented. A man with whole floors of himself closed off. An everyman, awfully. Not in the classic working-for-the-weekend aphorisms-as-talk way, but in the failed, yes married, yes career, yes unhappy style. Marcy liked him. He was familiar; like the lesser brother of a catalog model. Or a friend of this lesser brother. She asked Callie for Ben Silas's file.

For the past four years Marcy had been granted two interns. There was no schedule for their departures, promotions, exits. They were paid well, Marcy thought. In the current grouping Callie had seniority over Brent. Brent was currently compiling in a cubicle. The interns' main function was to presort all candidates for ones they thought Marcy might like. And one or the other walked Jet occasionally, if Marcy was stuck on a call or in a meeting. "Walked" wasn't right; Jet was escorted outside. Marcy's interns had a history of rising in the industry, was what she told them, without examples.

Ben Silas was one that Callie had told Marcy she was eager to present. It was the utter unlikeliness of Ben Silas succeeding with the approach he had chosen to take, paired with his clear self-delusion and jarring lack of preparation, that made him, in a sense, irresistible. Marcy had tasked Callie with continuing to find increasingly unlikely contestants; it was the directive she'd given her once she realized Callie was competent, around a year and a half previous. She'd told Callie increasingly unlikely contestants were what she needed in order to remain "Marcy." This understanding was unspoken at this point.

Ben Silas's submission video, even the way he completed the necessary paperwork, answering very applicable questions with N/A, N/A, N/A, was offensive. Marcy had no doubt that the show would know what to do with him; that wasn't the issue.

They'd rip him apart. Or they'd let him rip himself apart. In the room and in the edit he would most likely be ridiculed. Depending on Ben Silas himself, that process could be generally received in a myriad of ways. All that was out of Marcy's hands. Getting him on the show was the thing; there was not a more unlikely candidate to pitch than Ben Silas. He was so wrong, he could potentially be a way for Marcy to begin to create an exit for herself from the show. The mistake of allowing Ben to pitch could signal a weakening in Marcy's thinking, enough for her to justify a leave of absence that she might choose to make permanent.

Marcy sensed that Brent, too, was invested in Ben Silas. She knew he believed he would be able to take the Top Marcy Intern spot if Callie moved on; this was not the case, but it did not benefit Marcy to make that clear to the young man. Marcy believed Callie was planning on leaving, and offering up Ben Silas seemed to be confirmation of sorts—a last big swing. Marcy knew Brent was anxious to no longer be saddled with the bulk of Jet maintenance. Brent was afraid of dogs. He'd successfully hidden this from everyone except Marcy, and Jet, who for some reason had not exposed him fully. Jet interacted with Brent as if there were a layer of smudged glass between them. Marcy found their exchanges difficult to watch. The dog pitied Brent but would not lie for him. No affection was offered in either direction.

Marcy required paper contestant files in addition to digital. Everything was printed and grouped and placed in manila folders, one for each contestant her interns believed worth her time. As Marcy received each new member of her intern team, she gave a talk about how the recruitment and the sifting of applicants began not with herself, but with them, the interns. Interns who had heard the talk upon their hiring were required to sit in with the new hire to hear the message again. Callie had heard the talk three times. How their role gave them power and allowed Marcy to keep her job. Marcy's job security was their own job security. "Having interns at all," she said, "is an act of trust. But I don't want our trust to mean we keep secrets amongst ourselves—it does mean that, but I don't want it to mean only that. I want our trust to extend to the work we are doing, daily. By granting you first refusal on all applicants I see, that's trust. I need you to, and I know that you will, make the right decisions. You are here not because I think we can be friends but because I know that you can see what I see."

Marcy held the Ben Silas file against the window to write on it. She muttered, "Sun," as if she were from some dark Nordic plain and not from California. She did not specifically remember telling the lie that she was raised in Oregon, one she'd told more than once, but she was consciously vague about the location of her growing up. She could recall saying "Which West Coast city would you like me to name?" when asked directly about her hometown. As if constantly moving had formed her. She would not have been writing with the folder against the window had Callie not been in the room. She would not have been working if Callie had not been in the room. On the front of the file Marcy rewrote the name that was already written on the tab, BEN SILAS, and underneath wrote:

*sad?/kind?/failed/humbled?/dumb?*

The question marks followed the obviously relatable qualities. This approach was one she had conceived early in her career when she realized all that mattered was what the audience was able to perceive. Her contestants, the human contestants, needed their human qualities to be forefronted. Often, little amplification was necessary because her contestants inhabited their humanity wholly: wore it, spoke it, radiated it. It was there in their eyes, between their eyes, in their lack of salesmanship, in their quiet wrongheadedness and confident stumbling. But, occasionally this humanity could be underlined by asking questions. The questions were not reserved for any one stage of the process or any one person. Everyone in casting and ultimately production was wrapped up in the creation and delivery of the contestants. The questions were for Marcy, were for the interns, and eventually the rest of casting if a contestant progressed in the process, and occasionally for the contestants themselves. The questions provided a framework, a starting point, a shape to the creation of these people as they would exist within their pitches. These words on the front of the manila folder that Marcy punctuated with question marks were the qualities of Ben Silas she would further interrogate.

"'Failed' troubles me," Marcy said.

"It's troubling," said Callie.

"I don't know how relatable 'failed' is?"

Callie laughed. "Very."

Marcy scrutinized Ben Silas's image on her computer screen. The man looked physically uncomfortable: like his pants didn't fit but once had, and he could remember their past comfort, like he was a sufferer of deep heartburn, busy tonguing a cut in his cheek, stricken with itchy mud butthole. The discomfort he wore on his face spoke of ongoing failure, or even more damning: his being a failed man, having already reached an end point and now waiting for death. But his application, the attempt, however ludicrous, suggested ambition. Ambition meant hope. Hope would negate the finality of "failed." But this hope must be perceivable to the viewing audience to matter. If this hope solely existed within a small closet in the basement of Ben Silas's thinking, it was irrelevant. The application, the audition video, could not be the sole evidence of the man's ambition. There must be evidence of this hope originating from Ben Silas for him to not appear as failed. The effort, the pitch itself was not hopeful if it was received as pathetic. Failure and ambition needed each other. But Marcy wasn't sure if there existed an instant TV-relevant relatability to failure; at least not if it read as being permanent, a failed existence. Depending on whether Ben Silas appeared to the audience as failed, his presence on the show could play as irreparably feeble. And Marcy was thinking mainly of his physical presence, his face squinting needlessly, what she'd seen of his hurried movement, his garbled delivery—this was to say nothing of the pitch itself, the nonpitch. Or maybe most people felt they'd failed too—were failed. Persisting within their defeat. Ben Silas might think of his pitch as noble, hopeful, meaningful; but unless the edit framed it as such, his personal beliefs, ideas, convictions—he himself—meant nothing. It didn't matter what he said; what mattered was what he would be allowed to say. Marcy saw it clearly: his pitch might make sense coming from someone else but did not make sense coming from Ben Silas. Ben Silas was such a bad idea that Marcy believed if she chose to push him through, which she believed she was capable of doing, it would potentially show a very real crack in her judgment. Ben Silas possessed a narrower potential window for success than anyone she'd previously considered backing. By "success" she did not mean that the person would gain a deal or even coherently deliver their pitch. "Success" was defined by the Big Shots' ability to engage with the person pitching in an entertaining way that could be edited into an even more entertaining ten to twelve minutes for the viewers at home; it would be cruel to expect as much from Ben Silas.

And yet, Marcy was sure she wanted him. The reasons Marcy wanted Ben to pitch were threefold: 1. to prove she could do it, 2. because if he somehow was a success it would be stunning, and 3. because if he failed she could lean into that failure as being indicative of a personal softening and begin to make her exit into a different life while still holding onto the residual safety and reassurance of her past triumphs.

Simply quitting did not and would never occur to her.

# 22. CALLIE

CALLIE DID NOT know what she was going to tell Marcy the development with Hillis had been, the reason she had not sent an email update. Callie was mulling whether or not to introduce to Marcy the concept that Hillis had somehow become aware of her investigation. This would give reason for Callie to be able to mimic the anxiety that Marcy had, and allow her to use this anxiety, fear, as a way of potentially doing even less for Marcy and still maintaining out-of-office privileges. Seated across from Marcy while she wrapped her head around some idiot from Chicago, Chicagoland, Callie was busy remembering Miguel holding up the sopping mush of paper towels and asking her why she had flushed these paper balls. "What were you doing?" He'd been on his knees on the wet floor looking up at her asking. "What the fuck are you doing?" She liked that he'd again been speaking to her from his knees.

"I wanted to see you, Miguel," she'd said, and pulled him to her body, hugging him. He'd stood to avoid having his face directly in her chest. Both standing, Callie had patted his back pocket, his ass, where he kept his pocketknife, and gripped it though his jeans until he looked at her.

Miguel had patted her on the back once, in between her shoulder blades, using three fingers, in place of returning the hug, then asked her to please leave her own apartment for two hours and told her he would clean up the mess if she promised not to contact or touch him ever again.

"If you need help? I'm not the person. Please don't touch me please don't mix me in whatever this is."

Callie had felt she could trust the man now; Miguel's response seemed to prove he would be of no harm to anyone in the future. She'd nodded, agreeing fully to Miguel's terms, and left.

# 23. BRENT

BRENT WAS VERY aware that his cubicle was borrowed space, and that there was no time he spent in this borrowed space during which he was not being observed. He felt observed now, in his red Chucks, as he did every day. But the space itself, the cubicle, he felt no ownership of, and as a result, it was a mess. The mess was his attempt at ownership, in a way. The only decoration he had tacked onto the wall was a thick yet orderly pile of McDonald's receipts. There were so many receipts you could mistake the tacked wad of paper for a thermostat. Brent didn't get McDonald's every day, but when he did, he kept his receipt. He'd be going today; he was waiting for Marcy or Callie to close Marcy's office door so he could slip out without a conversation. Brent ordered the same thing every time: a large #1, no lettuce, with a Coke. His routine was to give the fries to the statue-like homeless man Frinz who waited near the street in a silver reflective jacket that read *FRINZ* over the left breast in red italics, then eat the Big Mac in the car, skipping the middle bun, idling in the parking structure before closing his eyes for twenty minutes, hitting his weed pen, and heading back in. Most of his workday was spent either waiting for the twenty-five minutes where he could close his eyes in his car or waiting to be tasked with some errand by Marcy, Callie, or Jet. He felt they all especially liked to boss him because he was so much taller than they were. A pleasing inversion. Or maybe because he was Ecuadorian American and they were white. Marcy's whiteness made Jet white too. His father had thought the name "Brent" would give him a leg up somehow.

Marcy's door was still open, and so Brent waited. Then, as if she knew he was waiting for her office door to close, Marcy called to him, "Brent, I have a simple question."

## 24. BEN

BEN, PARKED, HIS engine running, watched the cars gather, watched the blot clouds quickly pass, and clicked up the speed on his wipers. He had not eaten since the previous night and this morning had drunk three cups of coffee. The chunky, reddish eight-story building served by this large parking lot was not tall enough to jut into the gray sky. Ben thought, we are below the sky, keep that in mind. Small goals, small successes, baby steps, feet on the ground, below sky. CBAS. Ben was glad no one could read his thoughts. His jaw ached from clenching and grinding. He shut off the windshield wipers and hustled to join the rest of the invited inside the building. Exhaling wildly.

The open casting calls were not "open." They were invitation-only events held in LA, Chicago, Houston, New York, Miami. Every single person struggling to find parking in this rainy Rosemont office park, immediately northwest of Chicago, had been invited. It seemed *open* was the word used by production on subsequent emails following the initial invite for this stage of casting, to help articulate to invitees that they had not yet accomplished anything.

The second email had been very clear—further information on how to digitally submit the audition video and then an explainer of the audition day itself. There were going to be two sets of interviews with the invited potential contestants. Group A would be interviewed between the morning hours of eight and twelve central time; Group B between the afternoon hours of two and six. The email did not include how many total people were invited, did not give a sense of how many would be passed onto the next round, nothing of that sort. Each person or persons invited was given an Interview Number. The email stated that if you were not present when your Interview Number was called, you would be passed over, no questions asked, no second chances. It was not stated how many people were in Group A or Group B, or if being in one group or the other was preferable or an advantage or an indicator of any kind. Ben believed, without cause, there must be an advantage to going early in Group B, after lunch, but he would not have that opportunity, as he was assigned A-17.

Attached to the email containing Ben's Interview Number was a confidentiality agreement, a release form that when signed would grant Big Shot LLC the right to film the interview, and a background check approval form. The email explained that the background check would only be run if you were being considered for the next round of selection.

Required items for the interview were: a digital or hard copy of your Interview Number, signed release and background check approval, and two forms of identification (one including a photograph). And in bold, appearing twice in the email was the sentence: **Do not bring anything to the interview other than the required items.**

At the entrance to the stunted building, two young staffers both wearing headsets were holding tablets and looking over each person's copy of their Invitation Number. Each staffer would look at the Invitation Number held out to them on a phone or a piece of paper getting dotted by light rain, make eye contact with the person, look at their identification, check their information against the master list, then poke at their tablet before saying, "Okay. Second floor."

Middle-aged Black man in new white Nikes, plain sneakers that seemed to most likely have been obtained at an outlet mall; two tall white women, twins, with gauzy scarves and no rings, no nail polish; a crazed white woman in a green turban and green business suit like a one-episode guest villain on the Adam West *Batman;* a Latino man with gray in his beard wearing a blue blazer and holding a large tan umbrella; several men who looked similar to Ben: white, thirties, bellies. Ben was making his way to the entrance, faking calm with all the rest, gripping his phone, ready to prove he'd been invited, that he belonged. The staffers were working independently of one another, but each possessed a tense awareness of the other, as if in competition, though it was hard to understand what "winning" would look like within their current task. Ben, like everyone else, was told to make his way to the second floor and to find a place to sit, to wait for his number to be called. The unfortunate and sportsy smell of cologne pervaded the elevator. Ben's stomach groaned as he and the strangers were lifted up one floor. He thought about what passed for breakfast in modern America. His thoughts stalled on the three-word set: "passed for breakfast." If only the coffee he'd drunk too much of had actually been a meal—if only he were the kind of human able to make that problem into a business. Ben put his hand to his dumb aching jaw and smiled, thinking of his complete loyalty to nothing.

The second story was a completely vacated office floor. Where cubicles must have once stood, there was nothing, only two hundred or so plastic folding chairs all set up facing four large flat-screen televisions that had been hung on the wall. Each of the screens had the same message, white letters, Helvetica, against black:

> Invitation Numbers will be posted here
> and announced via loudspeaker
> beginning at 8 AM

The inevitable feeling Ben had possessed after receiving the invite had left him. The sheer number of people trying to do what he was doing was overwhelming. His confidence had shifted into quiet, defensive anger. Who were all these fucking people? Much harder to delude oneself in the presence of so many others trying to do the same, alone with a computer being maybe the most conducive situation for delusion there is—and Ben had had a lot of that lately.

At 7:29 a.m., a third of the two hundred chairs were filled. No one was sitting in the first three rows nearest the television screens. Ben had yet to see anyone else from the casting staff. He didn't anticipate the show staff would be wearing name tags and believed it was very possible he would not even learn their names due to time constraints. He didn't have a sense of what level of the staff would travel, if this open audition crew had any relation to the names credited on the episodes of *Big Shot* he'd been studying. But if a face that he'd seen online passed his field of vision, he'd know it.

Sitting in his chair, adjusting his posture and craning his neck as if looking for someone specific, Ben felt overmatched. These people looked fed. His stomach creaked its emptiness. Seeing the faces, the openly debauched, determined, shiny, terrified faces still streaming into the room, was stupefying. What had led these people to this room? Had everyone been recently fired? Ben felt momentarily, flatly ridiculous—not with any insight, for trying to get on a reality TV show—but, among the crowd, he also now wanted it more. He knew enough to know that they were all wrong; none of them should be here, no one should be in this room trying to get on TV. But they were already here, and en masse, and for that reason he wanted to succeed more desperately than at any previous moment. Get on the show. There would be another job eventually. But right now he wanted this. He thought of running sprints during high school basketball practice, suicides, probably called something else for the current youth, but looking to the boy next to him and thinking—I will beat him. That was his feeling. Though now, with speed having nothing to do with it, his confidence was less direct. He tried to reassure himself, thinking, physicality still matters. He thought, my body matters. CBAS. He added three letters. CBAS-UTH. 1. Confidence, 2. Belief, 3. Ability to convey 1 and 2, 4. Sex, 5. Unrelated to Hargitay.

The tall scarved twins Ben had seen outside were seated directly behind him and had shed their raincoats to reveal matching red dresses covered in white polka dots—modest, cutely retro, attractive dresses that made their horsey faces much softer. Their scarves were different colors, one blue, one gray. Ben thought, you must always have to dress well, especially because there are two of you. He thought, ugly has to compensate, and felt bad. Double ugly, double compensate. The twins watched Ben squint toward the throng of people finding chairs. Gray said, "And remember, this is only Group A, and only Chicago. LA is twice as big."

Blue said, "More than twice as big. Think about it: last year we were Group F."

The twins were smiling at Ben. He again noticed their bare hands, no rings, no polish. Ben thought, working hands? He was intimidated by their hands. He looked at his own hands and questioned his thoughts on physicality mattering. Ben said, "You were in LA last year?"

Gray said, "Last two years."

Ben nodded and tried to decide how to ask the obvious questions. The twins said they had decided to audition in Chicago this year to shake up their approach. Smaller pond, they said. He asked, "Are you coming this year with the same pitch?"

The twins looked at each other and Blue said, "Different pitch. Same product. You?"

"First year," Ben said. He noticed the twins relaxing; somehow, revealing this was his first attempt allowed them to interpret him as a non-threat. Later, driving home, he would misremember Blue mouthing the word "virgin." He asked, "Is it uncommon for someone to get through on the first try?"

The twins were taking turns talking, and Gray said, "The odds are never in your favor."

"Like the lottery," Ben said.

"Not quite," said Blue, laughing. "When have you ever been invited by email to play the lottery?"

They exchanged information, which Ben would lose before reaching the car, and shook hands as if being monitored by parents; Ben wished them well before turning around in his chair. Ben dumped his remaining $82 balance on the sportsbook app into an MLB three-teamer leaning heavily on underdogs on the road. He again muted his Somebodies I Used to Know/dads text thread, humming with more baby pictures, and ignored a text from Nguyen. The television screens all still held the same message. Twenty more minutes. The countdown before the countdown.

# 25. TARA

SHE'D BEEN LAX in filling out the journals for the other kids for about a week and a half. The painting had mostly replaced the journals in her thoughts, thank god. It did not occur to Tara that she did not have to keep these notes, that they were for no one.

Something about the news from Billy's parents about their extended trip, and her readiness to comply, had crushed her spirits around her job. What if these families were forced to make less money, forced to watch their own children without help, live in a different, more affordable state? Work less, acquire less, plan and save less. Forced to live unstructured days alongside their children. Forced to make sacrifices from the beginning of their child's life that money could not help them avoid. She thought, what the fuck am I thinking. She thought, of course, nothing would ever change for the better. Life is a slow descent. Life and lives. Individual lives. Slow descent from a heyday that is rarely recognizable. Childless life, maybe. No, kids or not, it was the same. American life. Descent peppered with relocation to warmer climes. If you had the money.

It was the upending of the boy's expectations that upset her. She feared the boy's expectations regarding his parents were already devastatingly based on careful observation and past letdowns. Maybe that was why he so regularly set himself apart in another room. A preemptive defense mechanism. Tara remembered herself as an oblivious girl—that is, that was her adult understanding of her past self: oblivious. Art school, give me a fucking break. Leap headlong into debt so one day if you work hard enough in an unrelated and crushing field you can eke out some time at night to use the education that has financially ruined you. She cracked her neck by dipping her head toward her shoulders. Trying to create a physical break from her previous set of concerns. Started singing along to the song that was playing. The past two songs had been Westerberg. Seated at the kitchen table, her legs were bouncing. *"Call me when your arms are empty/that's the only way it can be–"* She set to catch up on the other journals, inventing the events she was putting down.

- *Micah said, "The important question is: McDouble or Double Cheeseburger?" I have not yet told her of the lesser-known Daily Double.*
- *Jules is fixated on the size of her ears. She looks at herself in the mirror and yanks down on her earlobes saying, "Stretch, please!"*
- *Billy told me adult raccoons can see through walls.*

She went journal to journal, adding invented pieces of memory an invented day at a time. The light was starting to go. She didn't know where Ben was; she'd expected him much earlier. And yet, she thought, it's not even five in California. Not even five on an American Saturday in California. She looked up the name of the production company that produced *Big Shot.* There was a number listed on the website. Saturday, no one would be there, she would leave a message.

Tara set her phone face up on the table, put it on speaker, and called. The phone rang once and was answered by an automated system: Thank you for calling Big Shot Productions. If you would like to leave a message and know the extension, please enter the extension now followed by the pound sign. If you have a question about how to apply to appear on the show, please visit our website at bigshotshow.com. If you have a question regarding your application or audition, please visit our website and complete the "I Have a Question About My Application" form in the *Audition* section of the website. You will receive a response within seven to fourteen business days. If you'd like to speak to a member of our team and it is between the hours of 9:00 a.m. to 5:00 p.m. Pacific Standard Time, Monday through Friday, please stay on the line. To hear your options again, hit 9. Have a nice day.

Tara did nothing and the line began ringing. The phone rang three times and was answered by a soft male voice.

"How may I direct your call?"

"It's Saturday."

"Yes."

"Why are you working on a Saturday; it's five there, right?"

"We are in the office all the time. How may I direct your call?"

"I was hoping to reach someone in the casting department."

"Is this regarding your application or audition?"

"It's not. Not mine."

"How can I help you?"

"My husband auditioned. Today, actually. In Chicago. In Rosemont."

"Great. Bigger Midwest application pool than in previous years."

"Okay. Well. I'm calling to let you know that he should not be considered for your show."

"Should *not* be?"

"Right."

"Okay?"

"He has nothing. It may seem like his gimmick is hiding some actual value, that he is trying to be innovative, that he is being innovative, but there's nothing there. It's empty."

"He's misrepresenting himself? His application is falsified? I guess I don't understand what you're telling me?"

"No. In his application he is open about not having anything to pitch. He's not hiding anything. He's not lying."

"He's *not* lying."

"Right."

"Sure. Okay. Sure. And what is your husband's name?"

"Ben Silas."

"And your concern here is? Sorry, I'm not following exactly."

"He is what he says he is. When he tells you he has no pitch and that his only idea is to take the idea of *Big Shot* and to localize it, that's it. There is nothing else."

"All right, I will certainly make a note of that: 'He is . . . who he says . . . he is.' Mrs.—I'm sorry, is this Mrs. Silas?"

"Tara Silas. Yes."

"Okay. I will definitely pass that message along to the casting department."

"I'll make sure you do. What's your name?"

"This is Brent."

"Okay, Brent. Talk soon."

Tara hung up. She put her head on the table and imagined herself laughing at the situation but she did not laugh, she moaned. Billy peeked into the kitchen at the sound of her moaning and Tara altered the moan into a neigh directed at Billy and he smiled, hugging her from behind before running back upstairs.

She'd never stopped thinking of herself as a maker. A dormant artist who had made her own business. Strange now, because she'd always said she'd dropped out of art school because she found so many people there were businesspeople and not makers. People obsessed with cleverness and money. People who viewed the objects and images they were creating as potential tools to unlock the spoils of an even easier life. People who quickly found they lacked real aptitude for the creation of objects and images and instead their tool for an even easier life would be the talking around and talking into existence of dense realities surrounding and buoying these objects, images, ideas, gestures. People obsessed with masking their obsessions with cleverness and money and not working. More polished iterations of what Ben was attempting to do.

Tara could admit she was making excuses. School had taken hope from her. The paintings being made around her, the non-paintings, the theories floated—mostly terrible. No power and no light. No humans and no life. There were some bright spots, surely. But often the strongest work was not recognized as such. And so, she retreated. A sane and common response and also an excuse.

When they'd bought the house, Ben had set the guest room up for her to paint, worrying about ventilation and natural light, and Tara had effectively avoided the room ever since its completion. Ben had told her he hadn't made a space for her to paint as a recommendation for how she should spend her time. That he didn't know what was best. He told her he was not concerned with how she spent her time. Only that if she wanted to paint, he knew she'd need space. Instead she'd filled journals. She was a maker but not one who shared her work. Her career—a strange word in this context—existed primarily within the walls of her home. She could not paint, could not make anything if she felt it was a job. That she was clocking in and putting in her time. She understood that if she were open to such an approach, job-like, she'd have made far more work, but that wasn't important to her. She'd had jobs, all her jobs until her day care, where she'd clocked in and had to serve the demands of others. Real and debilitating and common. Physically and mentally eroding. Like most everything.

Over a decade of having to deal with people with enough money to lavishly eat out, carefree; making wild stipulations to their orders, their table location, the pace and tenor of their time spent within the confines of the establishment. Entitled honest-to-god motherfuckers. Motherfuckers whose teeth she'd wanted to kick in. And Tara knew this was nothing, and common. But still, dealing with condescending motherfuckers over and over and over. Day after day. Weekends, nights, holidays. For years on end. Those people and those jobs were what made her want a house. Separating herself from the sounds and demands and expectations of others. House living did not make her an ascetic, not at all, but Tara especially needed the opportunity to forget other people for stretches of time.

Tara filled her glass of water to the top and her cup of wine halfway and came back to the table. Maybe it came from painting, but she liked spending the day in one place. The forgetting began to allow her to invent the lives of others. Of the kids she watched. Her writing was given to parents who didn't ask for it and didn't know it existed until it was handed to them as a parting gift, and, she suspected, was probably rarely read. She was guessing. Only once had she received direct feedback about a journal. An email from a mother, the family had moved to Seattle, a single line at the end of a general thank-you note: "The journal gave me questions for my daughter I don't think she would be able to answer."

Since starting her day care, Tara's work life now stood less in opposition to her making life, and as a result her making life had faded. She did not retreat from her day care job as she had with past work; and Tara believed, in part, this was why she was imbued with less purpose in her own projects than when she'd served, bartended. That is, because she no longer had to struggle for time for herself, or work hard to find a space where she would be left alone, she rarely tried at all. She was already home, had a room set aside for her painting, and had no need to build a barricade between the day's events and her real work. The kids were picked up and her days would continue. Her life was easier now, and the making had become much harder. The journals were a place she could drift to—a place empty of the slights and daily stressors and the fighting for time with a painting she was working on. The making was natural to her, it had never left, but the ease of her journaling process, the lazy invention, the lack of rigor was unnatural. She'd lost something; she knew it.

The painting. The trees, the sky gradient, all done and dried upstairs, same for the street, the asphalt, the ghostly blocks of houses, but Tara could not settle on how flat or void-like to make the black of the enlarged snack helmet. Or how massive the helmet should be. Her instinct had been to make the snack helmet the size of a small car on the painted street. She'd been sketching the helmet, the depression in its crown, but could not settle on the nature of its color. She was at a natural resting place in the work; and so she would wait and not rush to determine what was to come for the enormous snack helmet and its future.

She was planning to give the painting to Ben. A sort of truce, a half step into a new place together. She'd never given him a painting before. Tara did not have any idea how he'd respond. He had always liked her work, but this felt different. She wanted him to take meaning from the gesture—wanted to make clear some of her intent, to move forward together, without having to explain everything.

Her plan was to take elements of the painting and have four small enamel pins made. A tree, the road, one of the ghostly block houses, and the black snack helmet.

She'd give Ben the pins with the painting and the following note she'd already composed in her head: "Take from this painting what you will. It's for you. Take pieces of it with you as needed. If you want."

This was less a test than a game for Tara. In her notebook ///, she assigned meaning to each of the pins. She wanted to see what Ben would wear and when, as if it would grant her secret knowledge of his actual inner life:

- *Tree: calmed by what has been and will be*
- *Road: illusion of changes made/illusory new direction*
- *House: false eternity*
- *Helmet: bravery/true madness*

Tara had been at the kitchen table for hours, for most of the day, sometimes with her head on the table asleep, sometimes drinking water, sometimes drinking wine, sometimes reading to Billy, sometimes writing in her notebooks. She'd made lunch for Billy and they'd walked to the park; then she was back at the table, watching pieces of movies on her computer, documentaries on anything. Mountain climbers. Factory processes. Video game record holders. Plastic in the ocean. Putting a thumbs-up on texted late-stage images coming in from Hank and Nguyen's kitchen remodel. She hadn't even heard Ben come in the house. She'd turned off her playlist and put on the radio. WNUR was playing. College radio. Tara liked the embarrassed-sounding DJs. Mumbling. She stood and stretched wearily and they hugged, swaying while some slow muddy electric-guitar riff started up on the radio. Billy had heard the door and ran downstairs with the snake coiled around his neck.

"What happened?" Billy asked. Tara had forgotten momentarily about the audition and realized Ben had been waiting for her to ask. It was the only question.

"Well, there were lots and lots of people," Ben said. He turned to Tara: "But I feel like it went pretty good." He turned back to Billy: "A woman in a green turban and green suit was kicked out for bringing a kitten dyed green in her purse. Escorted right out." Billy was beaming—he said, "What!" Billy had helped Ben prepare, sat with Ben as he went over his notes and the application packet. The boy was invested. Tara thought, Jesus, his notes. Mariska.

The boys high-fived clumsily and with complete love, though neither knew it was love or would ever know. These two ridiculous boys. "What makes you say it went well?" Tara asked, reaching out and grabbing Ben's shirttail, untucking. He slapped her hand away and began gathering hamburger fixings from the refrigerator as he answered. He opened a beer and continued preparations. She watched him settle into his hamburger routine.

Why was Ben doing this? Tara watched Ben with this thought in her head. It made no sense. She looked at him, trying to square her husband, this man beginning dinner, open, with her question. Did she need to understand? Was the point that she was trying to understand? Was the point to keep trying no matter what your spouse hands you to deal with? Could this man reasonably be a father? What was the line? What was the line she would not allow to be crossed? You can't know another person, but Ben seemed fine retreating into that truth in all ways.

She didn't believe what he'd written down to be indicative of how he spoke with other men, or his actual thinking—not really. Tara knew he'd had sex with only four women, including herself, over his whole life—that he didn't even like idle loose talk—and yet here they were. If he had written something else, not used the word *attacked*, it would have been different. *Attacked* felt too closely related to her own experience—both hatefully dismissive and also seeming to grant particular ownership of the evil thought to the person who spoke it, wrote it: Ben, in this case. He could have said, "Mariska Hargitay, vulnerable."

She didn't understand.

What she did understand was that the less control a person had, the more dangerous their thoughts became. And without trying, this Hargitay thought was what had poured out of Ben. And he hadn't run from it. He'd highlighted it. Was that actually good? His attempt at regaining control? Was he actually doing the right thing? Not everything is easy to highlight and have discovered. And it seemed true that he hadn't known anyone was going to read the journal, despite the fact that he'd handed it to her. Still, though.

She watched him with his burger components, sunk deep into his routine. Shirt untucked, tie loosened. Salt, pepper, gas on, set at medium heat. He had distinct and head-injury-simple routines for each of the five or so meals he could prepare. Tara wondered if she had ever begun as poorly as he had, with a thought so deeply sick, in any past pursuit of her own. Surely, she had. Daily, maybe. But she didn't write them down. Didn't highlight them. She watched him move around the kitchen. He answered her question about how he knew his pitch had gone well that she had forgotten asking.

"I was told they liked my pitch because they hadn't heard it before. Asking for nothing in that way. Taking their own idea. And they liked the tie-in with the seasonal aspect, that is."

"Pretty loose tie-in. What did they think of the video?" Tara asked.

"Less enthused about the video," Ben said, forming hamburger patties from the mound of 80/20 resting in its black Styrofoam platter. "They told me how to reshoot it. Editorial advice. If I do make it to the next round, I might need a new audition video. Maybe not."

"Why?" Tara asked.

"They sometimes use those audition videos on the show. You know, kids on the driveway, the inventor in the basement. The behind-the-scenes-type stuff. They want the videos to help paint a picture. They shoot their own explanatory background footage occasionally but need the submitted video to be of a certain quality as well." Ben pulled out his phone.

"Did you see anyone you recognized? Jabaree? Pipes?" Tara could tell Ben was gauging whether she was making fun of him. She was. Ben knew it too.

"None of them were there," Ben said. "Completely different staff."

"Who are you texting?" asked Tara.

"Forgot to tell Nguyen anything."

She watched him type: went well had them laughing. Less excited about video

"Is it the ones who can't tell their story using their pitch alone? Is that when they use the video on the show?" Tara asked. "I mean, is it the people with complicated pitches, muddled—"

"Don't know."

"They didn't have a problem with you not having a product? No business? With you coming out and asking for the Big Shots to invest in you?"

Ben was sternly salting, peppering. "No, I mean, I think they thought it was funny. Especially when I started quoting specific episodes where each of the Big Shots had used the phrase, 'I invest in people,' or, 'My decision to partner with you is a bet on you, not your company'—I rattled off the ones I'd memorized. And they liked the fact that I was also actually asking for money."

"They were okay with a gimmick," Tara said.

"Well, because of its basis in the Big Shots' actual language and my insistence on using the money to create my own *Big Shot* here in town. Not sharing in profit it will create. I told them, we all know your model works, let's see if it works in a different way." Four patties flipped onto the square skillet. Salt and pepper on the unseasoned sides. A small dash of Tabasco in the center of each uncooked puck.

"Didn't hear that part until now. You get fired and then decide to not profit from this?"

"When I say 'not sharing in profit,' I mean not in a major way. I'll pay myself, we'll make it work."

"Work. That's the word I'd like you to focus on. *Work*. To find. *Work*."

"There are remote accounting options I'm looking at. Working from home."

"Have you actually determined what it would take? Or have you searched whether such a thing existed and, when you found that it did, stopped? Also: maybe you don't remember, but *I* work from home."

"Come on."

Tara didn't believe that any group of people actually associated with the production of the show would have been so transparent with Ben. Why tell Ben anything? What was the advantage to encouraging him? Silence was much easier.

She turned to see what Billy's reaction to all this was, but he'd wandered back upstairs without them noticing. Maybe she wasn't ready for a kid. Maybe *they* weren't. The sex hadn't stopped even in the days after Ben had admitted he'd lost his job. She wanted a kid despite whatever dumb shit Ben was up to—wanted a kid with Ben. Maybe a kid would pull him out of all this lost-boy spiraling.

Tara generously changed the subject. "Did you know 'heyday' used to be 'heyday!' like, an exclamation, like 'what a great day!'?"

Ben watched the patties in the skillet for a few seconds and said "Hey-day" to the pink meat.

Tara said, "No, no," trying to smile.

# 26. MARCY

FROM THE WINDOW Marcy asked Callie, "Do you think most of our audience think of themselves as failed?"

Callie said nothing, seated across from Marcy's empty desk. Marcy knew silence was Callie's way of communicating she felt they were off topic.

Marcy sat back down at her desk with Ben Silas's folder and began playing the rest of the audition video without sound as she waited for Callie to speak. She'd watched it a dozen times already. There was something moony and youthful about Ben Silas. She watched him make his taped pitch from a park bench, a spring grass park behind him. What the fuck was this man doing? He seemed to think he was getting by on charm that he didn't actually possess. He was alluding to a misunderstanding of what he thought was his former charm; that was what he radiated. The man had been lied to about who he was and had believed every word he decided to remember. Marcy stopped the video on her computer.

"I don't think our audience sees themselves as failed," Callie said, putting her hands in her lap and then crossing her arms. "No." Marcy had forgotten asking the question. She looked over at Jet rolling on his back, offering his genitals to the world. The animal did this without the typical head-back, tongue-lolled, upside-down dog face; even luxuriating in a back-scratch, this dog was inscrutable. Callie continued, "Failure is universal. It doesn't matter how a person reads to our audience, we don't have to convince them this person has experienced some failure. It is about degree. But 'failed' sounds total in a way that most people probably wouldn't choose to bring into their thinking."

Marcy shook her head. "Depends on age. Nationality. Gender. It's demographics. For Ben Silas, for white, midthirties, employed American man"—she pumped her fist—"you know, middle-class with debt, I think many of his contemporaries would agree with what you said about 'failed' being too strong. We are talking about homeowners. People who take vacations. Run marathons. Talking about our audience here. Our bread, our butter. But even for them, failed becomes a distinct possibility. If you keep living, it's there like a monolith. A wall. Waiting. Like something ahead of you on the coast. *Planet of the Apes.* Haystack Rock. Much of our audience might qualify their answer, say they had 'failed in X department' or 'failed in Y department' and so on, right? Hope in isolation from all things. Have hope. Hope. Here's hoping. Current reality always understood as a middle phase. Nothing will dampen blind hope. But eventually they hit a wall. I mean, it's so much of what we do now that I'm saying it: failed people that do not recognize themselves as such. Like you said—these people are beautiful. So, maybe failed is the whole thing." Marcy realized Callie was on her phone, had not been listening, and returned to the list on the manila folder:

*sad?/~~kind?~~/failed/humbled?/~~dumb?~~*

Marcy knew audiences questioned the truest parts of themselves. Doubted the very existence of the truest parts of themselves. The truest parts being: ignorance, debilitating self-obsession, stubbornness, jealousy, vengeful thinking, general lack. In focus groups she heard voiced the insecurities that helped her to understand what it was that would comfort and frighten and last. Fear-based thinking. Lack of purpose. Lack of money. Money as purpose. Money as success. Often it was that a contestant wanted baldly to assume the life of one of the Big Shots: these contestants were no longer willing to work in obscurity, to not have their path be valorized, affirmed. Success could be as small as recognition of effort. In this way, appearing on the show was in itself an end of sorts for many contestants, regardless of what followed. The desire was to have already done the work. To already be living in the aftermath. Consuming the spoils. Living coastally. Open floor plan.

Contestants would cite examples from Suzanne Reinhart's book *Short Stack*: how she built her pancake-house empire into a lifestyle brand, cookbooks, cutlery, cookware, elastic-waisted pants, alternative dog foods: "You said when you opened the first Pancake Hill you were serving, cooking, cleaning, designing ads, and building menus, and what you had to learn was to delegate. Chapter five, delegate. I remember. Chapter five for me was a workout with the highlighter. Well, I've learned that lesson and have people as motivated as I am. I have the staff. Staffed and ready. Independent operators. They burn like I do. I need capital. Gas to flame. This is me asking for gas. Gas me up." Or they'd studied Sam Mackaday's recovery from alcoholism to start his motivational speaking career. They'd recite his branded motto to him: "What you think about plus what you do equals you.®" These narratives were reverse engineered into existence and were all similar, for all the Big Shots, in that each one hit verifiable checkpoints related to growing wealth. Event A happened, and as a result money was made. Event B, more money. Contestants would cite decisions, risks, strategies, circumstances, and by doing so were making their own decisions, taking their own risks, and with an audience. In perpetuity and with diminishing returns. Contrived, witnessed, edited, and ultimately false despite however large the subsequent profit became. Curated. And of course, also, real. Most of these never aired. Around 40 percent of what was shot, edited, and packaged was cut.

The way Ben Silas was mourning for himself felt familiar. A man with regrets, that's television. The way he created himself by having others participate, knowingly and unknowingly, in grieving for the enduring loss of his past self, one that had never existed, that was from TV. Especially if TV is taken to mean what it actually is: the condensed-void delivery of invented narratives. Actors had made careers off this self-mourning brand, his inherited brand, of specific self-hate and arrogance. Performative emptiness. His wants were not obscure, although he may have believed them to be. He wanted to be on TV; not obscure. He thought he made decisions that ran counter to the information he took in, but that wasn't true. Marcy thought: we've made him do every fucking thing he's ever done. By "we" she meant TV. She included herself inside her understanding of what comprised TV. Callie began speaking. Marcy watched her without hearing the words she was saying. Marcy thought of Callie as a hare. That is, a hare, as opposed to a rabbit. She seemed like maybe she'd been happily sent to boarding school, or, no—Inland Empire public school kid, K–12. Marcy could guess at her upbringing but would not ask: an only child who had read a lot. A picky eater with footspeed she'd wasted, and perfect eyesight. Had dated a series of much older men when she was eighteen, nineteen, twenty, but was done with that genre. Men with awful beards and opera tickets. Opera tickets? What the fuck was Marcy thinking? Callie kept speaking and Marcy heard none of it. Marcy guessed Callie felt she knew less about what it was to be a woman than other women. That she felt inadequate. That her hair, straight, oily, parted down the middle, was a decision made before puberty by her mother, in another state. Now she saw it. That she'd had one haircut her whole life. Marcy knew nothing about her.

Marcy said, "I see," after missing all of what Callie had been saying, and Callie said, "Right. So, the rules violation we ultimately ignore because who cares, we can reshoot whatever we want and make a new audition video if need be and ultimately the footage was our own, so two points, Ben Silas, yeah."

Marcy asked, "Where are we at with him?" Marcy looked up from her desk because Callie did not reply immediately. She was slow responding today; something was off. Marcy asked, "What are you not telling me?"

"His wife keeps calling."

Marcy watched Jet walk out her door into the open part of the office filled with cubicles containing other interns and the various lower levels of the production staff. She knew the dog would be largely ignored until he got to Brent's cubicle. And then, in his way, he would demand attention. She knew Jet would stand behind Brent's chair until the man sensed he was there and Brent would stand, quietly swearing, attempting to focus on his breathing.

Marcy said, "His wife keeps calling where?"

"She calls the general studio number and asks to be connected to someone who works in casting on *Big Shot.*"

"Who does she end up talking to?"

"Brent, mostly. He picked up the first time and now she asks for him by name. And when Brent doesn't feel like talking, I speak with her."

"Is she rude?"

"Not really."

"Why is she calling?"

"She doesn't want her husband to be on the show. She wants us to know that he doesn't have a business, really doesn't have a plan. His plan is to pitch *Big Shot* to the Big Shots. He wants to run his own local *Big Shot.* Whatever that means. She keeps saying, 'He will not surprise you.'"

"Why would she think we would understand his application, or the video, any of it, as anything other than what it was?"

Marcy again put her head against the window, looking straight down at the lot. Le Corbusier. The "Mother's horse" cock tattoo roommate had always been talking about Le Corbusier. Had full-color photo books, Le Corbusier, all over the apartment. Marcy had looked up what the dead architect looked like and was offended by his glasses. No idea what had become of the "Mother's horse" tattoo woman. More tattoos, surely; small and rune-like. Marcy said, "Why does the wife feel that way?"

Callie said, "I haven't asked her directly. My guess is that she thinks he'll look foolish. That she thinks he doesn't understand what it will mean to be on TV. That she's trying to turn us off so he won't pitch."

He does not know what it'll mean to be on TV, thought Marcy. That naiveté paired with his brazenly empty endeavor and taking into consideration that he was low-average white relatable and not handsome—that's good television. That's mashed potatoes. Turkey sandwich. Scrambled eggs. Buttered toast. Light beer. Lite beer. That's human: ignorance. Also human: his lack of preparation and making his lack of preparation a part of what he claimed was the appeal of the pitch. "I have nothing. No business. I want to take what is already proven: this show," he said, believing it was possible that things would work out for him. Ignorance, lack, and desperation folded into his own reframing of his entire effort: human. And he had no real plan for the money he'd receive should he win. Improve his community, or some other innocuous language that allowed for later developments, or not. That allowed for someone else to do the work. He could say he wanted to facilitate his own version of *Big Shot* locally, but, as Callie said, what in the ever-loving hell did that mean? Did that mean it would be filmed? If so, he would surely be leaning on production staff to hold his hand and organize and uphold the brand name and fund his endeavor in ways he wouldn't even be able to recognize as they were happening. His pitch, whether this man knew it or not, created more labor for everyone involved. The wife's fears were warranted. The wife seemed interesting. The wife was more interesting. If Ben was to be the opening move in Marcy's potential exit strategy, it didn't mean this couldn't be fun. She needed this wife. Success or not, she did.

"Callie, what do you tell this woman?"

"That the decision is far from made. That we're still waiting on background checks for hundreds of potential contestants, that her husband will not be forced to be on the show even if we select him as a potential contestant, that she is wasting her time worrying about it."

"That's really wonderful. And mostly true. But she keeps calling?"

"She keeps calling."

"And you let her vent."

"Brent too. He's good on the phone. I don't want it to seem all me."

"He better fucking be good on the phone. Does Brent tell her the same as you?"

"No. Brent asks her about the weather. Asks about her day. She tells him about the kids she watches. She said one of the kids makes fortunes, like fortune cookies, and hands them to the mail carrier. Little jokes written on them. She tells Brent lots. And he tells her he wishes he could help her, but even if he could, he's only an intern."

"Who does Brent tell her you are?"

"His boss."

The two women smiled. Marcy said, "I want to talk to this wife. I understand calling once. I don't understand the rest."

"You have time to call and get into the whole thing before your vacation?"

For a moment, Marcy forgot when she was leaving, or, when she had told her office she was leaving. Of course, she was never leaving the country, but for some reason now any movement, even to the other side of the city, felt inconceivable.

"I forgot about my trip. I mean, I know how that sounds, but I did."

Callie gave her a look. "Day after tomorrow, right?"

"I haven't actually booked a place to stay. Will you find something? I'll send you everything, and if you could pull the trigger for me. Pull several triggers. But I'll call the wife. I don't think this will be a whole thing. I'm going to call and try to give her enough information, or some words that will seem like enough information, so that she'll stop calling."

She asked Callie to book the fake cabin in Canada and a real place to stay in Venice, and plane tickets to Canada that she obviously wouldn't use.

She wanted Canadian charges in case she needed to defend her lie. Marcy had no problem delegating the details and machinations of her personal life to Callie. *Intern,* of course, in part meant *personal assistant.* That was fine. None of it was hard for Callie. Marcy would have Callie make all the arrangements and reservations and then have them occur without her participation. Easy.

Brent and Jet appeared in the doorway. Jet came first, tags clinking. Callie told Brent that Marcy was going to call Tara Silas, and the young man winced. He said, "I can call her. If we need to tell her something. I can call. I think it might be a waste of your time, Marcy." Brent audibly farted; he stood in the doorway with his mouth open nervously, farting. Jet sniffed wildly, spinning. Neither woman said anything though both had heard the ripping fart. Marcy almost asked Brent to leave but stopped herself.

"Why would it be a waste of my time?" Marcy asked.

"She's very stubborn. She's not interested in changing her mind."

"Are you interested in changing your mind, Brent?"

"Not when you put it like that," he said. Brent half gestured at the back of Jet's head, as if remembering mid-action that you don't wave good-bye to a dog, and went back to his cubicle.

Marcy said to Callie, "You know I like Brent. But I like him more when he's not in the room."

"Don't tell me negatives," said Callie.

# 27. CALLIE

"AND IN RETURN I won't tell you negatives either," said Callie.

"What do you mean?" said Marcy.

"I was able to get in touch with the woman who was working the desk at the YMCA the night that Hillis abducted Darnell Poole."

"You spoke with her?"

"She's been in touch with Hillis this whole time. He made it public in an early interview, one you've probably read and forgotten—he said 'And I apologize to the kid, the kid at the desk.' Well, he was talking about her, Kim Davis."

"And you spoke with Kim Davis."

"I asked her if Hillis ever brought up the family, the Lons. Specifically the children."

"Oh my god."

Callie was making up every word.

"Davis said, 'You mean the Pooles. His family had the same name as him. Poole.' She didn't even think to consider the homeowners, much less their kids. You."

"She didn't."

"She didn't."

"Did you correct her?"

"What?"

"Did you tell her to tell him that there are kids? The homeowners. That the Lons, the homeowners, have kids?"

"Am I misunderstanding what I am supposed to be doing? I thought the whole idea was to obscure the connection if possible. Make sure that you aren't linked."

"You're right, exactly that."

# 28. BRENT

BRENT BELIEVED THAT Tara and Marcy were too similar to get anywhere over the phone. Neither would back down in a way that felt like a victory to the other, and no solution, no natural resting place, would be achieved. This could impact Brent in multiple ways. He could receive more phone calls from Tara as a sort of ballast for her unfortunate experience on the phone with Marcy; or Marcy could become angry, and this would affect him at work because frankly he was already afraid of her on days when she was calm. He hoped that Marcy would relent and allow him to reach out, but he knew that her mind was already set.

# 29. BEN

ANOTHER THREE WEEKS had passed, and Ben had watched seventy-nine more episodes of *SVU* in that span. He was not even halfway through the series and could watch no more. The episode that had done him in was not even close to the most brutal. Season 7, episode 12, "Infected," opened with a mother being shot in the head by her lover as her son watched, hidden in the bedroom closet. The boy spends the night in the closet with his mother's body slumped lifeless against the door. Something about that opening was enough for Ben. It felt odd to abandon his project without focusing on Hargitay, so he decided to watch some interviews with the real person. He'd read some articles during his library hours, read some interviews too, but had avoided watching footage of the real woman speaking.

The first interview he watched was a red-carpet barrage from an Australian celebrity news outlet at the premiere for the sixteenth season of the show. Hargitay talked about being thankful for being able to play the role of Olivia Benson, being thankful for the platform she had been given to speak out on the issues of supporting survivors, testing rape kits, and believing women. She went on to say, "I always try to think that there are no accidents," and that she tried to deal with the reality of situations on a daily basis. "More than simply making the best of the day, I try to first see each day for what it is, and go from there." She had the ability to appear completely open with the interviewer and also seem to be reserving something of herself for those who knew her in her private life. The combination of openness/self-protection was so admirable to Ben, because in the midst of his appraising Mariska Hargitay as being able to inhabit that duality, she was also speaking with grace, wisdom, clarity. She had not only allowed a role on TV to inform her actual reality, she had changed reality and actual law and the behavior of law enforcement because of her ability to engage with the material and take it into the fabric of who she was.

And yet, what was he doing? What the fuck was he doing? He couldn't keep at it. If he saw a man doing what he was doing on a TV show, a character doing what he was doing and had been doing in the library, in some movie, some book, not only would he not believe it, he wouldn't understand it.

Hargitay had led to nothing, and for that he was thankful. Rather, nothing, the void, had allowed his pitch to exist.

The remainder of his normal library routine remained; Ben checked in on West, Wagner, Marcy's IMDB pages for updates and found none. The same credits, the same photographs. Imposing, anonymous, and deadpan, respectively. He'd not shed all his idiocy. Ben was searching for a new way in and failing. And yet, in a literal way, he was making progress, despite himself. He'd auditioned, openly admitting he had no business and no idea, or only the idea of taking *Big Shot* and claiming it as his own, and had not yet been eliminated from the process. He could account for none of it. He closed his computer on the interview and headed to the bar. He texted Nguyen to meet him.

The bar was called Dambo's and no one knew what that meant; it was not a real name, and for a fake one, it was poor. Gunmetal gray and dark-brown wood, matte finishes and some maroon cushioning along the bench that ran the length of the wall, large TVs looming and pitched forward hanging above the hard liquor, audio from the soccer on TV playing quietly. This was a bar for bankers, and other people looking to drink at lunch or after work before heading home. The food was forgettable but not offensive. Ben did not have money on the soccer game. He had looked at the line, Everton hosting Newcastle United. Monday midday game. There were fourteen minutes left in the match and no score. The crowd was singing "Leighton Baines, you probably think this song is about you." Ben hadn't had any action since his audition, and he hadn't even checked the result of his bet from that morning. He felt the outcome of that bet held an inherent double meaning; he did not want to know, either way. He was drinking his second tall draft beer. Ben knew nothing about soccer.

Nguyen stepped in off the street and Ben put his hand in the air, as if he weren't the only person seated at the bar. Ben could tell Nguyen thought he had money on the game and was refusing to acknowledge the situation beyond a small shake of his head. Nguyen put a hand out and Ben hugged him instead before they both turned their focus to the game. The bartender was watching the game with them from his corner; he seemed neither interested nor bored. There was rain in Liverpool too, apparently. The bartender caught Ben's eye, put both his hands up to his neck to indicate "choking," and pointed at the TV. Ben gave him a thumbs-up. It'd be okay.

"Most of upper management is in Tampa. The office is loose. I doubt anyone noticed I left."

"And still getting paid, that's beautiful," said Ben.

Nguyen did not turn from the game, asked, "So what specifically was it about the video that they weren't excited about?"

"They said … it felt like I was a TV pitchman, selling an empty promise."

"That's exactly what you are."

"I'm not selling anything."

"You're selling yourself, and that seems like an empty promise."

Nguyen was frowning. Ben had reached some end with him, and felt this was mutual. Nguyen ordered a gin and tonic and paid cash when it came.

"But you're through to the next round?" Nguyen asked, clarifying what was still hard to understand for Ben as well. Nguyen was drinking quickly.

"No one is through until they clear the background check."

"What's the next step?"

"I'll be in front of higher-ups. Be asked more questions. I don't know how many more rounds there are until the real thing. I don't even know if there are rounds. Next step might be the show."

"What are you going to say when they ask what you would do with the money?"

"I want to take their idea, *Big Shot,* and apply it locally."

"You're saying you want to make a TV show?"

"I'm going to let them understand my pitch in whatever way they want. However they want to interpret my idea that is most conducive to me actually getting on the show, well, that's my idea."

"You can't say that."

Ben looked into Nguyen's eyes. Nguyen looked tired.

"Your calling me 'Nguyen' is like calling me 'Smith.' No one with the last name Smith is called that."

"You want me to call you Thuan?"

Nguyen shook his head as if for an audience and looked elsewhere.

Ben watched as the extra time ticked to an end. A draw. He'd lost his bet.

"Why do you think you got fired? Why do you think any of that happened? It's like you weren't even there. You know that? For a long time, you weren't even there."

"It was downsizing. I got severance."

"In name only. Drop in the bucket." Nguyen did not demand his attention, was apparently past trying that hard. He went on. "You haven't gotten beyond the word *lottery.* How will the numbers work?"

"That's not my job, that part will get figured. Not by me."

"What are you willing to figure out?"

Nothing. Ben was unwilling to figure out anything. He felt that his idea that was not his idea and that he did not understand was enough.

They jogged through the wet city back to Nguyen's office.

A rainy day downtown near the lake; the whole city gone silvery blue. Ben considered apologizing to Nguyen but wasn't sure exactly for what. Ben felt like it was what Nguyen wanted from him. Maybe he could reassure him that the issues with the video were not his fault. Thank him for all his help. Tell him he couldn't have done it, any of it, without him. Never would have even gotten to this point.

They reached the office and stood cold and damp in the shining gray-stone first floor. A security guard seated centrally inside a large, round gold desk watched them. The man had a face like an owl. It was too late for workers to be returning from lunch, and they were the only people he currently had the opportunity to guard against. Pedestrians blitzed by outside the glass in the rain, but the lobby was still.

Nguyen said, "You aren't coming up, are you?" Ben waved across the lobby at the owl guard. He did not wave back.

"Real quick. Wanted to say hello to everyone."

Ben and Nguyen made their way to the gold bank of elevators. Nguyen was texting. Nguyen pocketed his phone on the elevator and said, "They aren't going to understand why you're here. It's only been a month and a half." Ben shook his head as if to say, doesn't matter.

They were off the elevator, and Ben was grinning and waving to his former coworkers as he entered the office, thinking about sweating while the TV lights would be on him. Nguyen quickly ducked into the bathroom. Ben thought, light clothing, less sweat, more confidence, more belief, better ability to display confidence and belief.

His former coworkers looked confused. A middle manager with a new haircut walked out from his office smoothing down his tie and said calmly to Ben, "You can't be here."

"I'm not doing anything," Ben said. Ben was smiling and looking around, trying to make eye contact with anyone. No one was meeting his gaze.

The middle manager said, "Not an option."

# 30. *NGUYEN'S ELEVATOR TEXT TO HANK, WHICH HANK SENT TARA, WHICH SHE CHOSE TO NOT RESPOND TO, ENDING THEIR COMMUNICATION FOR THE TIME BEING*

I don't think Ben's ok

# 31. *TARA*

"HOW LONG DO background checks take?" Tara asked.

Ben and Tara were seated in their backyard in low-slung lawn chairs as the sun was setting, fireflies blinking, no kids to watch. Drinking beer. Tara had gotten her period the day before, not pregnant, and had decided to have a drink tonight.

An unusually warm evening this late in the summer. Occasionally they'd have to brush an ant off a leg. None of their neighbors had fences, and everyone's yards opened into the others'. This is not to say there was any great communal notion between these houses, but the lack of fences was notable. There were fist-sized round lights strung up a few backyards away, a modest gathering with kids and dogs and parents. A small pit with a fire. Wonderful smell of woodsmoke. Detached garages and smallish stands of trees threw late shadows. There was music coming from speakers at the lighted gathering, but they couldn't make it out.

Billy's parents were home from Africa, and Billy, as a result, was finally home with them. Tara could not stop thinking of the boy. Of how independent his routine had been from her own, from Ben's, how Billy was like a small silent man tasked with completing a child's activities, daily. She pictured him laughing, darting around a corner in socks slipping off his feet. He'd already experienced willful abandonment, repeatedly, at the hands of his parents—and to make the pain sharper, whether he knew it or not yet, it was abandonment they would deny, smile in the face of, and never admit to.

She loved Billy. Maybe irrationally so, she thought. Actually, no. Rationally, rationally. Why question it? The feeling was as real as the grass at her feet. As real as her hair. Her fucking shampoo bottle. This love was not motherly, not really, though she'd played the role gladly—this love was thankful: thankful the boy was as tough as he was.

Tara hadn't heard Ben's response to her background-check question. She told him so and he repeated, "Weeks. Month tops. Depends on how much background they have to check." It had been almost two weeks.

Tara sputtered her lips and finished her beer. Ben asked if she needed another; she did. Ben walked away for more beer. Now, maybe because the music had been turned up, she could make out what was being played. That vocoder Lampchop record from a few years earlier. Turning over her shoulder and watching Ben reach the house, she thought the two words *stalks off.*

Tara needed Ben to realize she'd decided there would be a baby. She wasn't sure when it would happen, but it was going to. She needed him to wake up. She stood and placed her chair six feet nearer the music, six feet nearer the far unmarked border of their backyard, and then got up and placed Ben's chair next to her own. The sun was still not full down. She looked up from her sunken vantage and traced with her vision all the old two-story-tall telephone poles hiding in plain sight in these backyards, the wires drooping, the detached garages, the pines, the oaks, the maples, lit upper windows; again noted the fire at the party, its wonderful smoke, saw a glowing orange Frisbee snatched violently out of the air by a dark shepherd mix, heard one lone shrieking firework somewhere far off. All this in half a minute. Where was her husband. She thought, where is my husband.

Ben returned holding a small Ziploc and cradling two beers. Tara asked him, "What did you think of having Billy at the house?"

"Great kid. Quiet."

He handed her the Ziploc with her weed inside. "What took you so long in there?"

"I put two glasses of water in the bedroom. Your side, my side. I didn't know if you were smoking. I mean, I know you aren't pregnant if you're drinking."

"Slow down, detective."

"Night Moves" started playing from the party, and Tara began rolling a joint in the dark, her hands working near her lap. She rolled joints effortlessly. Art school. She let Ben's nonquestion fade out, shook her small lighter out of the baggie, took her first pull, and offered some to Ben, who declined. He was among the worst people to get high with and knew it. Tara had only offered because she was sure he would decline.

"How much severance is left?"

"Four weeks."

"Four," said Tara.

Tara felt glad to be talking with Ben about something other than the show, even if the topic was their money running out. The party several yards away was growing. A little boy in a bike helmet was trying to ride the shepherd dog like a horse in the dark. The boy was screaming a thin piercing note from atop the dog. His sisters were trailing in a ragged pack, laughing and falling over each other. One of the sisters kept yelling "BOBBY BUTTCRACK" at the boy.

Tara said, "We have the two credit cards with a balance and the third is okay. We have my student loans, which will never be paid off—yours are whatever, minor, at this point. We have the mortgage and we have my car insurance. Did you look at anything yet? In detail? How long we are okay for? I mean without going into savings. How long do we have health insurance through your work?"

By "savings," Tara meant the $2,000 they had in a joint checking account. The account had hovered at that figure for around a year and a half.

She watched Ben staring off as he responded. "Money-wise we are okay for two months. Health insurance for six more months at least. We can apply for longer, but there is no guarantee and the process seems complicated."

"Do you have a real plan to find a job?"

"I do. I do."

"I know you're lying. It's okay. You are. I believe you'll figure out something. But know that I don't want to take on more kids if I don't have to. Not kids I'm getting paid to watch."

She waited for Ben to turn and look at her. When he did, she waited until she saw in his face that he understood her; that didn't happen.

"I'm smoking this tonight and then I'm not smoking anymore. And I'm not drinking anymore."

"You're pregnant?"

"Jesus Christ, I'm smoking a joint. No. I got my period yesterday. But I'm going to get pregnant."

"We want to, yeah. We've known this."

Ben reached for her hand and she let him take it, their hands resting in the grass between them. Tara shook loose after six seconds or so, squeezing twice quickly before releasing.

The crowd at the party seemed to increase twofold over the next ten minutes. There were enough people at the gathering that the fire was mostly obstructed from Ben and Tara's view. They had their chairs facing the back of their yard. Tara thought, if one were at that party, it would be possible to think that their chairs had been positioned to watch the party's goings-on. Tara said, "You think they think we're watching them?"

"We aren't watching the trees."

"We are, kind of." Tara said. It was full dark now but not buggy.

Tara punched Ben in the shoulder. And again, hard. "Why is it you want this show? Come on." She would not mention she'd been calling the production office trying to dissuade them from considering him. Tara had been calling every day; she felt it was justified, considering his recent deception.

"I think I can do it."

Tara was trying. "Because you think you can."

Tara would not state the obvious, that that was not a good reason to do something, simply because you can, because the obvious didn't exactly seem relevant here. Ben wanted people to see him succeed. And success for Ben meant getting on the show. That was clear to her. But she felt he did not care to impress his true and only witness. None of this was for her.

Ben said, "I think this may be the hardest thing I am capable of doing."

"That would mean you don't want kids."

"That's not what I mean."

"You think that getting on this TV show is the hardest thing you are capable of doing?" Tara wasn't sure this was true for anyone in the world. No, she was sure. This was not true for anyone in the world.

Ben said, "It's not easy to do. Thousands and thousands, tens of thousands of people try to get on every year."

"Don't sell me. I feel like it's implicit in saying 'the hardest thing I am capable of doing' that you are actually saying 'the hardest worthwhile thing I am capable of doing.' I'm sure if you wanted, you could survive on the roof in the middle of winter for two, three nights, with items you found in the kitchen. A tarp from the garage. And if you did that, it might even be the most difficult thing you'd ever done. But that's a made-up thing. Like TV. TV is a made-up thing."

Tara flicked a lone ant from her arm. She watched Ben, who appeared to be considering the roof. She didn't want to have to say what a worthwhile difficult achievement would be: being a present husband, honest, supportive, patient, attempting to be happy in this life. Continuing to try without end. Spending time and effort on pursuits that mattered. On her. The real hard things can seem laughable when voiced; can sound too plain, clear. She went on with the lesser: "And so much of it is out of your hands. You would not be in control." She wasn't even sure if such an achievement, getting on the show, could be claimed; if the people who gained deals had enough agency within the process to even claim a victory. It was a business decision made by someone else, several someone elses. A corporate decision.

A figure from the party, long haired and short statured, started walking toward Tara and Ben. Tara couldn't make out anything beyond height, hair length, and speed: this person walked slowly. The figure appeared to stop and dance halfway between the fire and Tara and Ben. A new song had begun playing, "Thirteen," Big Star, and the woman's body seemed compelled to acknowledge this change. The woman shimmied out of the song's hold, barely, and circled toward the couple.

When the woman got close enough, she was revealed to be maybe in her early thirties. A devastating hoop in her nose. The woman asked, "Can I get a hit?"

Tara said, "You can smell this over there?"

The woman said, "Nobody said anything."

Tara eyed the woman warmly and handed her the joint. The woman took a deep drag. The lack of small talk, no greeting, and the sharing of the weed felt transactional, sexual.

Tara said, "Keep it," as the woman exhaled. The woman looked at her confused, said thank you, turned around, and began walking back toward the gathering.

Tara called, "Wait." The woman stopped. Tara asked her if she had ever seen the show *Big Shot*. The woman said, "Big Star." Tara said, "No. The TV show, *Big Shot.*" The woman said that she hated the one with the beard. Mackaday. "He never gives money to women." Tara asked the woman—everyone introduced now, the woman's name was Ricki—Tara asked Ricki to sit down where Ben was sitting and pretend to be a judge on *Big Shot*.

"Pretend to be a Big Shot," said Ricki. She was smiling. She had a wide face in the best sense.

Tara touched Ricki on the shoulder, and both looked at Ben and laughed like estranged sisters remembering how to get along. Mimicking a bond from childhood. Ricki continued smoking. Tara kept her hand on Ricki's shoulder and looked at her as if she finally remembered how they knew each other: "You're from Michigan?"

"How did you know?"

The women laughed, inadvertently touched foreheads, and turned to Ben standing in front of them. Ben looked confused; did not speak their language. He had his hands on his hips watching them, and his face was doing a lesser Michael Keaton. Ben told Tara and Ricki to keep in mind this would be for a spring episode. Ricki waved her hand to indicate, *Get on with it.*

Ben began speaking. "Everyone comes on this show looking to make money. It's the unifying thread between every person on this stage and stages like this all over the world: asking for money from yourselves, or people like you—"

Ricki whispered into Tara's shoulder, "Who is he talking to?"

"Not us."

Ricki said, "Done?" and Tara laughed openly.

". . . and maybe it's why this show is popular. We have the audience sitting at home thinking what would I do in his situation, in her situation? What is it that I have that could get me on that stage, would allow me to gain an investment, would make me the kind of money where I wouldn't have the kind of troubles I'm having now? Well, I'm not asking for money, not for my own gain, not for my own profit. I am asking for an investment from you, from you Big Shots, so that I can turn around and invest money into my own community. I'm asking for you to believe in me. Maybe you're thinking, I get it, it's the April Fools' episode, this is a joke—"

Ricki said, "You want me to give you money, you don't have a plan, but like, April Fools'?"

Ben started to answer, but Ricki went on, "That will never, ever work." She said bye to them both, as they had reached the natural conclusion of their game, and began making her way back over to the fire. Ben said, "You can ask questions. It's the beginning of a negotiation."

"No," said Ricki, and waved as she kept walking slowly away in large, lunging steps.

Ben sat down next to Tara and he drank his beer and they both watched the fireflies. Tara said, "If that is the pitch, it's going to be rough."

Ricki was walking back into earshot. She half shouted, "People pay money to see others believe in themselves. So, who knows?" And she was lost again to the dark neighboring yards.

Tara said, "That's the problem."

"What?"

Tara said, "You'd have to believe in yourself for this to work."

# 32. MARCY

MARCY HAD BEEN on the phone with Tara five minutes already.

"—I don't think you're hearing me. What I'm questioning is the starting point. Your starting point—"

"The submission video? His audition? Why does the starting point matter?"

"No. Your starting point. The criteria you are using to select contestants."

"The criteria with which the show is selecting contestants."

"No. You. People are choosing people. You. Unless there is a computer program you use in making these choices, which wouldn't surprise me. But even then, it's people. It's you. You called me. Brent and his boss never called me. I called them. You must be different. You are in a position to make decisions. That's clear. Am I right?"

"I am one of the people, the main person, in charge of making that call. Yes." Marcy felt an almost sexual thrill listening to Tara.

"Thank you. I watched this documentary. A man attempting to beat what he, for most of his life, believed was a world record that he held for points in an arcade snake game"—Marcy put her phone on speaker and motioned for Callie to leave and close her office door—"so you snake around the screen and collect dots, and as you do so the speed of the game increases and the length of the snake does too. His whole adult life, 'cause he'd set this record when he was a teenager, he believed no one had ever scored higher. This man had never left his hometown. Rural Iowa. So in his late thirties, working and working, he finds out an Italian man actually has the record for this game and not him. He finds out that in actuality he was the world record holder for maybe seven months when he was a teenager. This is twenty-something years later. The main identifier he provided for who he was, taken from him over twenty years previous without him knowing. So with his Thanksgiving days off he attempts to break the Italian's record. He fails. With his Christmas days off he tries again. Fails—"

"Please. Jesus."

"To what end?"

"Are you asking me a question?"

"To what end? This is a stupid man. A fucking fool. He wants a stupid thing."

"People have different interests? Is that so offensive? Because the thing he likes is obscure, it's foolish? I know the link you want me to make—"

"Ben is no different from that man. He is pursuing a stupid thing. Maybe even stupider, because it is not obscure. And at least this man, this arcade snake man, had a talent. Ben does not, not in any way that is relevant. His failure would be broadcast widely."

"There is a lot you don't know about this process. A lot you don't know about television. You don't know about our respect for the people we give opportunities to."

"Go fuck yourself."

"And also, who is to say he won't attempt to do something else you won't approve of. What I will tell you is that Ben is interesting to us. He is blatantly attempting to do something we haven't seen before."

"Go fuck yourself."

"What is your work situation?"

"Whatever I choose for it to be. I run a day care out of our house. I decide when I work, when I don't work. I can take time whenever I need it."

Marcy took a beat. She stood and put her head against the window glass again. She needed the wife. The wife would make this a better story. "When was your last vacation?"

Marcy heard a flat thud on the line. Some weight dropped from counter height. She heard Tara sputter her lips, then say, "Fuck you."

Marcy waited.

"I'm sorry. I'm sorry. I didn't mean to swear at you. I meant to, I take that back, I did mean to. You don't seem to be taking it in, though."

"When was your last vacation?"

No response. Instead the dull clomp. The felled heavy. Bag of flour. Work boots in a large shoebox. Marcy couldn't even guess what it was.

Marcy asked, "Are you cooking? What's the noise?"

"Making churrasco. Ecuador week. In Ecuador it's steak with a fried egg on top, fries, plantains, and avocado. Same word means something different in Brazil."

Her answer hadn't accounted for the sound; Marcy didn't know what was going on. Marcy said, "Come out to LA. Our secret. You can have a break. We can talk about all this. I'm already going to be renting a place. We'll pay for the ticket."

Marcy surprised herself by extending the invitation. She had not thought about the resulting implications. When she'd realized she needed the wife, she hadn't known what that could mean. She still didn't. Her objective became twofold. Tara and Ben. Even if it was still only Ben on the show, it would have to be Tara who was convinced. She only needed Tara because she already had Ben. Ben was easy. Threefold: 1. Sell Tara on the show, which meant sell Tara on Marcy. 2. Get Ben on the show. 3. And now get Tara to LA. Marcy would never admit it to Tara, to Callie, to anyone, but she didn't want to be alone. Not if Hillis was going to be on her mind. She needed to be thinking about something else; enter Tara.

"We don't know each other," said Tara. Again the thud.

"Free. A free vacation. What's that sound?"

"I'm dropping a fucking dictionary on the ground. We don't know each other."

# 33. CALLIE

CALLIE WAS TYPING on her phone while listening to Marcy, performatively engaging with the words Marcy was saying as they were being spoken—not really listening, but it was the expected style of conversation in this moment, the notation, confirmation, searching. Callie brought her eyes up every few seconds, showing Marcy she was with her. Marcy was telling her about Canada as if she were actually going, although she'd already told her to also book the Venice rental. "I'm going up there to have some time to read. I've said that to others, but not the pointed, the real reason behind the reading. I want you to know the full truth. I want to think of a next step, a next career, a next kind of life. I want to make a movie. You know some of that, I know you do, I can't hide it all. I'm reading some Duras, I feel like I haven't seen much of her work in film. Some Annie Dillard, others. Maybe some nonfiction. Children of murdered parents. Or witness stories. Murder witness stories. And I'm telling you because I think it's possible you'll be there with me for this next step."

Her eyes scanning her phone, Callie said, "Duras. I'm seeing Duras has over seventy film credits attributed to her work, or at least based on her work."

"There are other writers."

But the extension of the purpose behind the reading was a tentative offer to Callie; she knew it. The reading that would not actually be taking place. She'd never seen Marcy actually read anything longer than an email.

Callie's Burbank apartment did not allow dogs, and she was unwilling to watch Jet. Shedding bothered her. Her own shedding included. Peanut skins on wood flooring of suburban chain steakhouses; the dinners out from her youth in the Twin Cities. Flaking sunburn. Removing her clothes. She liked none of it. Regarding canines: Callie preferred photographs of dogs—being able to briskly scroll through deeply curated images of French bulldogs, pit mixes, mouthy terriers, and the rest of the not-Labradors—to the actual living animal. "A dog is a mess creator" was a sentence she had once spoken aloud to her therapist, unprompted. They had been speaking about her sister's children. Pretending to write something down in response to those words, her therapist had sternly etched a threatening horizontal line across the page in blue ink. Callie had watched the therapist's etching in the reflection of a squarish framed Lindsey Buckingham poster. Also, Callie didn't understand why anyone had to watch the dog now that Marcy was staying in LA. Marcy explained she needed her interns to be able to honestly say that, of course, this Canadian trip had happened, was happening, that's why Jet is still in the office with us. Being watched by us. But Callie was not interested in participating in the dog's take-home care. She was certain no one was going to ask where Marcy was.

# 34. BRENT

BRENT'S ONE QUESTION for Marcy after loading Jet's food, enormous crate, canvas bag of chew toys, and rose-gold-handled brush into the trunk of his inherited Subaru was, "How does a dog sleep?" They were on the top level of the parking structure on the studio lot. It was a sunset like the earth's core, orange, blinding.

Marcy said, "You mean, where does a dog sleep?"

"Where does a dog sleep?"

"I'll speak only for Jet, not for all dogs. Wherever he wants."

Jet was unfazed by the obvious apocalypse in the sky. He sat quietly panting with all the light at his back. Brent shielded his eyes with his hand, and Marcy wore large fashionable sunglasses. She stood next to Jet, and it seemed to Brent that their heads moved in unison for a few synchronous moments. Marcy scratched at the dog's neck while she gave Brent advice on living with Jet. Between the deathknell omen from the sky and Marcy's slowly offered Jet-minutiae, Brent heard nothing. He was very high; Marcy did not notice. This handoff was too ominous for Brent to take in any new information. He was spaced out within an auditory hallucination of a roaring furnace that the color of the sky had given him; he slipped in and out of its deep white noise. Pink noise. The one sentence that stuck in the days to come: "Hot dogs and rice can be thought of as the ultimate treat. However large you'd cut up a hot dog for a koi fish, that's the right size for Jet." He would feel as though he were misremembering this instruction, but he was not.

Brent began attempting to nod into his exit, opened the front passenger door and waited for Jet to hop onto the seat.

The dog refused. Brent opened the back door, passenger side, and same—the dog would not even acknowledge transportation was being offered. Brent opened the door behind the driver seat, and Jet yawned and slowly, in a two-part creaking sequence, leapt into the back row. Sitting alert, already staring at the driver's headrest in front of him. Marcy handed Brent four hundred dollars cash and said, "Do as little as possible and make sure he has food and water and it'll be fine. Take him into the office like normal. Walks morning lunch and night."

Brent felt like he might cry. "Enjoy Canada," he said. The women had not told him Marcy would be in Venice. They felt it would make little difference to Brent. Knowing the truth of situations did not seem relevant for his day-to-day life.

# 35. BEN

BEN WAS HAVING trouble sleeping since they'd started having sex with the intention of having a baby. Only he thought of it this way: "with the intention of having a baby." Tara wasn't as simple. Tara wasn't drinking and no weed and she was alert now, always, and that scared Ben. They'd have sex and she'd rock onto her back, pulling her legs toward her chest, and start humming. Ben would leave the room and, with football season approaching, head to the basement to watch whatever the Big Ten Network was airing. Michigan Football Classic. Purdue Football Classic. Oddly, Rutgers Football Classic. Nebraska Football Classic. Rutgers was eighties basketball to Ben, New Jersey crew cuts, and Nebraska was Big Eight. Big Twelve. Tommie Frazier. Stoic Tom Osborne. He'd set the DVR for the rare Illinois Football Classic. He'd put on a game and mute the TV and listen to *Purple Mountains,* skipping the first track. Eventually he'd listen to it, he wasn't omitting the opener entirely, but he preferred to start with the second song, as a rule. Or it would be *Time (The Revelator)* or *New Skin for the Old Ceremony* or *Bitches Brew* or *In the Dark* or *Paradise and Lunch*—it was endless. He'd listen to music, drink beer, and watch old football.

Ben's first year at the University of Illinois, the football team had won one game. Went 1–11. The team beat Illinois State, a division 1-AA school at the time, at home in Champaign. Barely a win. They'd chanted "I SCREWED UP" in the stands, which is what they said ISU actually stood for, awful really. That kind of hate-in-the-stands is love in a football context. The next week, a 6–3 loss at the Rose Bowl against UCLA. A bad year of football. Next year, three wins. Next, two. And Ben's senior year, again,

two wins. Over his four years, the football team had won a total of eight games. Ben understood and agreed with a lot of
the general anti-football takes, but, to be clear, he would never
ever stop watching his godawful alma mater. They barely had
fans, and he would never abandon them. It was all he could
focus on lately. Getting on the show and old football reruns. His
yearly hope was for eight wins. For the team to annually equal
their win total from his entire time downstate. Ben should have
placed that number at seven, but it felt wrong in his gut to be
so realistic. So he hoped for eight wins and a Rose Bowl appearance every twenty years or so. That was the loose pattern
recently and not so recently: 1947, 1952, 1964, 1984, 2008.

He'd heard nothing new from the show in two weeks
and they were trying to get pregnant. He did not have a job.
Chandra had never emailed a reprimand, apparently too classy
for that despite the choking gesture.

They were trying to get pregnant. They were trying. And
Ben was adrift, though he hadn't stopped to realize it.

# 36. *TARA*

There was nothing, strictly speaking, within the eligibility requirements of the show that would forbid Tara Silas from accepting the offer of a free vacation from Marcy Lon; she told Tara this was the opposite of what she wanted. She forwarded Tara the third tenet of the eligibility bylaws via email:

Neither you nor any of your immediate family members or anyone living in your household may be nor have been within the past one (1) year employees, contractors, officers, directors or agents of any of the following: (a) Big Shot LLC, any entity owned, controlled or affiliated with Big Shot LLC, or any parent, subsidiary, affiliated or related entity of any of the foregoing; (b) any person or entity involved in the development, production, distribution or other exploitation of the Series or any variation thereof; (c) any known major sponsor of the Series or its advertising agency; (d) any "Big Shot" or any entity substantially owned or controlled by any "Big Shot"; or (e) any person or entity supplying services or prizes to the Series.

Marcy explained in the email that Tara traveling to visit her in LA implicated no one technically, and that it would only be extremely strange and questioned if they were ever found out. That is, if Ben went on to actually appear, much less gain a deal, on the show. It would be suspicious, but not necessarily against the rules of the show.

Tara felt that even if provided with the context he desired, April Fools', and given the benefit of the doubt by the Big Shots, Ben had long odds at best.

Tara understood that Ben was less interesting in isolation than, say, if he were documented alongside a wife dealing with the fact that she didn't want her husband to appear on the show. She knew what Marcy must have been up to—that Tara herself was agreeing to be a pawn, a position she'd warned Ben against. But Tara was tired and wanted a vacation, regardless of what that actually meant.

From Marcy's email: "I want to implicate myself with you as witness. My desire is to give you the tools for blackmail, should you ever need them. I will be hiring you as a consultant out of my own pocket."

Tara reread the section of bylaws she'd been sent carefully and replied that she'd prefer to be referred to as "an agent." If events transpired that Tara felt were damaging, she would have the ability to expose Marcy as being insubordinate to her own show's structure.

How it was exactly that Marcy would involve or document Tara's experience leading up to the show, and what that would mean, she wasn't sure.

Tara closed her computer and went upstairs to look at the canvas she'd finished. The painting was still on the easel in the guest room. She hadn't taken down her lamps or removed her tarp. She intended to keep painting until they got pregnant. Then this room would be the natural nursery; oil paints don't mix well with pregnancy. But some kind of making would remain. She looked at the small canvas. She hadn't gotten the snack helmet exactly as she'd wanted. She wanted the helmet to be both a complete void on the canvas and also a shade more threatening than absolute black. She was content with the color she'd arrived at, a deepest gradation of brown-purple not immediately apparent as any shade other than black, but as for the void, Tara felt she might not have made the helmet large enough. The painting looked like the cover of a second album released by an indie rock band from a college town in the late nineties. Add the band's name written in Courier in one corner, album name kitty corner. A band with a recent one-hit wonder that had bloated this second record with strummy three-minute nothings. Songs that didn't fit the name of the album. An album with a name like *Wall of Death*, full of bright pop. That's what it made Tara think of. Her mind was trained to take down what it created. To doubt and self-sabotage and belittle. It was a good painting. One she hadn't seen before. Not what she'd imagined it would be, not even close, but that was to be expected.

# 37. MARCY

MARCY WAS BEING driven from her bare Silver Lake apartment to the rental that Callie had arranged in Venice. She rubbed her face with the flats of her palms in the backseat. The driver was bald. He whistled sparse, quiet notes as the traffic deepened its hold. In the back seat Marcy wore red pants, a red shirt, black sneakers. Unmatched shades of red. She was tired without cause.

Though she hadn't left the country, hadn't even left town, she had successfully removed herself from any potential San Jose murder coverage by staying put; this was her belief that she participated in like a game. The Hillis thinking may have been a game, but she was also actually frightened in a way she could not defend. She didn't want to be alone. Marcy was removing herself from the normal rhythms of her life. Not permanently, not yet, maybe not ever. But she was able to glimpse the possibility of erasing patterns. She'd been in the car for ten minutes and was already having thoughts this dramatic. Partly, she wanted to know what she could get away with. What she could pull off. She deeply wanted to get away with more than she ever had previously, and this was linked to the want to remove entire commutes, buildings, restaurants, bathrooms, as possibilities for herself. And she'd invited a stranger, making the terrain much more threatening in the process. The complexity was what would wreck her. Keeping straight: who knew about Canada, who knew about not-Canada, about Venice, who knew about Jet with Brent, who knew about Tara coming, her agenting, what Tara knew about Ben. And what did Ben know? Who cared? He knew nothing. What would the interns say if something came up? As little as possible, was what she'd advised. She was having trouble thinking her way out of what she'd sprung. Marcy looked out at the last of the day. Dusk here too; not just at the coastal Canadian wheat field in her mind. This driver was good. Calm in the red, jittery, shunting rush hour. The fucking hell of traffic. It would be over an hour, easily, from Silver Lake to Venice. Way over. Dark by the time they reached the house.

Marcy in the back seat of the car service, overnight bag next to her. Grand thoughts and regret, high-stakes anxieties all occurring behind a straight red mouth, sunglasses she had not removed despite the night. This vacation, the lie of it, seemed like the wrongheaded journey of someone who believed she might stagger her way into filmmaking someday. She could see that. But wrongheaded did not necessarily mean futile. She'd brought the books she had said she was going to read and would have a day to read them before Tara arrived. A day to muss pages. A day to make the house feel lived in, because she planned on telling Tara she'd already been there for three days. In reality, she would spend one night alone. It was important to Marcy that she appear deep within a routine, a way of life, a pattern of thinking. She wanted Tara to feel she was intruding. Or that she was invited into a stay that already had created its own weather. She thought, California without people. She couldn't picture it; but the traffic had given the thought to her. There need to be fewer people. There need to be fewer people in California. Marcy had taken a car service because she wanted to be left at the house and seem that she'd not left the house. That she'd arrived, been to the grocery store, and set to reading, to thinking differently than she did in her work life. For Tara, she'd reserved a rental car from LAX, the intermediate sedan offering.

The bungalow Callie had found in Venice had a short slant of driveway, a detached garage. There would be a place for Tara to park. Marcy had looked at pictures online. A neighborhood of wildly expensive and homey small houses. *Neighborhood* felt like the wrong word, really, because of the kind of money involved.

Marcy's phone buzzed in her pocket. A text from Callie:

Ben Silas is unemployed. Through background found out was fired over a month ago. Brent doesn't know if Tara Silas knows or not. Hasn't mentioned it and seems like she would have to help dissuade us.

Marcy texted back an emoji of a trophy and then an anchor.

To the back of her driver's bald head she said, "Can you imagine California without people?"

His large eyes showed roundly in the rearview mirror. "Wouldn't know. I've only seen it with."

The driver wore a gray sweater with a pink poplin collared shirt underneath. He lit a cigarette and cracked his window. This driver looked like Pete Postlethwaite, though American. He spoke with the voice of a former burnout youth quakily stepping toward steady work, regular hours, thirty years late. Marcy could call to mind the name *Pete Postlethwaite,* but instead asked the man, "Do people say you look like that actor?"

"No one's ever said I look anything except tired."

They drove in silence, full traffic the rest of the way as the night settled in. The rental was a one-story bungalow built in 1949. Two bedroom, two bath, 1,500 square feet, last sold at the turn of the century for $350k and now worth closer to two million. A common Venice story. To rent, $500 a night. The place was updated but not high end. A small flagstone backyard, lush. A tight kitchen. Three-minute walk to the beach down Rose Avenue. In two trips to and from the trunk the driver had set all Marcy's bags on the threshold with a cigarette in his mouth, but he did not attempt to place them inside or ask if she would like him to. Maybe he was protecting himself, especially this time of night. Marcy tipped the man in cash. He took the money with the cigarette still in his mouth. Observed her red outfit without obvious malice. Marcy made a noise like she was going to say something but paused. He folded the bills and put them in his back pocket, waiting to see what the noise she'd made was meant to signal. Marcy said, "Do you have access to fresh eggs?"

"Come again?"

"Do you know farm people?"

"Farmers?"

"Do you know where to get fresh eggs?"

"There are farms in Downey."

"I will give you an extra hundred dollars if tomorrow morning you bring me fresh eggs. Late morning. I don't care how many. And when I open the door say, 'More eggs. Good to see you again.' Something like that."

"Two hundred dollars. Paid now."

Marcy reached into her purse for the money. The driver looked up at her. She said, "Not going to ask?"

"Not until—okay, there, you've paid. Tell me."

"I need it to seem I've been here longer than I actually have."

He made mocking eyes at her—"To have been here and known it already." The man whistled airily and stepped away. He said, "Another way to make it seem like you've been in a place longer than you have, is to say so. But yes, I'll bring you magic eggs."

He tapped at his temple, holding his cigarette as he stepped away toward his car. They waved at each other dumbly from a distance of ten feet in the dark. Marcy could only guess at the intent of his comment. What the fuck did he care? She'd already paid; do the job and shut the fuck up.

The driver left. Marcy stood at the door and watched the dark street. Clean night asphalt. She spit as far as she could, which was not very far. Directly across from her rental was a pale green back fence covered in red bougainvillea. The flowers spilled over the fence and hung draped, partially blocking the sidewalk. Lit theatrically by a streetlight. She could not see into the yard where the flowers originated, even up on her toes, but could see three shaggy palm trees on its eastern border.

Could not see any house. This part of town felt different than her own. Cramped, fecund, terrifying in its monied particularity. It was hard to imagine anyone working here; Tara felt that in her own neighborhood too, though. A regally dressed couple in their seventies walked slowly out of the darkness and by with a very tall white dog. They wore what appeared to be expensive silver track suits. Their gaits were malformed and intractable. This neighborhood, this collection of houses, seemed capable of anything—that is, except work.

And then she was in the home, trying to learn its objects and furniture so she could move inside like someone with a past in this space. Walk the common routes until you know them cold. Learn switches. Side tables. Forks go here. Coffeemaker, okay. Glasses here. Water does not get hot. Still not hot. Still not. And cold, no, not cold. Not cold now either. The house was mostly one large open room, the kitchen against one wall, and against the wall opposite, in the respective corners, a bedroom with an attached bathroom and the second bedroom. Good, two bedrooms. In between, a living area. The couch pulled out. Marcy was thinking of her opening line for Tara: "Did you like the upgrade? No economy for you. No compact."

There was a knock at the door. She opened and the driver stood there, the looming green night of the neighborhood behind him and his car running, driver's side door open.

"If I'm going to help you lie, tell me some true things about yourself. I can't say why, but I need them."

"I am a television producer. Well, I get a production credit. I work in casting."

"What show?"

"*Big Shot.*"

"Is that a real show?"

Marcy made a face at him.

"Is me coming with eggs helping you to hurt someone?"

She had not considered this. If she was hurting someone, she didn't care. She wanted her victory to be unquestioned.

That was all. Were the eggs that this driver would bring to the house in the morning potentially going to hurt someone? She didn't care. Yes? No? She believed she needed the eggs to create the illusion that she had been a member of this part of the world for longer than she actually had been, and nothing else mattered, only the lie at hand. All parts of the game were real to her. The egg thought had occurred to Marcy, and so now it was important to her that it be realized. She cared less about the success of the lie than about needing the driver to agree to help her enact it. She stopped. Her thinking stopped. What part of the world was she actually a member of? Was it up to her? Was there an answer to such a question? The driver did not repeat his question to her as they stood in the green night. Marcy was leaning against the doorway and he did not repeat his question. Despite what you've just read, no time had passed. His question was still there: "Is me coming with eggs helping you to hurt someone?"

"Yes," she said. She never would have arrived at the word *hurt*. Or even something much more benign, like *trick*. What Marcy wanted to do was win. She did not ask the driver's name.

# 38. CALLIE

*MURDER GIRLS* WENT into hiatus after a cousin of one of the hosts was murdered. The cousin had been abducted from a Wisconsin rest stop, her body found in a nearby ravine three days later. The host was admittedly not close to this cousin, but was close to people who were, and that apparently was enough to jar her into consciousness of the reality of murder. The cousin was twenty years old, studying psychology, a former volleyball standout in high school. She'd been headed down from Eagle River to Madison to stay the weekend with friends and stopped at a rest stop near Coloma off I-39 to close her eyes for a half hour. She'd left Eagle River after work, 11:00 p.m.; she was a waitress at the Pine Brothers Supper Club. The man who'd killed her was described in the media as a drifter, but that was only accurate if they meant that he drifted around Coloma and the surrounding towns. He was a known quantity. He'd done sixteen years for previous heinous crimes. Anyway, it was too much for the host, apparently. They took down the archive of past shows, took down fan access to the message boards, shut down the website. Reality had intruded, and as a result they need to rethink their way forward. Callie received the kidnapping and murder of this complete stranger as a clear sign. Her time in LA was coming to a close. No more fucking with TV, at least not this kind of TV. Onward, soon.

# 39. BRENT

BRENT WATCHED JET take in his apartment. Mound of dirty clothes in the corner; three blue Dodgers hats, exactly the same, hanging on thumbtacks in a row over his mattress; two windows overlooking a broad alley with a mostly unfilled bookshelf set in between. Brent had a copy of Stephen Mitchell's translation of the *Tao Te Ching*, a large coffee table book that read *NOTABLE BRIDGES* on the spine, and the complete *Space Ghost Coast to Coast* in multiple formats. Coffee maker, mini fridge, two sleek bongs displayed. Brent followed the dog around the space from a distance, which was difficult in the rectangular studio. The dog went into the bathroom, spun, back out to the electric range, jumped onto the made mattress on the floor and stayed there. Jet closed his eyes. Ben was relieved the dog had stopped moving. He slipped his pillow off the mattress and lay down on the ground next to the bed. He hoped Jet would let him sleep for a long time.

Brent sometimes described his job as minor detective work and dog enabling. Over time his fear had shifted from blanket misunderstanding of the animal to specific comprehension of his lack of power within the relationship. Brent had recently been respectfully dating online. The dates were frightening to him, but less so than Jet. He could not see the dog apart from his imagined potential for violence. He feared a thrashing bite from the poodle based on no personal history. He would say to himself in the mirror and in the car prior, "I am not having dinner with Jet." This was an earnest tactic. "I am not having dinner with Jet." He would say this as he ate medicinal brownies, medicinal cookies, medicinal gummies. As he smoked weed. He would say this before getting out of bed on the weekend. He would say this

189

when he saw it was his mom calling on the face of his phone. When he had a flat tire. When his forehead broke out. The words had abstracted into a mantra reaffirming his existence, a pause, I am alive: I am not having dinner with Jet. The dating, though, was the chief stress lately. Problematically, many sane, dateable women owned dogs. There was a sentence on Brent's dating profile that he had cut, but which was true: *I hope one day to be a father.* Many people assumed Brent was gay, which baffled him.

Brent's apartment also did not allow dogs, but he was willing. As long as no one was yelling at him and he was not in danger of losing his job, he was willing. He was not afraid of being afraid. Daily he performed all of his life tasks from within a heightened state of tension. And now in a very real way, he would be having dinner with Jet.

He met the woman, June, at a crowded gelato spot. He'd seen tens of pictures of her in various outfits and had a sense of what to look for. As he looked for his date among the crowd outside the storefront, Brent was conscious of not telling June that she looked like Thora Birch. But there she was, and in person, yes, it was going to be even more problematic for him to avoid blurting this plain fact. The resemblance was alarming. They hugged like cousins and then exchanged the tamest of niceties based on the bullet-pointed biographical clips included on their respective dating profiles.

"Never been to Alaska," said Brent, joining the line that began in front of the shop.

"That's what everyone says," June said and smiled. "And then they say—"

"But I'd love to go!"

"Right."

They snaked their way through the line side by side. Brent was conscious of not standing too close and not brushing any part of his body against her body. She ordered first, a scoop of chocolate and a scoop of green tea. Ben ordered two scoops of pistachio and one of vanilla. They lingered without subtlety near a couple finishing up and then sat down and set to eating in earnest. June had been somehow reading Brent's thoughts.

"Who do people tell you you look like?"

Brent pulled his weed pen out of his pocket, took a hit, offered it to June who said "Maybe later," and then Brent made a long *mmmmmmm* sound.

"People have trouble coming up with celebrities that look like me. They'll say 'that one guy' from some show. Or talk about someone they grew up with. Famous people, famous enough to exist in easy shorthand conversations, don't look like me. What do people tell you?"

"I can tell that you know."

"You look like Thora Birch, yes. Exactly like her. It was distracting."

"Brent, I am Thora Birch. I use a different name on the app. I've had trouble with fans in the past."

"I am not having dinner with Jet," Brent said.

"June. But, that's right," said Thora. Another ten minutes and she took a phone call, mouthed "Thank you!" to Brent, and left. He was relieved. If she'd concluded he was a fan, she wasn't exactly wrong. He didn't care her reasons for leaving. He got back in line, ordered two scoops of vanilla for Jet (with a top so they would stay cold), and made his way back to his apartment.

# 40. BEN

AT A LARGE chain electronics warehouse store in an aisle with headsets and coffee-mug-sized computer speakers, Ben was being helped by a young man with terrible skin. He wore the collared maroon shirt all the employees did, and this especially highlighted his twin patches of cheek acne. Ben felt for the kid. He hadn't been in this store in years. Entire sections of the enormous space were cordoned off with dark-blue hanging gym-divider curtains. As if the store were being forced to exist in a smaller and smaller portion of the extant building.

Ben asked, "Renovation?"

The boy said, "Reduction of floor space for increased backroom storage, so we are heavy on the items that will move when we liquidate. Desks, TVs, office tables. Priced to move. Priced. To. Move."

"You guys are shutting down?"

"Eventually."

Ben's hypothetical understanding had been the reality; he hoped this phenomenon continued. The young man had walked him through computer monitors, ergonomic chairs, stood with him and considered various items with patience. Ben placed a sample headset on his head, raised his eyebrows and waggled his ears as if these moves were the true crucible.

The boy said, "You can get everything we've looked at much cheaper online. Including delivery, all this stuff. All of it. Easy. Really easy."

"Why would you tell me that?"

"I have . . . other incomes."

"How's that?"

"Herbal solutions."

"Weed?"

"Yeah, weed."

Ben looked around their immediate vicinity for any other maroon shirts and said, "I could be interested in that. I don't like to smoke it, though."

"Don't worry about other people hearing. Most of the people I work with sell weed to people they meet here."

"Most?"

Ben walked with the boy to his dark-purple Honda Civic parked in the distant center of the enormous lot shared by a stand-alone three-story gym. The car had completely blacked-out tinted windows. An orange wishbone "C" in the lower left of the rear windshield. Ben had purchased nothing in the store, instead had a list in his pocket of the boy's recommendations to purchase online. The clouds over the parking lot, over all of Harks, Lisle, Wheaton, were gray and massive, but it had yet to rain. "There aren't cameras facing the parking lot. Saves on liability and court appearances for when accidents happen out here. No one cares anyway. About weed." They sat in the Civic's two front seats. The car smelled like sport gel deodorant in a way that Ben didn't mind.

"Isn't it legal, mostly?"

"Not until January 1."

The boy reached into the back under the passenger seat and grabbed a small black duffel. Inside were gummies, chocolates, prerolled joints in plastic vials, and flowers in thick baggies.

Ben said, "Gummies. Do I need cash?"

"I take cards. The charge will come up as Buona Sera Hot Dog."

"Good evening hot dog?"

"Good evening," the boy said, taking Ben's card and swiping it through a reader attached to his phone.

"Remember, this is probably much stronger than you're used to. I drive out to Colorado to get the real medical-grade shit. No infrastructure in place out there. They can't track me going dispensary to dispensary. Every two weeks and I'm stocked up. But, seriously, not like how it used to be. Not what it was in your day."

"How old do you think I am?"

"Well, I'm twenty-two. So you have to be forty."

"I'm thirty."

"You're forty."

The boy recommended Ben eat half a gummy, wait two hours, then another half if he felt okay. Ben laughed and shook the boy's hand, then walked over to the Hyundai he shared with Tara. She was visiting Canada. Nova Scotia. Was maybe in the air already. Had found some unbelievable deal, under $200 round trip she'd said, staying with a woman from art school who had a cabin. Who had invited her out to paint after Tara had emailed her a picture of the painting she'd recently finished. Tara had told Ben the painting was called *Wall of Death* and that she had made it for him. He didn't know what to make of that; much less the set of enamel pins she'd given him with the painting. A tree, a house, a strip of road, a black helmet. The pins closely matched the painting; eerily so, in Ben's estimation. The note Tara had included with the pins said "take the painting with you as you want," and Ben felt like he didn't know what the fuck that meant.

Ben also didn't know what to make of her trip, but would have agreed and encouraged her to do anything she had suggested. He didn't have to understand. The painting was in their bedroom, resting against and facing the wall on Ben's side. Later on, he planned to drape a clean bedsheet over the painting in what he would call, if questioned, an attempt to protect it from the world.

# 41. TARA

TARA WALKED SLOWLY through the bright-blue-and-gray O'Hare. Every time she'd been here with Ben he'd say "*RoboCop*" to articulate his feelings about the place, and she knew what he meant—a possible definition of intimacy.

Tara stood in the Concourse C McDonald's line for a Diet Coke. Drank the Coke standing in front of the trash and threw away the cup. She'd apologized to Micah's, Jules's, and Billy's parents, saying, "I have a friend who needs help." The parents had received four days' notice. She'd given her excuse in a way that suggested attempted suicide by this nonexistent friend was a possibility without ever saying the word *suicide*. This might have been solely Tara's understanding of what the parents believed.

She arrived at her gate before it became her gate. Ben texted: love you proud of you. have fun send pictures. talk when you want. I bought weed from a kid at Fry's. sat in his car and bought weed. that might make you laugh. this is me not lying!

Tara didn't respond. She felt less and less like talking to Ben as the likelihood that he'd appear on the show seemed to increase. She was able to think of past and future Ben with love, but the man she was currently dealing with, that man's choices were troubling. She didn't know what her trip meant for his TV chances. Tara didn't feel she could swing the outcome wholly. But she might be able to alter the course of events significantly enough for her effort, and this trip, to be worth it.

Tara took her /// notebook with her. She was making notes occasionally at the gate, seated at the far window end of a bank of gray seating and allowing herself to nod off in between. She

195

boarded the plane and continued this pattern of nodding off, scribbling in her notebook.

- *Number of people boarding plane to Cincinnati is impossible.*
- *Dumb to not be afraid of air travel despite statistics.*
- *Statistics do not prevent deaths of individuals.*
- *Who can explain planes? If asked I'd say "thrust" and make a rising motion with my hand.*
- *Best meal I've ever been served on a plane was en route to Berlin. Food itself not memorable. What I won't forget: the small rectangular tinfoil serving dishes topped with clear plastic lids. Every component had its geometric jigsaw interlocking place on the tray. Fork and spoon clicked into place. Endless beer like aluminum.*

Tara sketched the tray and its blocky vacancies for bread, entrée, dessert, like a map of rectangular middle states with the rest of the country omitted. She drew rays of light emitting from the tray floating in her notes.

- *Getting on a television show solely to get on a television show is not worthy of effort. And despite any alteration to his attempt, that is most definitely what Ben is doing.*

Tara stopped writing from the middle seat. Three hours into the five-hour flight. The woman in the aisle seat had scoffed. She'd been reading over Tara's shoulder. The woman was drinking cranberry juice and continuing to read what Tara had written. The woman smacked her lips because of the cranberry juice. When Tara turned, the woman pretended to be reading her issue of *Self*. Tara said, "What part?"

The woman said nothing. She shook her magazine in her hand as if resetting her focus. Tara asked again, "What part?"

The woman said, "What?"

"If you are going to react to my, to my private thoughts, I want to know which of those thoughts caused you to make that little bitch noise. Were you up to the end? Were you reading along live?"

The woman calmly pressed the button above her for a flight attendant. Several other passengers turned and looked at Tara. The teenager in the window seat implored through her braces, "Please, no." Tara closed her eyes. She could hear loud whispering and the creaking of seats around her as other passengers craned to get a view of the woman who'd said "little bitch" to a stranger. With her eyes still closed Tara said, "I'm sorry," in a believable way. The flight attendant appeared and leaned in close to the aisle woman, apparently sensing the other passengers' ire, and asked if she was all right. The woman said that she had mistakenly hit the button, that everything was fine. The flight attendant hesitated and watched the woman and Tara for a moment, then left. An old woman seated in front of them made an impressed face, like she'd smelled something mildly unpleasant.

The woman said, "I didn't even read what you wrote. I'm sorry. I have a strong reaction to people writing in public. It's showy. Buying the little notebooks."

Tara put her head on the woman's shoulder. An odd regrasping of power, given what came before, but effective. The woman let it happen. Tara felt like she might soon pee her pants but would not under any circumstance ask this hateful woman to get up. Not directly. She figured that if she put her head on the woman's shoulder the woman might believe her to be needing special treatment. The woman patted her knee. Minutes later, Tara, still with her head on the woman's shoulder and wide awake, sunk into the role, made a small noise, and the woman got up, without ever being asked anything. When Tara returned, she continued intermittently writing her thoughts, napping, zoning out, listening to "Wrecking Ball" off *Soul Journey* on repeat at maximum volume in her headphones, and interacting consciously and unconsciously with the woman's near shoulder.

> *His wanting to be on TV makes me lose any understanding of who he is, who he was—*

The woman patted Tara on the knee. "I'm caught up now."

Tara thought, we can't leave these seats. We are on a plane. We both can't act like this. One of us must be the straight woman. You must be the straight woman.

"And?"

"That's why I stopped you. You have to tell your husband what it is that he needs to do. He doesn't know."

"You have no idea what you're talking about."

"None of them know. None of the husbands."

# 42. *MARCY*

THE NEAREST GROCERY store reminded Marcy of her youth. A 1980s suburban California grocery mostly empty an hour from closing. White linoleum, a broad refrigerated meat well fronting the butcher counter, wide aisles, red aprons, men in squarish glasses, middle-aged career cashiers, milky yellows, browns, station wagons, babies on hips in the parking lot. There was a man in dripping pants rolled up to his ankles parsing cans. He looked like he'd been walking thigh high in the ocean in another era. With gravity he acknowledged the cans: "Navy bean, navy bean, kidney, kidneys, Great Northern, Greatest Northern." The dripping man in short pants had a mustache and his hair slicked straight back and Marcy moved away from him like a weak actor would in a high school play. Thoughts of Hillis.

Marcy bought a red plastic container of coffee, she bought canned beer, she bought a whole kosher chicken, rice, haricots verts, Pink Ladies, blueberries, blackberries, a regional hot sauce called Tamber, salted Kerrygold butter, tinfoil, flank steaks, peanut butter cups, two bags of fingerling potatoes, a bag of unground coffee beans that she quickly ground in the store with the dripping bean man waiting behind her, peppermint tea, a scented candle called FRESHENING, soy sauce and tamari, pepper, salt, and two packages of center-cut bacon. Marcy had changed into bright-yellow gaucho pants and a man's gray undershirt with a pocket. Two densely packed reusable bags she had found at the house. She walked into the night, stopped, and then went back in for garlic, brown deli mustard, bourbon, soft wheat bread and ham and roast beef, a fifteen-dollar bottle of Cabernet Sauvignon. She had to pay for a third bag, which hung heavy on her shoulder for the trip home.

In the bungalow at a little after nine at night, Marcy emptied the coffee beans she had ground at the store into the trash. Then she made a pot of coffee with the coffee from the red plastic container. She cut the label off the bag of coffee she'd ground at the store and taped it over the label on the red plastic container. All this to show: coffee had been drunk, different grounds had been tried, mistakes had been made, time had passed, she had been in this house drinking coffee.

She put on the City of Prague Philharmonic Orchestra playing "The Harvest" from *Days of Heaven* on her laptop. She took a couple deep breaths in an attempt to stave off emotion, and failed. She wanted to be the kind of person that traveled to a cottage set on a Canadian wheat field to read instead of the kind of person that lied about being such a person. She wanted to not be afraid of a killer who wasn't after her. To not care that her life had none of the intrigue she hinted to others that it did. A man had been murdered on her lawn. So what? She'd never spent a day hungry, never been struck by her parents, shut in a closet, nothing. She was safe and had always been safe. She wanted to not be locked into continually creating her life and what her life would be, wouldn't be, and what others believed of her; she did not know another way to live. She could not accept that nobody cared.

She poured three fingers of the wine into a stemless glass and took a sip and then set the glass on the windowsill above the sink. Her intention was to leave it there.

She put two ice cubes into a water glass and half filled it with bourbon. She took two large gulps and let it hit her.

She lit the FRESHENING candle and set it in the bathroom on the apron of the sink. Once the wax liquefied, she poured some into the sink and then set the candle in the wax and blew it out.

She went into the kitchen with her bourbon and peeled a clove of garlic and ran it through the disposal. Coffee and garlic and their remnants, time spent. How small to fake what she was faking, how hard to believe anyone would make the effort for so little impact, too small to fake, exactly, she thought. She believed if she performed the tasks of having been in the house for several days in this abbreviated period, what would emanate was life lived, providing richness and density to her lie. Like vermouth in a glass then dumped.

Marcy took off her yellow pants and draped them over the back of the couch. She would leave them there. She considered what else she could do to the home to make it appear she'd been living and pacing around in this house. She could shave her legs, leave the razor on the side of the bath. No, she didn't want to do that. She could tape a note to the bathroom mirror. It could say: Eggs? Different coffee?

No, that work was already done. The note, should she leave one, should do other work.

Marcy tore a piece of paper from a pad in the kitchen. Across the top of the pad read: *I HAVE CATS BECAUSE I *AM* A CAT.*

She opened drawers looking for different tape and found none. Under the sink perched on top of a bottle of clog remover was a roll of black electrical tape. Marcy was crouched alone in an expensive and unprotected home near the ocean. The cleanliness of the house made it feel unsafe—like it had been prepped with awful intention or was not meant to be peopled. Alone by the ocean surrounded by homes filled with strangers. She considered crawling to the bedroom and grabbing the Maglite she'd brought from her bag. The thought of standing up in front of the darkened window above the sink made Marcy want to throw up. She stayed on one knee and became aware of her breathing and the taste in her mouth, bile. She began humming the song she'd been listening to earlier. She crawled on the ground over to the front of the house in rhythm to the song she was humming, what she imagined was in rhythm; crawled to a place where she could see out over the street when she stood, it felt safer; and bolted up with the tape in her hand, like a rock she was ready to throw. She looked out at the street expecting to see the tall white dog from before, passing by alone and untethered; as if deeper night was the dog's time for real living. She missed Jet. She could have brought him if she were less committed to this lie she was playacting. Marcy waited five seconds at the window thinking that maybe her imagining was enough to bring the image into reality on the street in front of her. A holdover superpower notion from childhood that she had never shaken. The dog did not appear. She went on. With four small squares of black electrical tape Marcy affixed the sheet of paper she'd torn from the pad to the back of the front door of the house. On the bottom of the page she wrote OCEAN and drew a line across the sheet above the word. Above the line, the falsely straight coastline, she made a small box to represent the rental. She stopped there.

Marcy turned on all the lights in the house. She began selectively cleaning and dirtying and staging the house further. Rearranging furniture. Washing and stacking dishes. Cupping handfuls of water that she would feed out around the small house: this specific action was not one she could consciously explain in the moment of its execution. Later it came to her that wet footsteps from a shower might be an explanation, a jostled glass of drinking water. She did not consider that the water would dry hours before Tara's arrival in the morning. She did think: something will remain. An echo. Her thoughts in isolation tracked, but inspected for relevance, coherence, maybe not. Maybe not. She could hear her thoughts spoken and racing, repeated in her head. Marcy caught her own reflection in the window above the kitchen sink, all the home's lights on and dark outside; she saw some trace of industriousness and effort in her face, traces of the expression she wore before she caught sight of herself and said aloud, "Shit."

Marcy made a phone call around midnight to Callie, who rejected the call, and left a message. "Hi. You're up. Tomorrow: please begin monitoring the *San Jose Mercury News* and the *San Francisco Chronicle* and the *East Bay Times* and the *Argus* and *SF Weekly* and anyone else you can think of in that region—see if they plan on covering the thirtieth anniversary of the PCKG murder. I have alerts set up but I think they might not be working correctly. You're better at this kind of thing anyway. It's hard for me to remember what we've talked about."

Marcy's books were on the bungalow's kitchen table, the Duras, the Annie Dillard. She'd left the Lowry at home, there was already a movie of *Under the Volcano,* and though she'd never seen it she was very impressed by the image of the Criterion cover she'd seen online. Albert Finney in sunglasses against stark black, a hazed-out skull below him. Another attempt would be silly. That cover would not be bested. She had yet to ask Callie to look into the rights situation for any of the unproduced Duras work or Dillard's. Owning the rights so she could tinker with what it would mean to film those works interested her, though she had no way in as of yet. A singular respected movie, one or two, a lazy California afterlife, being sometimes remembered and sometimes not, teaching and sometimes not, taking the money she'd earned in TV and becoming suddenly frugal, it all seemed possible. Owning a rental home like this one, further south in the state and much cheaper, being a tolerant, ever-present landlord. Because of the trip she was currently on she was deluded into thinking all she could imagine was possible to fulfill in the living, breathing world. It did not occur to her that the future she was imagining in the real world was a product of generational wealth, and for her would not come to pass. Marcy paged though *An American Childhood* and *The Lover* flat on her back on the couch. She held author photographs of Dillard's face next to Duras's and was moved by the grouping. Marcy squinted at the pictures in an attempt to see something new. She fell asleep on the couch.

# 43. *CALLIE*

CALLIE LISTENED TO the message Marcy had left immediately but did not respond. Marcy never remembers what she's told me because she doesn't care about me, thought Callie. Callie was a tool for Marcy. Articles from the time of the murder specifically mentioned that the Lons' children were not in the house at the time of the killing. Why would the killer want anything from Marcy? Marcy's past was not as hidden as she imagined; the reality was, very few people cared. No one cared. Callie felt that a thirtieth anniversary of an event widely unknown was meaningless; fortieth, same; fiftieth, same. There is no anniversary if no one recognizes its existence. No one cared about this murder. Callie spent a quick minute learning there had been 2,923 other documented murders in the state of California in 1987. 12,109 reported cases of rape. Add another 2,936 murders the year after. Another 11,780 cases of rape. That were documented. That were reported. These numbers were gestures toward the awful reality and not the actual awful reality; numbers cannot capture reality. And years mean nothing. Crime statistics do not exist isolated like baseball seasons. There is no separating of figures for any real reason that matters. Politics. Funding. The numbers get stacked and the individuals are crushed, killed again, lost, under the weight, the tonnage of death. Callie understood that. Marcy did not. Marcy understood the concept of death as it related to TV, repetition, and emptiness, the ever present and willing void, but not murder. Despite any familial proximity to murder and its aftermath, she understood none of it. Whatever hungover journalist had tried to force a Kitty Genovese connection had done a poor job.

The PCKG murder was less interesting, more gruesome, had happened in broad daylight, had featured more accurate reporting during initial coverage, and as a result provided less of a draw for people to learn the actual facts of the case. The actual facts were known. Follow-up reporting would be repetition, not revelatory. This murder was a one-off, the man murdered was Black, and the actions of the witnesses were reprehensible. The media did not care about murdered Black men, especially in the eighties. Especially ever.

Callie set up alerts for ten different words related to the murder but did not begin specifically monitoring any of the outlets mentioned. It was the most real work she'd done looking into Hillis. She then returned to cleaning out the corners of her apartment with Clorox wipes while listening to a podcast detailing the history of Sears, Roebuck and Co. Callie was originally from Minneapolis, as were her parents, and their parents, and their parents. She was compelled to know about the great successes of the Midwest. Wanted to apply this knowledge to her own life. She would not admit this to anyone, because such an admission was starkly ambitious in a way that Callie felt was off-putting. From Marcy she'd observed that different efforts yielded different results. Focusing elsewhere, say, on a retail corporation's success and downturn, and trying to apply an understanding of this trajectory into a personal life, this was not an obvious approach. Who is to say if this approach was actually useful; Callie hoped it could potentially yield a different context for her decision-making in the future. The scrubbed face and broad smile of a youth-group leader flashed into her head and she spat reflexively, cleaning the spit with a Clorox wipe and continuing along the baseboard. This was her Saturday night in Los Angeles, California, as her late-dinner salad was lazily being delivered from a restaurant a half mile away.

# 44. BRENT

BRENT IMAGINED ARRIVING for a second date, a canyon hike, with Jet in tow. Letting it slip that until recently he'd been afraid of dogs, of Jet, specifically. Telling the lie to his date that Jet belonged to a neighbor, and hell, maybe you could call this exposure therapy.

"Call this date exposure therapy?"

"Yes," he'd say.

The woman would walk for a while focusing on her steps, focus on not rolling her ankle in her hiking boots she rarely wore, ask, "Well, why aren't you afraid anymore?"

And with Jet tight at his side and unleashed, Brent would say, "It's not permanent. I could get afraid again."

## 45. BEN

HIGH ON FOUR gummies, absolutely buzzing, Ben was fixating on the words *internal radiation* and listening to the Bill Callahan song "Sycamore" in the basement. He had the Big Ten Network on mute as he sat with his computer. An old Wisconsin game. He said to the TV, "Barry Alvarez Penguin." Ben was wearing a two-hundred-dollar authentic reproduction of a 1981 Illini football helmet while he sat on the couch higher than he'd ever been in his life. He'd been looking for his snack helmet and instead found his replica. The snack helmet was missing. Ben suspected Jules, the child thief. Ben unironically loved gear. With the Callahan song droning and blooming in his head, Ben accidentally ordered eleven copies of *What to Expect When You're Expecting*. He then searched the phrases "pregnancy positive" and "Larry Bird beer video." He called Tara but she did not pick up. He kept trying and she did not pick up. He was crying but did not take off the helmet. The next song began and Ben did not move.

# 46. *TARA*

FROM THE NARROW window next to the front door Tara watched Marcy rise from the couch and lurch toward her, a tall woman in a wrinkled heather-gray undershirt pulling on roomy yellow pants. Maybe what was most frightening was she appeared to have no problem, no hesitation in coming directly to the door from the couch from dead sleep to meet a stranger. Tara was a little scared of this tall woman with the scent of warm sleep on her. The first words Marcy spoke after opening the door: "The convertible can't have been within intermediate?"

"I was upgraded because of some point system. Your points. They said, use it or lose it."

They both looked out at the rental convertible and then toward the bougainvillea across the street, the low pink home next to it in the bright morning. Humble pink million-dollar home. Multi-million. A tiny electric car, yellow, gleaming on the driveway. Tara thought this was a place she'd like to show her daughter. This bizarre set of self-conscious homes. The kind of place her daughter would instinctively understand as funny, being from the Midwest. Look at these people, Mom. A place that was not Chicago, not Chicagoland. A different country, really. Give her daughter some sense of the breadth and evil and wonderful lunches available out West. The nearby apocalyptic beach. The tidal hypnosis. Maybe the kind of place you'd want to show to a kid, hoping to blow her mind, and that the kid would probably have no interest in. The kid would have specific theme park requests. Tara was lost in it. The women watched the pink home for a few seconds and received no insight. The thought of weather occurred—the thought, that is, not actual weather—and Tara looked up. The sky was one that spoke of days that ran together, a life near an ocean that was informed and made laughable by the ocean. Slow and constant and inscrutable. The kind of life people kill for, themselves, others, but that will not save them.

Tara extended her hand and Marcy shook it. Tara wasn't short but Marcy had at least four inches on her. Tara laughed. Her thought was: I swore at this tall woman and she paid for my vacation.

Tara still wasn't sure, in general. She knew that this whole trip was a part of TV, a part of the show, a part of recruitment, because it had to be. What else could it be? She felt that Marcy was acting as if she were being filmed, despite this not being the case.

Marcy walked Tara through the rental in her bare feet, apologizing for the space not being cleaner. It did not occur to Tara to ask Marcy how long she had been at the cabin. Marcy showed Tara the still neatly made beds in both bedrooms. Tara was here on business, that was her mindset, at least while inside the home. She'd never traveled for business. Business travel to her was a genre of films from the 1990s. Baggy white dress shirts and ties visually reminiscent of potpourri. Ties colored with muddled brown-and-red swirls; eager clapping in that costume. Holding a credit card aloft with two fingers while seated at a restaurant, white tablecloth. American waiters that unintentionally slipped into English accents if they stayed with a table long enough. Or pacing a California kitchen barefoot in gold hoop earrings and a black dress with shoulder pads dressed for a party she would not attend. She was not a traveler. And she did not keep up with movies.

Traveling this far to have a conversation, in a setting that she was told was originally intended for one person, felt like an invasion despite her having been invited.

What was difficult for Tara was understanding how to learn how much of the situation was real. What was clear to Tara was that Marcy's energy was directed in places that were not easy to reconcile with her stated reasons for being in the house. She was not relaxed.

Tara was confident there was no potential benefit to Ben appearing on *Big Shot.* None at all. Her concern was only to understand what she could control, what would harm, what was real.

Marcy brewed peppermint tea and offered blueberries, blackberries, peanut butter cups. Tara said yes to all from the couch, and a beer if you have it. She was handed a cold can of the regionally popular Slade's and would eat the berries and chocolate out of a cereal bowl with her hands. Marcy stood by the kettle in the kitchen. "What did you tell your husband?"

From the living room Tara said, "I told Ben I was visiting a friend from art school."

"Age-wise that might track. If I'm a fifth-year senior when you're a freshman."

Tara did not offer up her age, though it seemed that was what Marcy was after. Tara said, "No matter what happens here, I can convince him to not do the show." Tara did not believe this.

Marcy asked, "Is it strange having Ben home more since he got fired?"

"Of course not," Tara said. "It's not like he sits at home all day." Tara had no idea if Marcy had known before she did about Ben losing his job; she hoped not.

"What if you both gave Ben's pitch?"

"Did he tell you he thought women were more successful in gaining investments?"

"I've never spoken to your husband. Women *are* more successful in gaining investments. We have more women pitch than men. For several reasons. Men want to watch women. Women want to watch women. Which is why I am asking you now; it's selfish. I care about myself more than I care about you. And married is even more desirable. Couples. But we could make it so you two were separate. Different deliveries of the same pitch."

Tara smiled. She didn't really know what Marcy meant and said nothing. She took a long drink from her can of beer and began eating the blueberries from the bowl. She'd eat the blackberries next. Then the peanut butter cups. The tea would get cold and she'd toss it.

"What if we document your resistance to the show? Ben doesn't even have to pitch. We have enough with you not wanting him to. A documentary half hour, or longer, about a woman with doubts about her husband appearing on reality TV."

"Why would the network want that?"

"Who said anything about the network? This could be made and released without their involvement. Online. Or elsewhere. My own project. We could package it for festivals. And the show need not be mentioned by name. People will know what we're talking about regardless. Or we can bleep the name of the show. Any number of artful ways around that. Or we could name the show, release it, and see what happens." Marcy shrugged.

Tara looked at Marcy, trying to understand what she was after.

"I'm not following. Is it already decided that Ben is going to be on?"

"It's not. But in the same way that you know you can make him do as you please, I know I can make him happen. The spring shoot. That's happening."

A knock at the door. Marcy opened the door for a ruddy-faced man to enter holding a small wicker basket filled with eggs. The man stepped into the cottage and said, "More eggs."

The exact words Tara was thinking were *The fuck is eggs man doing?* She turned on the TV in the living room to remove herself from the interaction. Tara changed channels until she hit *The First 48* and stopped. Someone had been killed in Memphis. A Sudanese refugee who owned a clothing store called NY STYLES. He'd been gunned down standing at the register of his own store. He was the father of two little girls. His wife spoke no English. In Tara's direction, the driver said, "Terrible."

Without turning around, Tara said to the man, "Wall of death." The man said, "We all hit it." Marcy said nothing; stood holding the basket of eggs. Tara continued to watch TV. The man didn't seem offended at being ignored. Tara didn't know who he was, but he'd probably purchased the eggs at the grocery store and placed them in a basket he'd found on a forgotten shelf.

Marcy told the man, "Thanks again," and shuttled him out into the day. Tara noticed a hand-drawn map taped to the front door. The word OCEAN was written comically large at the bottom of the sheet of a rectangular sheet of paper with a cat on top—as if Marcy were continually forgetting the word for the nearby body of water. Tara said, "Nice map."

Marcy ignored the comment. "I met him a few days ago. He's a farmer in Downey who was with his son down on the beach. We were talking about what kind of TV he watches and I asked if he could bring me fresh eggs in the mornings. This morning."

"What the fuck are you talking about?"

Marcy shook her head in a friendly way and put the basket in the kitchen.

In this room so far removed from her actual life, Tara began to feel a deep anxiety about her actual life: they could handle two months of the mortgage and student loans and three credit cards and car insurance without going into savings. Savings didn't really feel like the right word; they'd saved so little. Beyond two months, she didn't know. Maybe less than two months. She wasn't actually sure; Ben might have been lying. There was precedent.

Marcy opened a couple windows and set a lit candle that smelled like dryer sheets on the coffee table in the living room. She sat down on the couch and watched the TV with Tara. The show was going into detail about the shop owner who'd been killed.

During a loud commercial for a personal injury lawyer, Tara said, "He was able to figure out that you were one of the people who make decisions from staring at the show's credits."

Marcy looked at Tara. Tara kept speaking.

"He figured out your name. Wrote a whole bunch of names down and arrived at you."

"Wrote down names where?"

Tara gestured toward the duffel she'd set by the entrance to the bungalow and instantly regretted it. She didn't want to talk about Ben's notes. She needed another beer, more chocolate.

# 47. MARCY

MARCY MADE LUNCH while Tara continued watching *The First 48* marathon in the living room. Marcy cooked the flank steaks in a large skillet, butter in the pan, salt and pepper on the meat. Fried the eggs in Kerrygold, salting and peppering, more pepper than salt. She quartered some of the fingerling potatoes, purple and red and yellow, and took six cloves of garlic and chopped them. She mixed the garlic and potatoes in olive oil and placed them on a shallow baking sheet with a lip in the oven. It was 11:30 a.m.

Without turning from her show, Tara said, "I like knowing that my dinner will be late." The televised murder at hand had happened in Nebraska. Early-hours Omaha. A cop seen driving in profile described the area where the murder took place. A young man had been killed near the former site of Omaha Tech High School, the "largest high school west of Chicago when the school opened in 1923. Bob Gibson being probably the most notable alumni. Johnny Rodgers." Tara went on, "I like getting all this ancillary information. This cop knows what I want."

"I like when they are a little more direct," Marcy said. "There's comfort in a large lunch because it usually orients the day toward a late dinner, and a late dinner often means you have the luxury of eating a late dinner, knowing you don't have to wake up early and work. I think. For me, that's a comfort."

"Lots of people who eat dinner late have to get up early. You're wrong on that one. And this is work, in a way."

"You don't believe that," said Marcy. She liked cooking for Tara; liked disagreeing with her and having the day go on, not knowing what she'd say. Different from speaking with an obedient intern.

Marcy minded the steaks. "How much would it take for you to give me the journal Ben took notes in while he was planning his audition, and for you to agree to be on the show?"

"Why?"

"You looked like you wished you hadn't mentioned it. That makes me want the notes. And since I know you don't want me to have them, I am willing to pay. But if I'm giving you money to read a journal whose contents are entirely unknown to me, I need something else too—I need you to agree to be on the show, in whatever way I see fit."

Tara said nothing, waiting.

"How much would I have to pay you?"

"I can't."

Marcy made a face and killed the heat under the skillet. She took out the potatoes from the oven, and the whole kitchen smelled even more powerfully of garlic. "Do you not need money? Ben doesn't have a job."

Tara pulled out her phone. Her silence indicated that whatever she was doing on her phone was related to the conversation she'd been having with Marcy—a step further into what they'd been discussing, not avoidance. Marcy watched as Tara intently punched at her phone.

Tara said, "I will appear on the show in whatever way you want and let you have the journal for forty thousand dollars."

Marcy wasn't fazed. Her expression gave away nothing. "Of course not," she said.

"Make me an offer."

"Five thousand."

"Thirty thousand," said Tara.

"Ten."

"Eighteen."

"I can do fifteen," said Marcy. She noted Tara's relief, then immediate masking of that relief.

"In that case, I can do it for sixteen," said Tara.

# 48. CALLIE

AN ALERT WENT off in her phone that MIGUEL GALARRAGA'S thirty-eighth birthday was the next day. Callie had asked the property management company when Miguel's birthday was back when she had been actively building a file on the man. Callie made thirty-eight sopping wet softball-sized paper towel balls and laid them on the bathroom tile in a pattern that left room for her body. She tacked a string to the ceiling and tied a loop on one end for her phone to dangle overhead. She got completely naked, put on makeup, set the camera on self-timer mode, and arranged herself amongst the pulpy mess on the floor. She digitally marked up the photograph on her phone, writing "Happy Birthday Miguel!!!!!" across the top of the image in red cursive. She did not send the picture.

# 49. BRENT

JET GROWLED AT anything on Brent's television that moved too quickly across the screen. No televised sports, no action, and so for the duration of Jet's stay Brent put *Murder, She Wrote* on a loop. They'd tried *Midsomer Murders,* but the dog preferred American. The dog would pant and track Angela Lansbury's eyes. Brent would get high and watch the dog become Angela Lansbury. He'd say "Angela," and Jet would do nothing, pant and watch the glowing screen. Brent's wish was that he and Jet could get high together, decide on pizza toppings together, laugh. The dog would fall asleep with Angela Lansbury exclaiming, detecting, listening wide-eyed, and Brent would have already been out for a long time.

# 50. BEN

ELEVEN COPIES OF *What to Expect When You're Expecting* were on the doorstop when Ben stepped into the late morning. He'd unknowingly selected next-day shipping for books he didn't remember buying. Hoped he'd put it on the credit and not the debit. Ben watched his aged neighbor walking in green rain boots through his dewy backyard. The man appeared to be following some line, losing it, then finding it again and continuing. Ben waved, but the neighbor ignored him.

Ben tried calling Tara again. She picked up.

"How's Canada?"

"I'm in California. I lied."

She could have told Ben she was anywhere and his reaction would have been largely the same. She wasn't home, wasn't with him, and it seemed to make little difference where she actually was calling from.

"How's California?"

"I'm with Marcy Lon. From the show. The casting producer."

Ben sat down next to the boxed books on the cement porch. "Is everything okay?"

"Of course."

"Well, what then? What are you doing with her?"

"I was going to come out here and convince her to not have you on the show."

"Hey, what's the neighbor's name? The man. I know they're the Krenslows, but what is the guy's first name?"

"Ken. Does he have the pellet gun?"

"No, no gun."

"Ben, listen. Now that I'm here, I think I might be able to get

219

her to pay me, pay us, if I agree to go along with whatever she has planned."

"Pay us for what?"

"She wants to have me included on your appearance."

"Am I on? Am I going to pitch?"

"It's not decided. Not totally decided yet."

Ben began walking down the length of the finely cracked driveway and then down Prairie beneath the canopy of trees slowly beginning to lose their leaves. There was the first sign of fall in the air, but that was no promise; humidity could be back tomorrow. Seasons reached in all directions now. Ben was wearing sweatpants. He looked lost. Like a man who had misplaced his house. He kept walking down the sidewalk.

"What does 'included on my appearance' mean?"

"She wants to document my opposition to you being on the show and incorporate it into some supplementary footage that will air either with your pitch or online or something. An extra wrinkle for the promotion of the episode, maybe. She doesn't really seem to know, which means I definitely don't know."

"Okay. But not on the show with me, you're saying?"

"I didn't say that. Like I said, I don't know the parameters. If we take the money, it's giving up control. You see? It's not just you they have, then it's me too. But I want to tell you, I think we should do it. Take the money."

"I thought your whole thing was you didn't want me on the show because I wouldn't be able to have a say on what that meant?"

"I didn't think you had any chance of making any money. You said yourself you weren't interested in the money. This is up front, guaranteed."

"How did you get to her?"

"I called the office and kept calling and then she called me."

"Were you calling to reach her specifically?"

"She also wants the journal. That's the deal. Me and the journal."

"What journal?"

"*Mariska Hargitay, attacked* journal."

"I don't understand."

"I'm talking money up front. What could she do with that journal? Nothing that was actually damaging to us. You can't say, 'Mariska Hargitay, attacked,' on the show in a way that makes any kind of sense. You've proven that already."

Ben thought, have I?

He said, "Now that we're going to get paid, none of what you said before holds?"

"I am here in goddamn California. This is us taking control. This is you and me against this fucking show."

Ben stopped walking. He was standing on a corner looking at a house with three identical signs posted in its front lawn: "DRIVE LIKE YOUR CHILDREN LIVE HERE." Black background, yellow lettering.

"How does she even know about the journal?"

"I told her that you used it to take notes to get on the show. I brought it. How much is on the two credit cards with balances?"

Still on the corner, Ben watched the garage door open on the house with the three identical signs. A woman emerged from the garage in a purple sweatsuit holding a sign seemingly identical to the three others in her lawn, walking as if about to join a rally. She walked onto her grass and placed a fourth sign, black background, yellow lettering, that read "DRIVE REMEMBERING YOUR CHILDREN COULD DIE" on the lawn. She waved at Ben, but he stood still, reading and rereading the fourth sign.

Ben asked, "Did you take a test today?"

"Not pregnant."

"On both cards? On both, together, it's seven. Little over seven thousand."

"If I can clear that, clear seven, and we have the mortgage and car insurance and student loans only, and we have health insurance from your work for another five more months or so, that would help, right? That would be worth it?"

Ben turned around and started walking home, jogging now, breathing harder. "Get that money."

# 51. TARA

THE NEXT DAY was blank and the women woke late for it. They roasted a whole chicken in the oven and steamed the haricots verts and ate their lunch drifting into and away from each other in the house and the green backyard, holding mugs of coffee until noon. They spent the afternoon walking Venice Beach, drinking margaritas in various restaurants along the boardwalk, and talking about Linda Ronstadt and O. J. Simpson. These subjects arose naturally; the margaritas helped. Tara looked at the white sun over the ocean and thought, infinity apocalypse. The women found they had the same favorite Linda Ronstadt song, "Willin'."

Tara believed that Marcy could have been agreeing on the song as her chief favorite as some ploy, but she did know the words, sang them with Tara as they walked: "*smuggled some smokes and folks from Mexico, baked by the sun,*" being passed by rollerbladers and creaking beach cruisers. Passersby could have easily mistaken them for a couple; Tara wondered if this was what Marcy wanted, to be mistaken for lovers, to have their relation to one another be understood as something other than it was. Strangers.

Tara would have kissed her. Maybe sex.

After the transfer of $16,016 into Tara's checking account, an exact number drunkenly agreed upon while seated on the patio of a bar called Crunch Sue's, Marcy said she believed an interview would be the best way to document her resistance to Ben being on the show.

Marcy told Tara the interview would happen the next day. Lucidity had returned to Marcy's eyes. Even drunk, Tara could see she had been fooled in a more complete way than she'd known to be possible. Still, Tara believed the predicament to be worth losing all control of the situation. The money was worth it. Another blue frozen margarita in front of her, Tara eliminated her family's credit card debt by punching at her phone. Not all their debt, only credit card, but still, this was rarely an American option. She was drunk and happy, half listening to Marcy's agenda for the next day. Tara was an agent. A businesswoman. The fix felt too easy. But she'd won, despite whatever was coming. Tara smiled behind her margarita, her tongue deeply blued.

As the sun was setting on the boardwalk, they talked slowly, yes, another round. Another blue round. We'll begin tomorrow. A funny affectionate handshake across the table done several times. Marcy already had the interview questions ready, and sent them to Tara as they sat on the patio, night coming on, so she could read along off her phone as they sat faded doing business.

1. *How do you feel reality TV could negatively impact your family if your husband was to participate on the show?*

2. *What is your favorite TV show?*

3. *What is an activity, if any, you would wish for people watching the show to be doing instead?*

4. *If the show is merely business negotiations being filmed, what is the harm?*

5. *What is the last book you read? Did you like it? Can you remember it? Can you remember one thing about it? The name of one character?*

6. *Have you ever purchased a product you first learned of through reality TV?*

7. *Do you believe in hell?*

8. *Did you vote in the last presidential election?*

The questions were asked the following day before the lunch hour in the glass corner of a steak restaurant that overlooked the ocean. Tara found the restaurant high end and classless, the kind of place where men attempted to initiate conversation at the bar that could lead to paying for luxury rental sex. There was a fish tank behind the bar, and all the waiters' ties were teal. Tara and Marcy had been picked up in a rented black Lincoln driven by Callie. Brent sat quietly tucked against the back window with Jet. Brent was trying to sleep, but the dog was sitting on him. Tara tried not to be surprised at what Brent looked like, or acted like, off the phone. He looked like a tired, stretched-out boy in men's clothing. Like all his daily energy must have gone into those phone calls. Callie drove. Tara understood in meeting these people, putting faces to names, that her previous understanding of who they were had been wholly flawed.

Tara was positioned in the restaurant with her back to the water, her chair touching the window, floor-to-ceiling glass. Callie had found the restaurant, she'd said, after scouting ten. She required an indoor location that without alteration could make it seem in frame that Tara was sitting on the water.

The staff had given them space, seated the few scattered early lunchers on the other side of the restaurant, and seemed generally uninterested. This was a town of public striving and projects that went nowhere. Lunch would not be halted for anyone nameless. Brent told Tara he was framing her from her midsection up, and after learning this as she was getting situated in her chair, she removed her shoes.

To avoid trouble, Jet was wearing the red SERVICE ANIMAL vest that Marcy had purchased online. Jet sat idly next to Brent in the restaurant, yawning.

Callie told Tara after hearing a question to answer as many times as she'd like, one response was fine too, and to start and stop as often as she pleased. She was told that if she did stop and begin to answer again, to take a couple breaths and reset. Callie asked the first question.

1. *I have no idea. That's the point. The point is I have no idea what is going to happen. The point is the lack of control. For someone to question what is threatening about having a family member filmed making a laughable request and for that footage to be broadcast nationally, internationally, is ridiculous. Broadcast and shaped and given context beyond your control. That's a threat. His participation is not what bothers me. It is the portion of the appearance that he would not participate in.*

2. Route 66, The Rockford Files.

2. *Most of what airs on Bravo. And* Law & Order. Arthur.

2. Terriers.

2. *I only watch the White Sox.*

3. *Anything that wouldn't cause people to ask this question. I don't know. A slow walk.*

4. *The harm is: "business negotiations" is not what the show is. I can't tell you what it is, but it's not that. The harm is that a large portion of the viewing audience believes that it is as you describe it. The show is not business negotiations filmed. That is a reduction. A misleading reduction. We receive an edit.*

5. *I checked out* The Death and Life of the Great Lakes *by Dan Egan because of its perfect title. And because I know so little about the bodies of water nearest me. Any bodies of water, actually. But I did not read it. I let my borrowing period lapse and am now deep, deep, months, in fines. And I read Dana Spiotta's last novel. I did like it. I remember upstate New York. I remember two girls. Phone sex and movies. I remember less than I should. I'll read it again.*

6. *No.*

7. *No.*

8. *Yes.*

In the car on the way back to the Venice bungalow, Callie started in again. Tara was agreeable, payment received. Appearing game was on the forefront of her thinking—or, actually cooperating, as it were. Tara and Brent were in the back seats, Brent filming Tara with a small handheld camera. There was the ocean, there were other cars.

Driving, Callie said, "I'm not going to run through all the questions again. But I would like you to answer any of the questions you remember from earlier. Either clarifying your responses or elaborating or whatever you'd like."

Tara said, "I lied about hell," and turned to the passing landscape, the dark Pacific, failing to remember anything else she'd been asked a half hour earlier.

Brent stopped filming. They drove on in silence. Tara watched him let the small camera sag to his knee and rest. Despite all the times they'd talked on the phone, he seemed to be intimidated by her in real life, afraid, maybe. Callie put on the radio, but then shut it off after cycling through a few unlistenable offerings. Marcy was silent in the passenger seat, with Jet dominating her lap.

Brent again trained the camera on Tara and asked, "If *you* had to make a pitch, what would it be?" Callie intermittently watched Tara in the rearview, and Marcy turned her head to listen.

Tara said, "Escape plans. An escape provider. Clients supply a wish list, what they require out of the vacation; they give employment information and rough guidelines as to what is realistic for them in taking time off work, or in some cases best practices in preventing their work from knowing a vacation is taking place. How to take a vacation under the guise of extended sickness. Clients provide preferences in travel accommodations. I'd like to be on a plane and Xanaxed. I'd like to drive and have a case of Coors in my trunk ready to be iced for when I arrive at the hotel. I'd like to be driven by someone else. Destination requests. Island. Midwestern chain hotel with a view of a shallow body of water. Montreal apartment living. I'd like to be in a cramped New York hotel room with a barbershop on the ground floor. With a bar on the ground floor. Surf bungalow in Big Sur. Partner preferences. I would like my significant other to be there waiting when I arrive. I would like to be alone. Food. Curated restaurant recommendations. Fridge stocked to your liking. Full-service travel agenting plus personal assistance as needed. But, potentially very hands-off."

From the front, Callie asked, "And for you? If you used this service?"

Tara closed her eyes. "I'd wake up one day and there'd be a text message on my phone. Today and the day after and twelve more days after that. No work. The company has called and let my employer know that I am going through a family emergency. It's summer. My daughter doesn't have to be at school. We go downstairs and I find our bags are packed, a suitcase and a backpack. My daughter is excited. I've combed her wet hair straight back. She's six years old and not wanting to be elsewhere. We walk out of the house, and parked on the street is a car that isn't ours. A white 1974 Dodge Dart. I look into the car and see a thermos of coffee. A bag of honey-roasted peanuts on the passenger seat for my daughter. Her favorite. A sheet of stickers for her. There is a note on the steering wheel that tells me to put my cell phone in the glove box and to use the map I find there. There is a blue highlighted route on the map that leads us to Knoxville. When we get to Knoxville there will be another map waiting in the hotel room already reserved for us. We will be alone for the next two weeks. My daughter falls asleep before we hit the highway. We drive and drive. We reach Kentucky, it is green, green forever—"

# 52. MARCY AND CALLIE AND BRENT

TARA KEPT TALKING and Marcy and Callie and Brent all thought but did not say that the life she was referring to in her trip bore little resemblance to her own. She did not have an employer. She did not have a daughter. Her daughter did not have a favorite nut because there was no daughter.

# 53. BEN AND TARA

BEN WAS PULLING up curbside at Arrivals. Tara had flown out of O'Hare and come home Midway. Two expensive one-way tickets; the round-trip deal had been another lie. She'd been gone two days and it had felt like two weeks for Ben. He'd seen their credit card balances erased, gotten the alert on his phone, but he hadn't asked what that meant for him being on the show or what it meant Tara had agreed to do. He'd tried to call her again and she wasn't picking up. She'd texted him flight information earlier that morning.

She waved once and Ben stopped; she got in, and she held him in a hug from the passenger seat until the car behind them honked. It was raining lightly. Ben didn't know what to say. He was choked up.

He put on his right turn signal, made a right turn on a red light, and immediately merged into the far-left turn lane to begin making their way west and home. "Tell me what it means that the credit card balances are gone."

"It means we won," she said. "That we have to hold the ball until the clock runs out. It means that Marcy Lon paid me six thousand dollars"—she realized only as the fake number came out of her mouth that she'd been planning on pocketing the difference all along—"for my participation on the show and your notebook. I already filmed an interview with Marcy and her interns."

"What is she going to do with the journal?"

"She wants to understand your thinking." Tara was laughing.

"Seems unnecessary."

"You mean like paying for a trip to California for the wife of a potential contestant? You mean like paying that wife six thousand dollars?"

"Her process is messy."

They were driving through the near western suburbs. Auto shop, Czech bakery, bar, Dunkin' Donuts, McDonald's, bar, auto shop, over the highway and onward into progressively less city-oriented suburbs. The night had a blue neon hum.

"Expect a phone call from *Big Shot*," Tara said.

Ben smiled. He couldn't help it. Tara punched him on the shoulder three times as hard as she could as he drove. Lunging out of her seat as she struck him. They both were smiling as she hit him. Ben wanted to tell her to hit him in the goddamn face, but he was driving. Three more. Ben winced each time. His arm dead now. They passed more low, darkened businesses. Fast food and ancient townie bars, Miller Lite and White Sox bars, were the only open establishments. Tara pointed at a McDonald's and said, "Do it," and Ben pulled into the drive-thru. Ben ordered for both of them. He didn't have to ask what Tara wanted. Ben got two double cheeseburgers, a large fry, and a Diet Coke. For Tara he ordered a McDouble, small fry, Diet Coke. They pulled into one of the parking spots. Ben wasn't even hungry. Going through the drive-thru and not ordering anything was anathema to him. He watched Tara eat a fry and said, "I love you, thank you."

"For what?"

"I'm not even sure how to say it."

Tara put her fries back in the bag and set the food on the dash. "Are we doing this?"

"Yes," Ben said, stepping out of the driver's side and getting into the back. Tara crawled over the center console and began shimmying her pants down. Ben was unconcerned and focused, expecting and incapable of anything but quickness.

# 54. TARA

TARA PUT HER day care on a more extended hiatus. She'd made the equivalent of two and a half months' pay instantly and wiped out her family's credit card debt. There would have to be new kids in the near future, or some different source of income. She wanted some time to reassess where she was. She wanted some time. She called each set of parents, apologized quietly and said she understood their frustration before allowing any of them to voice their frustration. Over the phone she told Micah's mom, a short blinky woman from Cleveland, that she was trying for her own child. Micah's mom said, "Of course," several times in response. Tara helped to find each family a new day care. Sent over three or four suggestions for different childcare providers to each family. It was easy. She had the internet. She wrapped and mailed the journals she'd kept for Micah, Jules, and Billy to each respective set of parents. She wanted to say good-bye to the kids somehow, but was at a loss for how to do so. She wouldn't figure out how to with Micah and Jules. Billy became a regular phone call.

# 55. *MARCY*

MARISKA HARGITAY, ATTACKED. Definitely fucked up. But this was not a record of something that had happened. It was nothing. Substitute in any name, any perpetration. John Candy, caged. Sara Trimbel, beaten. Otto Graham, bound. Denna Wortley, murdered. Callie Olson, pushed off boat. Brent Harmsa, fed to dog. Jet Lon, released into wild. Words on a page. There was no real action. Misguided words on a page. Marcy heard worse ideas spoken in production meetings weekly. Heard worse spoken about people in the office daily. Heard worse on TV. Much more casual and ingrained hate. She participated in and benefited from much of it. She was willing to exploit any of it. Unlike Ben, she was smart enough to not write down her ideas in that realm, and would admit as little of her actual thinking as possible. It wasn't clear to Marcy what Ben was admitting to. He didn't seem predatory. Didn't seem to be much, other than lost. Marcy knew what to do with Ben. And now that she had Tara bought, she could see a plan. She did not know that Ben and Tara were aligned. The money was nothing. She had a slush fund supplied by the show for dart throws and various coercions if need be. Annually, thirty thousand was deposited into the fund, and so sixteen was not insignificant. She would have gone to twenty. She needed a number high enough that, when revealed to her superiors, or found out by accounting and reported, it would be alarming. A number large enough to aid in her departure.

# 56. CALLIE

CALLIE AGAIN MADE thirty-eight softball-sized paper towel balls and laid them out on her bathroom floor spelling out I'M SORRY. She was only able to make the first six letters with the thirty-eight balls and had to make eleven more to complete her apology. She kept all her clothes on, stood on the toilet, and took the picture. She texted the number to Miguel's work phone, and he responded four hours later as she was eating dinner: :) please no more flushing

The smiley face reminded Callie to call Ben Silas and let him know he was going to pitch. She logged into her computer so she could make a call from her office phone number and dialed Ben Silas's cell phone. It went to voicemail. "Ben, this is Callie from Big Shot Productions. If you could give me a call at the office at your earliest convenience, I have some good news to share with you. My number is . . ."

# 57. MARISKA

"THAT'S FINE, LIKE I said, two hours is no big deal. What I want to be sure of is that this is not another Palmer House. Right. Don't want to feel ambushed. Listen, if he's a fan, and me being there could potentially help him, right. Two hours—yes, on the long end, fine. Beyond the usual claims, seen every episode, watches with his wife, reluctant at first; right, beyond that I'm going in with nothing. I'm going to listen and try to be appropriately encouraging and if his idea is good, sure, maybe I'll throw some money his way. Maybe there is a tie-in for the foundation..." Her manager's phone dropped the call, and Mariska didn't call back. She put her window down and watched the empty sidewalks as the driver carefully drove them to Culver City. It was not a prerequisite that she check in with her manager before an event, but for this one, Mariska wanted her to know she did not want her time wasted, and that she knew going in that that was a distinct possibility. The call had been a warning. This was business.

# 58. *BRENT*

BRENT WAS IDLING in front of a Marriott ten minutes from the studio lot in Culver City. Three weeks had passed since they'd informed Ben he was going to pitch. It calmed Brent to imagine the set ready and waiting. Dressed, prepped, the crew eating breakfast, waiting for the next group of pitches. Seatbelt still on, he reached down and loosened his shoelaces, keeping his shoes floppily on his feet as he waited. He smiled dumbly at the bright empty street. This Marriott was being remodeled and had been being remodeled for the past eighteen months. Production used this hotel exclusively. Staying permanently under construction, appearing to be striving, was a part of the hotel's charm, Brent believed. He was not privy to any actual information regarding the hotel's appeal to production. Maybe the hotel retained the production's business because of a scarcity of decent lodging nearby. Brent didn't know. He had been told by past contestants who'd stayed at this Marriott that there was a disarming quality in constantly being apologized to for the dust. One woman had told him this. She had not gotten a deal and her segment had not aired. Brent could have told her what the result of her pitch would be as she made her way from the hotel to his car. He was usually right. He didn't keep any ledger of guesses, but his intuition on success or failure was in the ninetieth percentile. He had the right eye, an understanding of what mattered, though he rarely shared his insights with anyone. His private wagers hinged on what the contestants did with their attention between exiting the hotel and attempting to locate his car. If there was even a flicker of visible uncertainty as to where they were headed, he believed they would fail. The presence of uncertainty was fine if it was hidden, but Brent didn't want to be able to perceive doubt. If he could read fear from thirty yards away sitting in his car, think of what a viewer at home would be able to understand in a close-up. Several of the most successful people he knew excelled at hiding their feelings and also understood they were performing from the moment they woke up. Marcy, for example. And so he waited and watched and meted out determinations on the contestants he ferried.

Brent believed that since he'd watched Jet, his car now permanently smelled like dog. It had been almost a month since watching Jet, and yet he would always believe the dog's mark was present. Brent smiled, remembering Jet watching the programming of his choosing. And the dog had chosen. It felt wonderful for someone else to choose what to watch. To have a partner.

Brent put the driver's side window down and slipped his socked feet out of his shoes. He deftly hit his weed pen. Two of Marcy's contestants were filming this morning, and one in the afternoon. The first two would shoot between nine and noon, and the third after that. All three staying at this hotel. The first two had befriended each other instantly and had never been to California. The third was Ben. Brent didn't know where Tara was. No one knew where Tara was. They hadn't heard from her in two days. He knew she was in California, and had at some point checked into the hotel, but that was all. Their surveillance abilities were limited, which was potentially a problem. But, a problem above his pay grade. A problem for other people.

Contestant One was pitching a wall-mounted storage system designed to reside in the upper corners of rooms. A grown woman with braces. The material that cloaked the storage system received light in such a way as to nearly camouflage the hanging container. Essentially: lightweight, sturdy, perchable storage boxes for apartment living. Easily maskable storage for spring cleaning. Contestant Two was selling seasonally scented natural deodorants. Contestant Two lived and manufactured the deodorants in a tiny two-hundred-square-foot house near

Boise. Spring brings us out into the world, no more snow, we will be sweating, deodorant. Spring, Brent thought, right.

Both One and Two exited the hotel in their own personal frenzied style, eyes on their phones. One wore a pink turtleneck and took comically small steps, and Two wore a floral-printed tank top he was perpetually tugging on to hide the reality of his body. They were standing in front of Brent's car to look up the street for the car they believed had not yet arrived. This was their day. He let them sweat for a half minute. Neither would gain a deal. Ben and Tara were both supposed to be at the hotel. This was known to all involved, though neither Ben nor Tara quite actually knew what they would be walking into. Brent felt uncomfortable around Tara. He'd dealt with her aggrieved on the phone so many times that meeting a more sedate and resigned version of her made him feel like she still might be somehow trying to trick him into injury.

Brent dropped One and Two back at the hotel after their shoots, and though he should have picked up Ben at the same time to be efficient, he did not. He had time to kill. He returned to the studio. He parked on the top level of the three-story parking structure and then made his way along a far perimeter wall of the lot toward the soundstages. It was a bright, weatherless day. The studio lot was bounded by a sturdy tan wall you might find gating a militant golf course community. Brent made his way along this wall up against where the trailers for contestants making pitches were located. Brent weaved around all the milling staff, the fanny-packed and headsetted and walkie-talkied. Wagner and West's underlings. The clipboarded and purposeful. Brent walked in the narrow alleyways between the soundstages. He reached the soundstage and opened the heavy security door that said CLOSED SET. He walked onto the set, darkened, past the outer chairs and folding tables and wires bunched and lights hanging and cameras into the inner lit aura where performances occurred and were filmed. He looked at the Big Shots' chairs, plush, and sat down in the one on far stage right. This was expressly forbidden. He turned in the chair and admired the blue largeness behind the maroon chairs the Big Shots sat in. Today this chair would be occupied by Mariska Hargitay. She had requested to sit on an end. Her only request. Brent thought Hargitay was a surprising choice, but had been told she was a big fan of the show. As likely as anything else he'd witnessed while working for Marcy. From the chair, Brent admired the deep-red cherry wood of the set, the enormous crane set-ups, the cameras looming. A dressed but vacated set was an ideal place to be alone. Brent thought of *Mrs. Doubtfire.* His phone went off. Callie had texted: Ben knows.

Brent did not know what this meant. He knew some of the possibilities. Osmosis usually triumphed over his inattention, but not in this case. Ben couldn't know that Mariska Hargitay was one of the Big Shots for his shoot. But then, what else could Callie be talking about?

Brent felt that maybe Callie was with Ben because of how vague the text had been. Maybe she'd even wanted to lead Ben off the trail of what was actually happening by sending such a text. As if he were looking at her phone as she typed.

Brent called Callie. She declined the call. Brent closed his eyes in the chair on the empty set. He did not know the complete history of this place, of this lot, this soundstage, but did know *Big Shot* was filmed on the same studio lot as *The Night of the Hunter.* This was something he'd been told and remembered, not a piece of information that meant anything to him. Regardless, even though he'd never seen it, this fact lessened the unseen movie for Brent somehow. He'd read a description of the plot on his phone. He hit his weed pen again, keeping his eyes closed. He began to consider what he'd get tattooed on his knuckles if forced to choose.

A door opened to Brent's right, and a production assistant walked onto the darkened set with Mariska Hargitay. They walked slowly over to Brent, who stood from the chair before they reached him and shuffled a few steps in the opposite direction. The production assistant knew Brent's name, but Brent had no idea what the pudgy man's name was. He would have guessed "Keith."

"Mariska, this is Brent. He was warming up your seat for you."

Brent waved to Mariska Hargitay from about six feet away. It never would have occurred to him to even attempt to shake her hand. He would have been insulted by the suggestion, actually. Brent was surprised at how attractive she was and tried to hide this surprise. He felt, with what he understood as just cause, that if he made the wrong move or said the wrong thing he might end up in jail. That he was in danger of being outed as a deviant by this television cop. Despite nothing in her bearing projecting Olivia Benson, Brent felt power emanating from this woman and was unable to separate this feeling from a sense that he might be arrested by her. Mariska Hargitay smiled warmly and raised her hand in a motionless acknowledgment of Brent's wave. Like a shy student wordlessly stating "here" for roll call. She said, "Call me Mariska, please." The production assistant said that he had to go grab a key, and asked Brent to take Mariska over to makeup for him. The production assistant jogged away, and before he was out of sight began walking, limping.

Brent asked, "Where is your assistant? Are you alone?"

"I have a friend who lives nearby. I was there this morning and then came right here."

Brent said nothing. No one lived nearby. He had no idea what she meant.

"I guess that's not an answer," she said.

"Let's get to makeup. I don't know where that is exactly, not my area, but I am certain if we walk in this direction we will encounter someone who knows where you are supposed to be." Brent should have known where makeup was, but truly did not.

Mariska laughed as Brent began walking. Brent was trying to stay ten or so feet ahead of her.

"You don't have to do that," she said.

Brent didn't have to ask what Mariska meant. Both knew exactly what was going on. Both knew that Brent was being

demonstrative in avoiding her so that there was no misunderstanding. He slowed his pace but took an additional step to the
side to widen the gap between them. He was technically walking next to her, but also providing a wide enough berth that no
observer could ever reasonably say he was walking next to her.
They were at the outer edge of the dark set, making their way
to a set of double doors. Brent held open the door for Mariska,
and they were in a dim hallway. A comically long dim hallway.
The hallway was lined with posters for the films and TV that
had been shot on this soundstage. *Kindergarten Cop*. And *Ghost
Dad*. Odd they hadn't taken that one down.

Brent said, "This hallway feels very nineties to me." What
Brent meant was a blank gray hallway of an unknown slick material that he could imagine Arnold Schwarzenegger running
down at quarter speed holding an automatic weapon while
looking for a particular door in pursuit of another man with a
gun. Mariska said, "I think I know what you mean."

Despite what Brent had initially told Mariska about running
into people who would know which way they should be going,
they had not seen a single person since the production assistant had left them. Brent had taken her down one long hallway
and was surprised they'd not encountered a crowd.

"A key to what, I wonder?" Brent said, growing increasingly
anxious.

"He didn't say, did he. It's good, though. To say, I need to get
a key, and then leave."

Brent smiled. Mariska smiled back. Luckily, though, her eyes
did not flash as they so often did onscreen. She looked like someone's mom. Someone's stunning mom. Brent was walking pressed
against the wall and Mariska was acting much more normal.

Brent said, "I have weed."

"In what way?"

Brent handed Mariska the pen, which she hit and then
placed in her pocket.

Brent laughed. "You can't have that."

# 59. CALLIE

IN A GOLF cart Callie and Marcy came to a rolling stop in front of Brent and Mariska Hargitay. Callie wore a dismayed look. She'd watched hundreds of hours of Olivia Benson solving crimes, powerfully making choices to defend victims, taking no shit. Callie revered Olivia Benson, but knew less what to do with this woman taking a casual hit off of what looked like Brent's vape pen. Callie had no real knowledge of Mariska Hargitay, did not know she spoke several languages, was an activist, none of it. Watching her take a small pull off a vape negated something for Callie, for whom TV was much more real and tangible than the shaggy mishap of real life. Brent and Mariska were standing apart from one another, Mariska now in sunglasses, Brent shielding his eyes with his hand, looking around as if he were waiting to be picked up. Callie and Marcy looked at each other. Brent was staring into the sky with a pained face. Callie got out of the golf cart and Marcy drove Mariska to makeup. Mariska did not say good-bye to Brent. No wave.

Brent made a weak motion with his hand toward the departing golf cart and said to Callie, "That woman is a thief."

"What?"

"You texted me, 'Ben knows.'"

Callie pulled out her phone and looked at the message. "I meant to say 'nothing.' 'Ben knows nothing.'"

"I knew that."

Callie made a face. "Are you fucking high?"

"No."

Callie made a face. "What were you doing with Mariska?"

"Walking, keeping my distance because I was told with

upper celebrities to treat them like dangerous zoo animals. Like you're in the cage with them. Keep your distance and stay in sight and stay calm and generally leave them alone even while interacting with them."

"Upper celebrities? Who told you that?"

"Marcy, day one."

"What made her tell you that?"

"There was a photograph of Bernadette Peters behind me at the deli where we were eating."

"Bubbie's. She took me there too. Same, day one. I did not receive this advice, though."

"What did she tell you?"

"I remember her saying 'At all costs,' and lifting her roast beef sandwich into the air."

# 60. MARCY

MARCY HAD NEVER seen an episode of *SVU*, and if anything knew less about Mariska Hargitay than maybe anyone working in American TV. She was impressed with how the woman emanated success despite not being dressed in any obviously monied way. She was wearing black slacks, a modest black top. The kind of clothes one might describe as "well made" or "chic." Other than thanking her for coming on the show, Marcy said very little to the woman. She did not want to appear to be a fan. After dropping off Mariska, Marcy circled back from makeup in the golf cart looking imperial, and told Brent, staring again— or still—into the sky, "Go get Ben. And remember, he doesn't know his wife is one of the Big Shots today. And the reason he doesn't know is because she doesn't know. Right? And of course: no Mariska talk."

Marcy knew that Brent didn't know enough to do any real damage. Even if he had the information he should have had, he could only ruin so much. Brent didn't know what it meant for Mariska Hargitay to be present; neither did Callie. Not really. They'd been told Ben was an outsized Mariska Hargitay fan and so her appearance might pair well with his pitch. Which was as true as anything else.

# 61. *BEN*

BEN STOOD WITH Brent on set, sweating. Ben was wearing a light-gray suit, not particularly well-fitting. On his lapel he wore all four pins Tara had given him. Tree, house, strip of road, black helmet. He had no understanding of what the pins were meant to be but wanted as much of her with him as possible. He would be able to say as much, if asked. The set was crowded and loud, though no one was standing near Ben. He was in makeup, sweating with his suit on, his own gray suit from home. Brown shoes. Ben was standing at the head of the dummied-up hallway that led to double doors opening onto the main *Big Shot* set. He did not know the configuration of judges for his pitch. He did not know who the judges were. His hope was for Mackaday and Reinhart, some weak guest, and another throwaway, like maybe a past contestant made good. Someone he didn't recognize and could ignore. Brent gave Ben a thumbs-up and a little pat on the back and walked away. There were five cameras being operated by humans that Ben could see. Another man with a Steadicam would be with him walking down the hallway. Ben didn't know if there were other cameras hidden. He felt watched in more ways than he could account for, though. He did not know where Tara was.

# 62. *TARA*

TARA HAD WALKED in twenty-five minutes before shooting began. That morning, as she had many mornings the past month, she'd taken a pregnancy test. Peed on the stick. And after peeing on four more different tests to make sure, she knew she was pregnant. She was anxious, doubly so because of the impending shoot, and had not allowed herself to fully realize her new reality. She was pregnant. She wanted to tell Ben. On this morning, and maybe in an ongoing way, she didn't give a shit about controlling what she let Ben know. Control, at its best, only led to more control. And no matter how many people it ended up being, Tara wanted a family, not control; she hoped she could remember this. They'd asked for separate rooms thinking it might help portray that they were not on the best terms, that Ben was making an honest effort, and that Tara was not attempting to interfere in any way with his pitch, because her opposition was clearly known to production. Separate rooms helped to articulate that there was no collusion, though it was difficult to parse what exactly that would mean in this context. They wanted to minimize the possibility that the money they'd been given would be taken away. It felt inevitable to Tara that the money would be reclaimed. But now Tara wanted to see Ben, wished she had woken next to him and pissed in their shared bathroom with the door open and yelled to him that they were pregnant right away, right in that first moment she knew. Yelled to him, and had him come running, yelling too. What was different this time was that Tara had lived enough years to know in a less obscured way what she wanted. She wanted a family and to have more that bound them, their family, together. A different work life for Ben would help; he'd be more alive. A kid would help too, despite "making Ben more alive" maybe not being in the top hundred changes a kid would bring. She wanted daily consequence and less drifting. Tara wouldn't say anything until this day was over, but she was ready to tell Ben, have him share in whatever was to come. All their life together from before dropped away; how could it matter anymore? What a relief. They could be single-minded together, she hoped they could, please god, and raise this child. She wanted their life to become daily: for them to live inside the days together and stop projecting hopes and losses outward in all directions. Fail and cry together; wake up and do it again.

But first she had to get through witnessing Ben's pitch. She watched the Big Shots on the dais and the still-empty chair. Mackaday was probably late, off the wagon. And then, Mariska Hargitay was standing next to Tara. Tara stuck out her hand, beaming. Mariska shook her hand and they said their names to each other. Tara laughed like a girl when Mariska Hargitay said her own name. But Tara's giddy recognition fell through the floor when she understood that Mariska was here because of Ben, because of Tara.

"Are you shooting today?"

"I'm here for *Big Shot*. One of the people pitching is a fan. I'm a guest Big Shot."

Tara looked around for someone who could change this situation. None of the crew was familiar. She wasn't sure what was going to happen, but whatever was going to happen wasn't good for Ben. As she'd always known.

Mariska made her way toward the dais.

Marcy and Callie walked up to Tara, Callie holding an earpiece. Recognizing what the expression on Tara's face meant, Marcy said, "We agreed on your participation in the shoot in whatever way I saw fit?"

Tara looked to Callie and then back at Marcy. Tara said, "Are you asking me a question?"

"I'm reminding you of our agreement."

Callie said, "I'm going to put this on you so production can communicate with you. You will be able to hear them; they will not be able to hear you beyond the microphones on set."

"What is that?"

"It's called an IFB."

Marcy said, "I have you right there in that empty seat," nodding toward the chair next to Mariska Hargitay onstage.

Tara said, "You couldn't have given me any warning?"

Marcy said, "Do I really have to say that I owe you nothing?" and walked away.

Callie began telling Tara how to put on the earpiece and how to adjust the volume, but Tara wasn't listening. She said, "I'm not fucking wearing that." There was still a remnant in Tara's thinking that Callie was a boss of some kind, and she was getting off on starkly defying her. Callie walked off. Tara was about to sit next to Mariska Hargitay and was thinking about how exactly it was that such a thing came to pass.

It was Marcy who was in control; Tara was not delusional enough to buck that reality. Not in this moment. Not with the credit cards paid off. Another reality: all this was still worth it, worth the money. Tara was sure. She reminded herself she was sure. No matter what was about to happen.

Mariska Hargitay couldn't know that she was a tool within this scenario; it would have been shocking if she had known anything and still agreed to be here. Tara did not see, could not remember, that her own plan had at one time been nested inside Marcy's; Tara had given herself over at this point. All Mariska Hargitay probably knew was that her agent had been contacted by *Big Shot*, by a casting producer named Marcy Lon, and that she had agreed to appear for a single pitch. Maybe she'd been told a man who was a big fan was pitching. April Fools', your favorite actress is hearing your pitch. Who knows what she'd been told?

The soundstage was bustling. The two short women quickly

touching up Tara's face as she sat in her chair on the dais were sharing a lie that had been disseminated throughout the set from an unknown source, that the man about to pitch had Mariska Hargitay's most famous character's name, Olivia Benson, tattooed squarely on his left ass cheek: *OB*. Tara whispered to them, "That can't be true," but they weren't listening.

Tara was made up and set in between Mariska Hargitay and Suzanne Reinhart. Mariska Hargitay leaned over and began to say something, but Tara cut her off. "I know."

# 63. MARCY

BRENT, CALLIE, AND Marcy stood huddled together in the dark on Mariska's side of the set. They could see the Big Shots that Ben could not yet see from his position, and also see Ben about to make his way down the false hallway. Callie whispered to Marcy, "I called the papers earlier today. No one is covering the anniversary. The thirtieth. No one is running new coverage."

"Not the *Mercury News*?"

Callie shook her head, avoiding eye contact. She said, "No one cares, Marcy. No one gives a fuck."

Marcy patted Callie's forearm, then gripped and released it—a gesture Marcy didn't exactly understand. She was embarrassed. She felt like crying. She decided to grab Callie's arm once more, hoping that Callie would imbue the gesture with meaning. Callie again allowed her arm to be handled. Marcy was much more afraid of not being pursued by Hillis, of never having a murderer after her. She was another woman with a job, hoping for different circumstances. She did not have memoir-material levels of pain in her past. She'd been a kid in Ohio eating soft serve when the murder happened.

Marcy sat down on the floor, leaning back on her elbows like she was watching a distant outdoor concert from a rise in the land. Callie and Brent were standing, watching Ben fidgeting before his cue. Marcy could see Ben visibly sweating; everyone could. Callie whispered to Marcy that Tara had refused to wear the earpiece. Marcy smiled. Attagirl.

Ben looked like he might pass out; that was apparent even from this distance. Jet trotted over, tags removed because they were shooting, and pressed his head against Brent's leg. Marcy did not resent their recent bond. Jet had been wandering the lot for the past hour. In the soundstage, on the set, with everyone gathered, it seemed impossible to Marcy that Ben was going to be able to go through with his pitch. He was about to look Mariska Hargitay and his wife in the eye and restate the idea for *Big Shot* on *Big Shot*, asking for a substantial amount of money in the process. Human.

# 64. BEN

EVERYONE WAS STANDING by. Waiting. Ben was waiting. He pressed his first three fingers to his jaw. He was given his cue and began walking down the false hallway, a cameraman backpedaling in front of him setting a slow pace. He was already sweating, impatient to know what was going to happen. It was clear to everyone watching that Ben was thinking about each step he was taking. Walking with this cameraman in front of him, bent over and backpedaling, Ben thought of Billy, was surprised to think of Billy's face watching the moment he was about to live in some future, Billy sitting on a carpeted floor in the dark, in front of an always-glowing bright suburban basement TV. He thought of Crant bleeding in the stairwell and later hawking his stain remover; could not imagine what Crant's violent thoughts had been in this moment before the pitch. Ben continued down the hall. Sweating.

The doors opened and Ben registered the women who would be hearing his pitch—saw Mariska Hargitay sitting next to his wife, basketball star Lisa Leslie, and Suzanne Reinhart— and he turned around and began walking back into the hallway. Not thinking about his steps any longer, shaking his head. The director yelled, "Take it again from the hallway."

Ben looked toward where the director's voice had come from and said, "I don't think this is right." He received no response. The director said, "Okay, take it again." Ben went back to his original starting place and again slowly walked down the hallway with the cameraman shuffling backward in front of him. He thought CBAS but could not remember what it stood for. He reached his mark in front of the Big Shots and stopped. Beads of sweat at his temples and on his brow as his minute-long staredown began.

As previously instructed, he stood for a full minute as a production staffer held a large countdown clock, indicating how much more silent standing he'd have to endure. He could not look at Mariska Hargitay. Not a chance. He respected this woman. And why his wife was a Big Shot, and with what money she'd be able to negotiate, if any, he didn't know. What was happening? She'd told him she'd be on set, but Ben had not understood that this was what she had meant. He didn't know if she had been obligated to keep the specifics of her participation quiet as a condition for payment. Jesus. Tara shrugged demonstratively at him.

Mariska Hargitay's presence was more distressing. Ben looked at her. She was a real woman. Looked like she could be someone's healthy mother. She probably was someone's healthy mother; he couldn't remember if she had kids or not. Ben had intellectually understood she was a middle-aged woman, but had never actually considered that she was a real person.

Still, why was she here? Did she know what he'd written?

If Ben was confronted with what he had written, he would deny it. If shown the journal and then also shown another sample of his handwriting to corroborate the source of this text, he would shout it down.

Staredown complete, Ben cleared his throat. He was not thinking about confidence, belief, or the ability to display either one. He was not thinking about sex. He was only thinking about what the women in front of him knew. And how much of who he actually was, what he'd thought and was thinking they were able to perceive; certainly more than he could.

He was also thinking about his wife.

Seeing Tara on the dais, seeing her participation on this level, he understood that she was somehow responsible for Mariska sitting in front of him. Tara did not look angry; she looked strangely peaceful. No, not somehow, it was that she was responsible. And not solely because she'd accepted the money. Tara had read Ben's journal, and as a result Mariska Hargitay was now seated in front of him. The shape of events had begun forming, and now the shape was closing. Ben was galled at his own stupidity. He wished the shape that Tara had helped him to form had been anything else. And maybe one day it would be. He wished he had wanted something different, my god he saw a bit of what Tara had meant. Want something different. She meant I can fucking help you. I can fucking help you if you listen to me. But if this is what you want, so be it. And now the reality, the end point of the start he'd created, was facing him. The first shape dictates the later shapes that become possible. It's not be careful what you wish for, and it's not be careful what you write down, what you allow to be found out, it's be careful what you allow yourself to think.

Ben spoke.

"Hello, Big Shots. Jesus Christ. Hello, Big Shots! I originally came here today seeking $500,000 for a stake in nothing. I was going to use this April Fools' context to my advantage, well, maybe to my advantage, and use language spoken by past Big Shots to bolster my request that you invest in me, the man, and not any specific business. I have no idea. I have no idea. But, as I stand before you now, I can't actually do that."

# 65. *BIG SHOT* ANYONE IN THE room paying attention knew
that something was going very wrong. Somehow, a sort of gag
pitch had slipped through, and either production had not realized the extent to which the gag was going to bomb or, possibly,
there had been a long series of such miscalculations.

A cameraperson leaned back from her viewfinder to see this
idiot with her own eyes and found one of her colleagues was
doing the same fifteen feet away; the two put their hands up
like you might if watching a child run into traffic.

Tara dropped her head when she noticed the pins; she was
overcome that Ben had worn all four she'd given him. Exactly
the kind of loving misunderstanding and perseverance that was
central to the best of who Ben was capable of being. Wearing all
four seemed to say: I'm here with all of it, good, bad, you.

Mariska smiled, her eyes flashed, and she looked over at
Tara and then at the other Big Shots. Mariska was laughing.
Lisa Leslie had no expression on her face. In her earpiece, Lisa
Leslie was told, "Ask him why he can't do what he'd planned to?"
Lisa Leslie took out her earpiece and let it hang down the back
of her neck. Only Suzanne Reinhart was listening to the pitch
with sustained focus.

Tara stood up from her chair, and all the women on the dais
turned. Their looks stopped her. Tara sat back down. Tara's instinct had been to stand up and hold Ben until everyone went
away. A protective movie embrace.

Ben started talking again. "I'm up here and I'm looking
at my wife. I'm looking at Mariska Hargitay. Olivia Benson!
Suzy Shortstack. Suzanne "Shortstack" Reinhart. Lordy, Lord,

Lordy. And Lisa Leslie. What have I done to deserve your time? Nothing. I've got nothing. But I am actually here to ask for something. And it's not money. I am asking for each of you to tell me, to say, that you believe in me—"

Tara said, "Noooooo—" Again the other women all looked at her, but she continued to moan her opposition.

Ben said, over his wife's moaning, "Ms. Hargitay, do you know what I said about you?"

Mariska didn't even shake her head. In her earpiece she was being told to let Ben explain himself before asking any questions, but Mariska was able to ignore the noise in her ear and also the pitch being delivered to her all while appearing to be absorbing every word. She looked incapable of being surprised by anything any man could ever say to her about herself. Tara was still saying "Noooooo—" Suzanne Reinhart gently touched Tara's knee. Tara closed her eyes and stopped. She took a deep breath. Her new goal was to mar the shoot enough for it to be unairable, while also hiding the pointed nature of her efforts enough that Marcy wouldn't consider going after the money she'd paid them. She knew full well she'd probably be unable to walk that line.

Tara stood again and started walking toward Ben. Jet started barking and darted in between Ben and Tara. The dog was spinning and barking, ferocious. Brent skipped into the fray, horrified—he was not a runner and had never had to physically respond so quickly to a situation, so skipping was the result, and he caught up and bodied Jet to create a barrier. Brent shouted, "April Fools'!" as if this explained anything and guided the dog back off the set.

The director called out, "Enough. Let's take it again from the top. Begin again, but this time, Tara, don't come in, just sit there and let's let Ben get the whole thing out. And Marcy, hold that dog unless I signal you."

"His name is Jet," Marcy said to the director.

Tara didn't know what to say. She hadn't known she was being directed. That her actions would be received as a performance. Her actions were a performance. She sat back down.

Ben began again, "Hi, Big Shots. I came here today seeking $500,000 for a stake in nothing. I have no business. I have no invention. I have no idea. No plans. I am asking for you to believe in me. Invest in me. In what you see before you, a foolish man, a confident man, looking to take the money he is given and better his community not with any idea of his own but with the idea of *Big Shot* itself. I want to take this show, a version of this show, and localize it. Who knows? It could work on a smaller, humbler, lower-stakes scale. Have people who aren't camera ready come out and make a pitch. Maybe the diner needs a new water heater. Maybe the park district needs three more lawnmowers. And that's nothing! The impact could be enormous. Not money-wise, but quality-of-life-wise. And this could be replicated. Localized and regionalized versions of this show, that you all invest in to make a different kind of impact than you typically make here."

Lisa Leslie said, "How did you go about getting to this moment? To get on the show. What was your starting point?"

Ben cleared his throat and stared at his wife for a few seconds. This well-lit and recorded moment stretched and deadened. He laughed. She laughed. A moment of understanding. Ben spoke: "I started by thinking about if I were a Big Shot, who would be the person I would be most inclined to give money to? Who would most effectively cause me to invest, regardless of pitch? I was trying to remove the pitch aspect because I knew I wouldn't have one. I have nothing."

The director called out, "Ben, stop saying you have nothing. Your idea is to modify an existing idea. That is not nothing. Stop saying you have nothing." He was not frustrated.

The director was a bald Latino man, maybe forty years old, with a perfect dense mustache. He looked like a man with job security. A man who could cook. He said to Lisa Leslie, "Ask your question again but more succinctly, please, and Ben, answer more directly."

Lisa Leslie asked, "Who inspired you to think you could get on the show without having a pitch?"

Ben said, "Mariska Hargitay."

Mariska Hargitay made a charming confused face. The director asked Ben to answer again, exactly the same way, and then for Mariska to have a "bigger" reaction. Ben did as he was told, and this time Mariska gave no reaction at all, instead looked at the palm of her hand at the mention of her name.

Ben continued, "I knew I wasn't going to have a pitch, so I tried to think about if *I* were a Big Shot who would I most want to invest in, give money to, devoid of any business opportunity. And the answer was Mariska Hargitay."

Lisa Leslie asked, "How does that make sense?"

Suzanne Reinhart laughed and looked at the ceiling. Tara had her eyes closed again. Mariska's attention was waning.

"I'm not saying any of this makes sense. I started with Mariska Hargitay; was inspired by her."

Marcy knew this wasn't going to be able to go much longer. She watched Brent and Jet on the floor next to her. Brent's arm around the dog. Blue-lit faces in partial profile; both open mouthed watching the scene. Tara was going to crack or the director would end things or one of the Big Shots would leave the set. Something was going to happen. Marcy was still on the floor too, hugging her knees. Marcy knew that Tara thought she cared what happened here today, but it wasn't true. Marcy was past caring. Callie had moved as close as she could to the action, standing. She had lied to Marcy earlier. She'd received a letter from Walt Hillis's lawyer with a communique from the killer for Marcy two days earlier. She handled all of Marcy's mail sent to the office. Walt Hillis's lawyer had typed out the dictated message for Marcy sealed in a small envelope within the larger envelope. Callie had read the message and destroyed all evidence of its existence. Walt Hillis had the following message for Marcy Lon:

*BARRY BONDS BONDS THE BAY*
*(I'm sorry for any pain I've caused your family.)*

Callie shook her head thinking about how fucking idiotic it

was of Marcy to trust her. Fucking idiot. She could have killed Marcy if she wanted. Easily. She watched the dais.

Suzanne Reinhart asked, "Why Mariska Hargitay?"

Ben said, "She's someone you want to like you. In part, yes, because she is beautiful"—Marcy, reflexively, could see the two-shot of Hargitay and Tara reacting to that line on TVs in homes around the country—"but lots of actresses are beautiful. Lots of women are beautiful. What's unique about her is that if she weren't an actress, she could believably be a person who had gone through trouble in her life. She doesn't seem insulated from the world. When she's not talking, in quiet moments, you can see that on her face."

Mariska Hargitay said, "What is going on?" She was speaking to the entire room. Speaking to the cameramen, the PAs, the director, the other Big Shots, to Ben. No one answered. She said, "Seriously? What is this?"

Tara stood and said, "Ben, April Fools'. None of this is real. It's all April Fools'. I'm pregnant. Well, that's real. I'm pregnant is real."

The camera caught Ben's face—several cameras did. He put a hand on his head like the quiet and private celebration of witnessing someone barely catch a ball he'd thrown some great distance, witnessing the leap to make the catch, too far away to do anything but put his hand on his head and take it in. What a catch.

Tara wanted that footage, her husband learning he would be a father, hand on his head like a boy, and though she'd try, she would never get it.

There was rustling and resetting and confirming whispers from the production crew, but it only lasted a few seconds. The director left the set. The camerapeople again threw their hands in the air—the child loose in traffic.

Brent got up and began walking outside and Jet followed. Once they were outside, Brent kneeled next to the dog's ear and said, "I knew that was going to go bad the second I picked him up today. That man has no shot. No shot at all. Sweating, sweating. No notes, no nothing. Confused. He's silly. Let's forget him." The dog didn't seem to disagree and held Brent's gaze. Jet's breath smelled like rotting meat.

Callie turned from the devolving scene and looked at Marcy on the floor. Marcy frowned. She stood and walked slowly onto set clapping. She felt she'd gotten away with something, though she didn't know what. Gotten away without losing her job; no, gotten away with quietly laying the groundwork to leave her job. She wasn't sure what she'd done. A PA who looked like a Halloween burglar said to Marcy, "Not the human."

Callie was watching, eager to leave. Brent and Jet were still slowly walking farther and farther from the soundstage, toward the looming parking structure. Marcy looked directly into Camera A and asked, "Did we have you?" The crew watching that monitor were not sure what Marcy was referring to; one said "Keep looking." Suzanne Reinhart began speaking to no one in particular, and then, spotting Marcy, directed her words at her: "Is this a Make-A-Wish type situation?"

Mariska took Brent's weed pen out of her pocket, hit it, and passed the pen to Tara. Tara whipped the pen as far as she could into the darkness. Mariska smiled—"Oops, forgot"—stood up, said "Congratulations," and left. Everyone was vacating the set. From her chair, Tara shouted to Ben, "Okay?"

Ben was soaked, sweating. He had sweat through his shirt, through his suit. Continents of sweat visible on the gray jacket. Ben had already been forgotten in the room. A failed audition. And yet, he'd turned his Mariska thought into nothing, had done less harm than he might have. Failed? No, couldn't be. The room had been so ready to forget him, to leave for other rooms. Tara was speaking to Ben from the chair on the dais, and though the soundstage was still crowded, it was as if they were alone. No one cared about them anymore; they'd been used and dispensed. They were lunetted for each other.

Ben yelled, "Pregnant," and smiled insanely at his Tara, taking off his jacket and his tie, then his shoes and socks, leaving a little pile on the floor. He walked over to her barefoot in his gray undershirt with a pocket and hugged her where she sat. He leaned back and looked at her from close range. Tara shrugged hugely. She said, "You're out of control." Ben nodded like a watched and repentant new believer, thanking his sponsor for a second chance.

The on-set psychiatrist approached Ben with her arms folded. Ben waved her off. Shook his head at her like a child deep in tantrum until she walked away. Tara watched this moment and felt proud of Ben. A minor victory. As if somehow all this had led to this moment with her pregnant and proud of her husband; he needed so much help.

He needed a moment. Ben walked off the soundstage barefoot and into the last of the day on the studio lot. He was crying. He let the blacktop burn his feet. Orange fading sky, pink buildings, black ground. He couldn't wait to be a dad. Give his life over to someone else.

Tara stayed in her chair and watched everything begin to shut down on set. He'd done it. Not in a way that made sense, was repeatable, admirable, or understandable, but he'd done it. That is, she'd allowed him to do it. Enabled him to do it. Had fabricated situations to make it possible. She would let him have a moment to himself outside in the California gloaming, then convince him (he'd need no convincing) to do what she wanted to do once she determined what that was. Pizza. Pizza at the hotel. Pizza with soda and garlic knots. But only one soda for Tara. One or two. In her room. She wanted to be careful with caffeine. With the shades pulled down and drapes drawn and all the lights burning. A recent feature film they'd rent off the TV and pizza and soda and garlic knots and all the shades pulled down. Out of her chair on the dais, Tara walked over to where Marcy was lying on the floor and lay down next to her. They shared a look, but didn't have words for each other.

Brent and Jet were walking along the top level of the parking structure. They reached Brent's car and Jet hopped in the driver's seat with Brent. The dog cradled in the crack between the door and Brent as he drove.

Callie walked from the soundstage to the offices and began altering her resume at her cubicle. Marking the current month, the month she was presently alive, as her last listed at Big Shot Productions. She considered purchasing a dangle cross earring like Bonds used to wear to commemorate the day.

Marcy was prone on the soundstage floor as it was being vacated. Next to her, Tara had her arm over her eyes, maybe asleep. Marcy's phone rang. Brent was calling from his car, asking if he could keep Jet overnight. Marcy laughed. She said, "See you tomorrow." Marcy decided she was going to Canada. Real Canada. To Nova Scotia. To the cliff house. To a cliff house. To a house and a foreign wheat field on the coast overlooking the Atlantic where she'd wait for work to call. Wait for work to realize she was gone and for someone to call and figure out what was going on. She would not answer the phone. She called Callie from the floor to have her reserve a flight and a cabin, to begin to reclaim what she'd never had. Callie did not pick up. The phone rang and rang and rang. Marcy stayed on the floor. She tried calling again, no answer. It occurred to her that if she wanted to leave soon she might have to make preparations herself. The prospect of booking her own travel, finding her own cabin, telling the tiniest truth about who she was, did not feel possible.

Ben walked back onto the soundstage barefoot, looking like an extra from a bloodless zombie movie. He walked over to where Tara and Marcy were lying and got on the floor next to Tara. Marcy, propped on an elbow, looked over at Ben and stuck out her hand. He didn't take it. Ben said, "I was right about you. From the first. I saw your picture. Dead-eyed. You looked nuts. I thought: either she runs shit or kills people."

Tara kept her arm over her eyes and mumbled at Ben, "It's okay."

Marcy said, "Listen to your wife, Ben."

Tara said, "Now you shut the fuck up."

The day was over.

# 66. *BEN*

BEN DID NOT appear in the spring seasonal episode. It was determined that his pitch would need too much scaffolding to make sense within the context of even an April Fools' episode. Not to mention the lack of usable footage. His inclusion on the show was then reduced to appearing in a gag reel of sorts. In the initial rough cut of the episode he appeared briefly in a forty-five-second pre-credits reel titled "April Fools" that included clips from failed pitches not featured in the episode. In this reel he received three seconds of airtime, uttering the sentence "I have no idea." The look on his face supported these words. Standing sweating in his gray suit. Not shown was Tara's reaction, Mariska Hargitay's, anyone's. Mariska Hargitay had asked her attorney to make sure she never appeared on the show, and that her footage was destroyed. Not shown were Marcy and Brent and Callie and Jet watching Ben fail from behind the scenes. Three seconds of Ben believably saying, "I have no idea," and then a quick cut to him with his hand on his head, having just learned Tara was pregnant, though her saying so was not included.

It was beautiful.

And would have been beautiful on TV, because he meant every word and his reaction had been genuine. But the reel was cut. More time was needed for the following week's episode's promotion. Ben never learned that for a span of several hours there was a chance he was going to appear on the show, in the reel, or what it was that reel might contain, or even that it had ever existed.

# 67. TARA

Ben was supposed to be in the basement working, one of the many remote freelance accounting jobs he'd taken, on a Saturday, but instead Tara found him speaking to the TV. Ben was watching his alma mater play Nebraska in Champaign. Tara sat down on the couch. "Poor Illini," she said, continuing the sketch she'd been working on of a boy-sized pocketknife set open and standing next to a house cat on a front lawn. She liked having Ben home. When the football game was over they'd probably watch TV they'd recorded to watch together. They watched network bullshit, streaming dramas, reality dating shows. Still watched *Big Shot* too. There were no hard feelings, really. They remembered their time with the show like a mugging, in both directions. Marcy had dropped off the credits recently. Ben looked at Tara's sketch and asked, "What's that knife's name?"

Tara's phone started ringing from where she'd dropped it on the floor. Ben picked up.

"Billy. No, we still didn't move yet, no. We might? We might. Are you with your dad and mom right now? That's great. Yes, she's right here. Okay."

Ben handed the phone to Tara. Billy would call a couple times a week to talk to Tara. Ben muted the TV and Tara put the phone on speaker. She'd been watching new kids recently. A brother and sister. Bronko and Sloan. They were terrible, and their parents paid terribly well.

"Billy, how are you?"

"I called to tell you my dad started reading me the book you wrote, the notebook of stories with me in the stories."

"I love that. Thank you for telling me." Tara put her hand on

Ben's head, her fingers in his hair. Ben let his head fall to her shoulder. He put his hand on her stomach, though there was no bump yet.

Billy said, "I asked my dad which ones are true and which are made up?"

As the boy asked his question, Tara already had Ben in a loose headlock. Ben wanted to answer for her, but the hold she had on him was enough to prevent that. She tightened her grip. Ben, red faced, strained his head backward in an attempt to make eye contact. His vision was dimming. She released him and Ben rolled over to face her, his head still in her lap, gasping. She held up her index finger to signal *shhhhhh*. Ben tried to understand the expression on her face as she answered the boy's question.

# *ACKNOWLEDGMENTS*

Thank you, Monika Woods; a friend and the reason I have a writing life. Thank you Willie Fitzgerald, Emily Adrian, Miranda Popkey, Dan Hornsby, Lindsay Hunter, J. R. Lennon, Adam Price, Justin Taylor, Catherine Nichols, Isaac Butler, John Wilmes, Bryan Woods, Erika Stevens, Zoë Koenig, Lizzie Davis, Abbie Phelps, Mark Haber, Laura Graveline, Jeremy Davies, Christina Vang, Drew Marquart, ST, RB, my family, CHP, and the people I forgot.

Coffee House Press began as a small letterpress operation in 1972 and has grown into an internationally renowned nonprofit publisher of literary fiction, essay, poetry, and other work that doesn't fit neatly into genre categories.

Coffee House is both a publisher and an arts organization. Through our *Books in Action* program and publications, we've become interdisciplinary collaborators and incubators for new work and audience experiences. Our vision for the future is one where a publisher is a catalyst and connector.

LITERATURE
is not the same thing as
PUBLISHING

# Funder Acknowledgments

Coffee House Press is an internationally renowned independent book publisher and arts nonprofit based in Minneapolis, MN; through its literary publications and *Books in Action* program, Coffee House acts as a catalyst and connector–between authors and readers, ideas and resources, creativity and community, inspiration and action.

Coffee House Press books are made possible through the generous support of grants and donations from corporations, state and federal grant programs, family foundations, and the many individuals who believe in the transformational power of literature. This activity is made possible by the voters of Minnesota through a Minnesota State Arts Board Operating Support grant, thanks to the legislative appropriation from the Arts and Cultural Heritage Fund. Coffee House also receives major operating support from the Amazon Literary Partnership, Jerome Foundation, Literary Arts Emergency Fund, McKnight Foundation, and the National Endowment for the Arts (NEA). To find out more about how NEA grants impact individuals and communities, visit www.arts.gov.

Coffee House Press receives additional support from Bookmobile; the Buckley Charitable Fund; Dorsey & Whitney LLP; the Gaea Foundation; the Schwab Charitable Fund; and the U.S. Bank Foundation.

# The Publisher's Circle of Coffee House Press

Publisher's Circle members make significant contributions to Coffee House Press's annual giving campaign. Understanding that a strong financial base is necessary for the press to meet the challenges and opportunities that arise each year, this group plays a crucial part in the success of Coffee House's mission.

Recent Publisher's Circle members include many anonymous donors, Patricia A. Beithon, Theodore Cornwell, Jane Dalrymple-Hollo, Mary Ebert and Paul Stembler, Kamilah Foreman, Eva Galiber, Roger Hale and Nor Hall, William Hardacker, Randy Hartten and Ron Lotz, Carl and Heidi Horsch, Amy L. Hubbard and Geoffrey J. Kehoe Fund of the St. Paul & Minnesota Foundation, Hyde Family Charitable Fund, Kenneth & Susan Kahn, the Kenneth Koch Literary Estate, Cinda Kornblum, the Lenfestey Family Foundation, Carol and Aaron Mack, Gillian McCain, Mary and Malcolm McDermid, Daniel N. Smith III and Maureen Millea Smith, Vance Opperman, Mr. Pancks' Fund in memory of Graham Kimpton, Alan Polsky, Robin Preble, Ronald Restrepo and Candace S. Baggett, Steve Smith, Jeffrey Sugerman and Sarah Schultz, Paul Thissen, Grant Wood, Margaret Wurtele, Jeremy M. Davies, Robin Chemers Neustein, Dorsey and Whitney Foundation, The Buckley Charitable Fund, Elizabeth Schnieders, Allyson Tucker, and Aptara Inc.

For more information about the Publisher's Circle and other ways to support Coffee House Press books, authors, and activities, please visit www.coffeehousepress.org/pages/donate or contact us at info@coffeehousepress.org.

**ALEX HIGLEY** is the author of *Cardinal* (nominated for the PEN/ Bingham Award) and *Old Open*. He is a founding editor of Great Place Books. Raised in Colorado, he currently lives southwest of Chicago.

*True Failure* was designed by Abbie Phelps.

Text is set in Bodoni PT Variable and Helvetica LT Pro.